WAVE HER HOME

KEN GAGNE

WAVE
HER
HOME

A NOVEL

ALSO BY KEN GAGNE

You're Gonna Miss Me Someday:
A Memoir

This is a work of fiction. All events depicted in this story are a product of the author's imagination. Some characters are based on his friends, who are far more interesting on these pages than they are in real life. This book contains strong language, alcohol use, and mature situations. It may not be suitable for children under fourteen.

To daughters everywhere,
to the women they'll become and the girls they once were,
and to fatherhood, friendship, and fate.

"Grief is the grenade that always goes off."

—Amanda Gorman,
"Pre-Memory"

"Sometimes you win, sometimes you lose, sometimes it rains."

—Crash Davis,
Bull Durham

PROLOGUE

"BE LIKE THAT tree, Izzy." That's what Papi used to tell me.

And I still hear his voice whenever I look at the old painting in our living room, the one hanging crooked above the couch, the one in the gaudy plastic frame. The painting is beautiful because the araguaney tree is beautiful—tall and sprawling, full of tubular flowers, deep yellow, the color of a honeycomb, or a wheat field at sunset. The national tree of Venezuela is tough and strong and can grow almost anywhere, no matter the soil or terrain. I used to think one could take root on my block, outside on the sidewalk, right below my bedroom window. But nothing much grew in our part of the Bronx.

The araguaney is a long-lasting tree, statuesque and impressive, with wood as solid as rock. But it's not always attractive, not always aglow in bronzed brilliance. Its flowers bloom for only three days each year, after the first rains of the dry season. The rest of the time, the tree is green and dull. Just another tree, ordinary and unnoticed.

"Be like the araguaney," Papi used to tell me. "Be strong, and when the time comes, show off your colors, bright enough for the whole world to see."

DAY ZERO

ITHOUT MY FATHER'S voice to fill our small apartment, other sounds take over the space. The rattle of the air conditioner, the buzz of the kitchen light, the Sunday hum of Mami's hairdryer, the everyday click-clack of her rosaries, the clunk-clunk clunk-clunk of the elevated train, the laughter of children outside on Barker Avenue, the chatter of old heads out on the stoop. But on the night my mother told me about her cancer, all of the sounds fell away, and it was just the two of us on the couch, holding hands, her voice wavering in the low light.

"Forty-three, Isabel," she said, a tear creeping down her face. "I'm too young. And what about your sister? How will you take care of Ava?" She broke down and let go of my hand.

"It'll be okay," I said, rubbing her back.

She picked up a framed photograph from the coffee table, a picture of Papi standing outside our restaurant on the day it opened, more than twenty years earlier. She ran a finger along the edge of the silver frame. Her hands trembled. "We have no choice." She took a deep breath and set the photo back onto the table. "We have to sell Café Isabel."

That night in my bedroom I lay still, staring into the darkness. In her bed by the window, Ava slept. On the couch down the hall, Mami sobbed. Fear covered me like a heavy blanket as I tried not to think of the losses we'd suffered, and all of the losses to come.

I'm at the office the following evening. As I collect my things to leave, my boss stops by my cubicle and hands me a thumb drive. "I need one more story out of you," Kay says.

The monthly magazine where I work, *Mature Living*, is going out of business in a few weeks. We've almost finished putting together what is likely to be our final issue, and the last thing I want is another assignment. I stare at the drive in my palm. "Seriously? The issue's full."

"It's for the next issue, if there is one," Kay says. "Just check out the movie on that drive and come up with a decent story angle. If anyone can find one, you can."

She hands me a corporate credit card and a scrap of paper with a name and a number. I fold my arms and look at the ceiling.

"Give that guy, Sal Rucosa, a call," she says. "The team leaves tomorrow. You should be on that bus. Think of it as a chance to relive your softball glory days."

I peek at the paper and cringe at the thought of reliving those days, which would only remind me of my father. "Wait. What?"

Kay is already gone.

I slump at my desk and plug the drive into my computer. The "movie," entitled *Bull Slurham*, is a homemade mockumentary about a group of old men in Walnut Gap, New Jersey, who play beer-league softball for a team called the Aging Bulls. As I watch, my main thought is that I'll never get these fifty-five minutes back.

Bull Slurham is quasi-entertaining and well-produced in an amateurish kind of way. Over a soundtrack of AC/DC, Willie

Nelson, Bob Marley, Miley Cyrus, and Run-DMC, among others, the Bulls describe each other's questionable abilities and wacky personalities, while playing up their camaraderie. The slapstick commentary and lowlights make me crack a smile once or twice, and the structure is creative, but I doubt anyone will care about this story other than the guys on the team. Also, it'll have to be a puff piece, which I hate. If I wrote honestly, it would be the story of a team founded on hollow, self-congratulatory "brotherhood" whose players confuse drinking buddies with true friends.

After the final credits roll, a co-worker informs me that our publisher belongs to the same Elks Lodge as a few of the players. Turns out the coverage is basically a favor, and I suppose Kay figures as long as the ship is sinking anyway, why not go along?

I dial Sal Rucosa, player/manager of the Bulls. Over the phone, Mr. Rucosa sounds upbeat and nonchalant, like he doesn't have a care in the world. He tells me the squad "miraculously" won the Northeast regionals of a 45-and-over softball tournament and, in less than a week, will be one of eight teams battling to represent the U.S. in the Senior Men's Softball World Championship. The kicker: the competition will be in Las Vegas. The rest of our phone call plays out like a scene from *The Twilight Zone*.

Sal: So, what'd you think of the movie?

Me: Well, I'm not bold enough to tell you the truth, so let's just say it was amusing.

Sal: How so?

Me: Honestly?

Sal: Sure.

Me: You're just over-the-hill buddies doing the weekend warrior thing. You care more about drinking in the parking lot after the games than actually winning, or even playing.

Sal: Yeah, pretty much sums it up.

Me: So where's the story there?

Sal: I dunno. A bunch of old dudes on a road trip, busting balls, drinking beers? You'll figure it out. Bus leaves Walnut Gap at 8 a.m. I'll email you the address.

Me: Wait, Mr. Rucosa—

Sal: Please, call me Sal. And listen, Isabel, I get it, old-man softball isn't as sexy as celebrity look-a-like rutabagas.

Me: Hey, I just write what they tell me to.

Sal: No, I understand.

Me: And Dottie Willoughby is the sweetest lady you'll ever meet.

Sal: Believe me, I get it. You could squeeze Yoo-hoo from a stone. That's what makes you such a good writer.

Me: Hold up, don't patronize me.

Sal: C'mon, Isabel, you know me better than that.

Me: What? I have no idea who you are.

Sal: Join the club.

Me: Wait. What? Sal, hang on a minute.

Sal: Yes?

Me: This is crazy. It's just that—

Sal: Just what?

Me: The thing is—

Sal: Yes?

Me: Ugh. Never mind. See you tomorrow.

Sal: Sounds good. Oh, and Isabel, one more thing. Don't bother bringing beer. We've got plenty.

After Sal hangs up, I consider quitting on the spot, or at least asking Kay to give the assignment to someone else. How can I go on a road trip to Vegas? I need to look for another job and help my mother run our family's restaurant, keep it afloat till her health improves, try to convince her not to sell the only piece of my father we have left.

But with the magazine closing its doors, the staff is down to a skeleton crew, and I need the paycheck more than ever, especially as the cost of Ava's insulin increases. Also I feel indebted to Kay; she gave me a chance at a career when no one else gave me a second glance. Still, the prospect of traveling 2,500 miles with the Aging Bulls and writing a story about it seems pointless. We don't produce many sports pieces at *Mature Living,* and the fifty-something Bulls skew twenty years younger than our average reader.

I'll go on the trip for Kay, but she better not expect a miracle. As for the Bulls? Like all upper-class, middle-aged men, I'm sure they expect nothing from me. And that's exactly what I plan to give them.

I pack up my laptop and leave my desk. While I'm waiting for the elevator—and scanning a printout of the Aging Bulls roster—Kay yells to me from down the hall. "Hey, Izzy. I know this isn't your dream assignment, but please don't phone it in." The elevator door slides open. "You're better than that."

The next morning, an electrical issue at Penn Station delays my departure from New York, and I'm late getting into Walnut Gap. But not late enough.

When I step onto the platform, I immediately recognize Sal Rucosa from *Bull Slurham,* his thinning white hair, his ice-blue Sinatra eyes, his Buzz Lightyear chin. He's holding up a sign written in red crayon: *Welcome to the Team, Izabella Domingez.* I shake his beefy hand and try not to smirk. "Nice to meet you in person," I say. "You kind of butchered my name."

"Sorry about that," Sal says. "One of our players, Slate Hetan, made this sign himself. I'm actually surprised he came that close with the spelling, since no one's ever confused him with a poet laureate, or with anyone able to string together a sentence. You'll understand soon enough."

Sal loads my suitcase into his Camry and drives me to the Stillwater Softball Complex, where the Bulls play their league games and hold marathon drinking sessions in the parking lot. Again, from the mockumentary, I'm familiar with the place: three unkempt diamonds, overgrown grass, and a neat row of porta potties lined up behind one of the backstops.

As he pulls into a spot, Sal beams and says, "We spend twice as much time in this parking lot as we do on those fields."

Across the lot, team members heave luggage, beach chairs, and equipment onto an orange bus that looks like a giant sleeve of peanut butter crackers on wheels. Hand-drawn on the side panels: a pair of dice next to green block letters spelling out *Gamblers Anonybus*.

"Sweet ride," I drone.

"It's a reclamation project from the department of corrections down in Trenton," Sal explains. "We got a guy on the Bulls, Vinnie Shalers, who's got a guy who knows a guy who had a cousin who used to work there. They were gonna junk the bus, so Vinnie's guy bought it and gussied it up. Now he rents it out to college kids for drunken trips to Atlantic City. But for today, we just need that baby to get us to Chicago."

"Wonderful."

"Yeah." Sal grins. "Vinnie says as long as the bus stays in one piece, he'll stay in one piece." One of us laughs. As we haul our bags out of the trunk, two other players approach, and Sal grabs my suitcase. "I'll load up your stuff while these chowderheads give you the scouting report on the other chowderheads."

The guys introduce themselves as Mac Lervacci and JC Strait, the only Bulls not going to Vegas due to family commitments. I feel badly for the team because, from the looks of them, Mac and JC might be the only players who are any good. Unlike the others, they look younger than fifty. Also they're in full uniform, wearing baseball pants, stirrup socks, belts, and royal blue jerseys with *Bulls* in bold orange letters stretched across their barrel chests.

"If you're not going on the trip," I say, "then what's with the uniforms?"

JC flashes a broad smile. "It's a solidarity thing, just showing support for these clowns. Also, I'm the newest member of the team, so I'm brown-nosing for playing time."

"And I'm the starting shortstop and best player," Mac says. "Gotta look the part, you know?"

"So what can you tell me about the team?" I say, finding the voice recorder on my phone before Mac and JC indulge me with a thumbnail sketch of each of their teammates.

JC: See the fossil in the Dipsy Doodles T-shirt? That's Leo Tarriso, a good-natured public defender, born and raised in Jersey. Leo's got three things going for him: a distinguished head of silver hair, an unquenchable thirst for Yuengling, and a disgustingly philanthropic heart. He splits time with another guy at first base, and when he's feeling frisky, he performs a lot younger than his fifty-eight years suggest.

Mac: The burly dude standing off to the side is Bo Loth, a lumbering outfielder and talented Mr. Fix-It who, legend has it, once built an entire house using only Elmer's Glue and a coat hanger. He speaks slowly and infrequently, but don't let his quiet eyes and drowsy demeanor fool you. Bo knows anger! At the plate, he takes violent swings and inflicts incredible pain on the ball, when he's lucky enough to make contact.

JC: The bald guy with ferret-like eyebrows is Henry "Hank" Sornecki. He's the CEO of an IT company and the youngest Bull at forty-six. He also looks like the villain Gru from *Despicable Me*. But Hank's an anti-villain, a great dude, and not-so-great player who possesses an inhuman amount of kindheartedness and back hair. He's an overrated hitter who plays the outfield like a blind grizzly in high heels swatting at horseflies.

Mac: Isabel, beware of Slate Hetan, the guy with the Joker grin and tatted arms, who's cursing and hugging everyone and drinking tequila straight from the bottle. He founded the Bulls and runs a chain of restaurants in NYC called the Blue Moose, despite any business acumen or standard etiquette. Slate's a power hitter who holds down third base like he was born on it, and he tortures all of us with an endless barrage of verbal abuse and flicks to the groin he lovingly calls "nut taps."

JC: The sketchy shirtless man who looks like an overgrown Lollipop Guild munchkin is Clete Shuheg. He's a staunch Staten Islander pushing sixty, sporting a cement-filled beer belly and an elephantine memory of his career stats. Clete's a trusty pitcher and outfielder who works in personal finance, which is odd for a guy who looks like he just broke into your duplex and stole your Labradoodle.

Mac: Everyone's favorite Bull is Rodney Pittbase. He's that handsome fireplug of a man oozing charm and charisma. And believe me, he smells as good as he looks. He's the sweetest guy on earth, or at least the sweetest from Trinidad, who's mastered the steel drums and the ability to single-handedly win games for us by *not* playing. Rodney exudes an effervescence that shines brighter than his million-dollar smile, or his twenty-dollar earrings.

JC: The pasty dude who just showed up, wearing shades and basketball shorts, is Biff Nerby, a lanky infielder whose name is easy to remember because it rhymes with *spliff.* He's a local realtor, we think, and the son of Walnut Gap's beloved mayor, Ed Nerby. Biff battles the double curse of living in his father's shadow *and* owning a Howitzer of a throwing arm that never met a mitt it couldn't pulverize.

Mac: The skinny guy in the faded Celtics hat, cackling uncontrollably, is Benny Eggan. He's a fifty-four-year-old outfielder and children's book illustrator whose softball skills and art career are neck-and-neck in a spiraling race to the bottom. Benny's best known for needlessly diving for flyballs, spitting beer through the Alfred E. Neuman gap in his front teeth, and egging on Slate Hetan's nonstop Bull-on-Bull abuse.

JC: And there's Webb Ucho, the athletic Asian stud wearing the stylish golf outfit, probably just got off the course. He's a high-achieving Princeton alum, and head of a mysterious pharmaceutical company, who's usurping the leadership spot in our outfield, leaving Benny Eggan pining for his youth. Webb's one of those guys who always looks like he's in charge, especially when he wears his glasses.

Mac: The debonair African-American fellow attached to the hip of Leo Tarriso, pretending that they're equally talented first basemen, is Darryl Shonjon. He's a genial gentleman in his mid-fifties, Brooklyn-born, who owns a laugh so infectious we all had to get vaccinated before he joined the team. Darryl works in human resources, but we call him "The Accountant" because he always gets stuck calculating our bar tabs.

JC: See the guy getting on the bus with his guitar? That's Bryson Lowdan, a poor man's Rob Lowe who can strum and sing at least one verse of every classic rock song ever written. He's an outfielder recovering from multiple back surgeries, undoubtedly caused by the way he corkscrews himself into the ground like the Tasmanian Devil after each of his Ruthian swings.

Mac: We should also warn you about Rocco Rupacava, our catcher, the human bowling ball sitting on his Santa's sack of equipment and running his fingers through his thick mane of hair, which is the only thing about him I envy. Rocco gets a little out of control now and then, but he's got a huge heart that he wears on his sleeve and a huge cup that he wears in his pants.

JC: Of course there's Sal Rucosa, whom you've already met, our masochistic manager who keeps us losers in line and has a Jabba-the-Hutt-sized appetite for aggravation. Sal's a real guy's guy, an Italian stallion from Jersey City, who can play any infield position and fills in wherever he's needed. We really only need him to fill out lineup cards and bring extra beer to the postgame parking lot.

Mac: The stiff with the movie star looks, puffed-out chest, and dark sculpted hair is Nick Chinsola. Reminds you of a foosball player, doesn't he? Nick's a heavy-hitting infielder with an eye for expensive real estate and a nose for fine wine. He hates Slate's merciless teasing, but he's learned to live with it, like the kid in *The Sixth Sense* learned to live with seeing dead people.

JC: The guy waving at us is Harold Hapnets. Don't worry, he's completely harmless, just ask any pitcher we've ever faced. Harold's a right fielder, web designer, and craft beer expert who carries a growler at all times in case he happens upon the elusive Westvleteren 12 ale brewed by the Trappist monks of Belgium. When he's into something, he's all in. Look, he's still waving.

Mac: The shady character in the Foster Grants and guinea tee is Vinnie Shalers, our number one pitcher and public enemy number one on the west shore of Staten Island. He doesn't look tough, but what he lacks in stature, he makes up for in moxie. And he operates a crane for a living, so that kind of says it all. If you need anything in Vegas, anything at all, just ask Vinnie. But ask everyone else first.

JC: Last but not least, depending on who you talk to, is Wink Sillano, the guy with the well-groomed whiskers, great hairline, and smoky blue eyes. Looks like a bearded James Dean if you squint really hard. Wink's a college professor and literary editor who's retiring from the Bulls after the tourney. He's really smart and really quiet, not exactly an open book.

On cue, Wink looks at us and nods.

I thank Mac and JC for their scouting report and say good-bye. Then I trudge across the lot and join the other Bulls. Sal introduces me, they all say hello, and we file onto the bus, out of the early morning sun.

DAY ONE

SOFTBALL IS LIFE. At least that's what it said on the T-shirt I wore to bed every night when I was a little girl. Back then, traveling to a tournament across the country on a funky bus would've been the coolest thing I could imagine, but only if Papi was with me. That's the biggest difference between then and now. When I was a kid, I believed that softball was life, but only indirectly, because softball was my father, and my father was life.

I was eleven the last time he saw me play ball. That was thirteen years ago, but it feels like a hundred. We won the New York City championship that day. Papi was coaching third when I scored the winning run. I remember him waving me home. I remember running as hard as I could, deciding not to slide, and the catcher tagging my leg. She dropped the ball, and the umpire called me safe.

The celebration was insane. I'd never seen my father so happy. He kept shouting, "Izzy, we did it! We did it!" He picked me up and squeezed me so hard, I thought my ribs would crack. His beard scratched my face as he spun me around and around. I was excited and angry at the same time. I messed up. I should've been out. I failed, but no one noticed.

The tournament director gave me the MVP trophy. It came

up to my waist and was too heavy for me to lift. After the game, Papi took our whole team to McDonald's. He told us to order whatever we wanted. I got fries and a strawberry sundae. I didn't finish either.

Before I went to sleep that night, my father kissed me on the forehead, then he picked up my crumpled uniform and tossed it in the hamper. He pulled the chain on my lamp and stood in the doorway, my trophy glowing next to him on the dresser, his eyes not as joyous as they'd been during our celebration.

"Goodnight, Papi," I said.

"Goodnight, Izzy. Congratulations, my love." He hesitated for a second. "You're becoming a great player, but sometimes you play it too safe. You have to be daring, especially on the bases. You have to be bold. And next time, you have to slide."

Then he forced a half-smile and closed the door. And as my father hit the switch in the hall, snuffing out the last sliver of light, I wondered if I'd ever make him proud and fell asleep hanging onto a secret hope that, someday, I'd be good enough for him.

Stepping onto the "Anonybus," I feel like Alice stepping through the looking glass into a world of nonsense, where nothing is what it is because everything is what it isn't. The interior of the bus is tricked out, in an acid-trippy kind of way. The floors and walls are lined with purple carpeting, old seats have been replaced with plush couches and swivel chairs, plaid drapes hang over the side windows, a TV is mounted high up front, and two disco balls dangle from the ceiling. It's as if Reuben Kincaid hired Austin Powers to redecorate the Partridge family's bus.

I sit alone up front. Behind me, chaos erupts as the Bulls throw open coolers filled with beer and sandwiches and more beer. They giggle like schoolboys hiding in the girls' locker room. They swear like rednecks picking fights at a biker rally. They argue over the societal importance of pub cheese, debate the nuances of Chris Elliot's performance in *Cabin Boy*, and contemplate the hidden meaning behind the '70s classic "Afternoon Delight." It's hard to imagine them appearing in a magazine with *mature* in the title.

The bus engine grumbles. I flip open my laptop, create a Word document, and start taking notes for my Bulls story. The first angle that comes to mind: a story about how they're doing what they love, with whom they love, and piling up memories that will last a lifetime. If Papi hadn't been killed, I could relate to a story like that. But the thought of trying to take the Bulls so seriously is more than I can stomach. I narrow my eyes and cast about for another angle, trying to freeze out the lunacy around me, but there's too much distraction, here and at home, and I can't believe Kay's making me do this. While the flashing cursor waits on the blank screen, I eye the disco ball swaying above me and wonder how far this bus will take me from my dream of being a serious writer.

As we pull out of the parking lot, the guy wearing the Dipsy Doodles T-shirt taps me on the shoulder and plops onto an adjacent seat. "Hi, I'm Leo Tarriso."

I nod. "I'm Isabel."

"Nice weather for a drive, huh?"

"Yeah, hey, sorry," I say, pointing to my laptop. "Gotta finish a work assignment."

"Oh, sure," Leo says. "Sorry about that."

As he scoots off to rejoin the calamity, I open my backpack and remove my security blanket, a book I bring wherever I go, the novel *All That You Had*, about a young girl's search for her father who went missing the day she was born. The paperback cover is faded and stained, fraying and curled at the corners. The pages inside are dog-eared, marked-up, yellowed. Beginning the story for the hundredth time, sinking into the words, I try again to find what I've been searching for: a way away.

Behind the wheel, Wink Sillano navigates the tree-lined streets of Walnut Gap and zips onto Route 78, kicking off our twelve-hour drive to Illinois. While settling into my book, I sneak a peek at Wink. He's focused on the road, a Chicago White Sox baseball cap tugged low over his eyes, a wave of dirty blond hair covering the back of his neck. His manscaped ginger beard is flecked with gray. Something about him seems familiar, and I wonder how I might know him—other than from *Bull Slurham*. I'm sure he's not from the Bronx, maybe Brooklyn, the gentrified part with the hipsters and vegan bakeries. He has a kind face, looks like someone who has a lot to say but keeps it all inside. *Is that what I recognize?*

I put my book down. "So, what kind of name is Wink?"

The well-groomed man keeps his eyes on the highway. "It's a nickname for William," he says. "My mom gave it to me when I was a kid."

"You a White Sox fan?"

"Not really."

"You live in Walnut Gap?"

"Next town over."

And our conversation ends there.

Four hours into the drive, we pull into a truck stop near Nowheresville, Pennsylvania. The Bulls ramble out of the bus and into a convenience store to buy snacks and desecrate the men's room. I follow far, far behind. When I enter the store, a couple of the other customers shoot me looks. I try to keep a neutral face, but the place smells like a Lower East Side subway station on New Year's Day. After grabbing a bottle of water and a bag of trail mix, I wait to pay behind Hank Sornecki and Darryl Shonjon, who are giggling over their purchase of a box of pepperoni nachos they found under a dim heating lamp. The cashier is a heavyset man in overalls and a *Take Back America* ball cap. Darryl ignores the guy's frown.

Behind me, a stubby woman with a neck tattoo grunts, and I assume she thinks I cut her in line. "You fuckin' people," she mutters under her cigarette breath.

The cashier rings up Hank and Darryl's nachos, snatches their cash without looking up. After I place my items on the counter, the man lifts his head and stares at me. He doesn't say a word, but I know exactly what he's thinking.

Back on the bus, I return to my book while the boy-men return to drinking, shouting, and laughing. Vinnie Shalers has taken over at the wheel and, for three hours straight, won't stop talking to me about the challenges of pitching, the dangers of operating a crane, and the yoga retreat his wife has planned for their anniversary. I barely say anything, but not because he's a bad guy. I'm just not in the mood for banter, plus he doesn't give me much of a chance to speak.

Like a gift from heaven, a ruckus in the back of the Anonybus disrupts Vinnie's storytelling. While he spies the antics in the rearview mirror, I pop in my AirPods and listen to *Cancer Out Loud*, a podcast I downloaded featuring conversations with cancer survivors, loved ones, and the bereaved. Five minutes later, I doze off, either from sadness or exhaustion or both.

I'm dreaming that my apartment's on fire when the bus fishtails, and my head bangs against the window. I open my eyes and ears to an unbearable clatter as frozen ball bearings pelt the bus and litter the highway. A sleet storm? In June? The Bulls hoot and holler, pressing their noses against their windows, in awe of the anomaly.

"Hold onto your hats, kids!" yells Leo Tarriso, now behind the wheel.

Leo drives the bus like Keanu Reeves—on speed—in *Speed*. I chuck my AirPods into my backpack and secure my seatbelt.

When I look out the windshield, my jaw drops; sleet is the least of our worries: coming directly at us, in the blur of weather, what looks like three rolling tree stumps challenging our bus to a game of chicken.

"Watch out!" I scream as Leo fiddles with the radio dial.

He looks up, yanks the wheel, and pumps the brakes, tipping over a napping Biff Nerby and a cooler of Miller Lites in the rear. Then he accelerates again, and we whiz past a highway sign reading *Entering Toledo*.

"What are you doing? Slow down!" I yell as the stumps rumble closer.

Leo grips the wheel with both hands. "Brace yourself, Isabel!"

I cringe as he veers across two lanes and slams the brakes. The squeal of tires stings my ears. *Or is it the squeal of pigs?* As the bus skids, a trio of wild boar dodge out of harm's way. Leo swerves onto the shoulder, steers off the road, and buzzes into a cornfield. After he mows down forty yards of maize, the Anonybus hisses to a halt.

"Way to go, Tarriso," Slate Hetan slurs in a fake British accent. "You didn't doink any oinkers, and you found the *Field of Dreams*."

"More like nightmares," replies a sweat-soaked Leo.

From the back of the bus, Benny Eggan shouts, "No way you're getting behind that wheel again, Leo. You'll be lucky if we let you use the TV remote. New rule, no one's allowed to drive if they're old enough to remember when there weren't any cars."

As the sleet turns into rain, Bo Loth goes outside and checks the Anonybus for damage. The other Bulls are either too drunk, too disinterested, or too disinclined in the ways of machinery to help out. I slump in my seat and bury my face in my hands. Will we make it out of the cornfield? Will we make it to Vegas? Will I make it to my twenty-fifth birthday?

After ten minutes, Bo reports that the Anonybus is in decent shape, other than a tangle of cornstalks wrapped around the axle. Bryson Lowdan and Harold Hapnets assist with the untwisting while the rest of the team celebrates with whiskey shots. Running my fingers over the bump on my head, I wonder if I'd been knocked unconscious, or if I'm still dreaming. After deciding this is all really happening, I go back to my book and pray I'll be left alone.

Before I finish a paragraph, Leo sits in the swivel seat next to me. "You okay?" he asks.

I nod.

Leo the lawman squirms, shoots looks in all directions like a bobblehead doll. When he finally stops moving, I get a good look at him. His eyes are bright but tired, like they just got home from an all-night dance-a-thon. And his nose looks like it belongs to a man who forgot to bring his arms to a boxing match.

"Might be a while before we're back on the road," he says. "Feel like chatting?"

"Ugh." I reach for my phone. "Mind if I record our conversation?"

He leans back, chuckles, and laces his fingers behind his head. "As long as you don't use it against me in a court of law." He crosses his legs and seems totally relaxed, except for the jumpy foot jiggling off his bouncy knee.

June 23 notes:

How to begin my story about the Bulls? Maybe like this... Dear Reader, my name is Isabel Dominguez, the last staff writer left standing at *Mature Living*. I'm a nobody who's going nowhere. But first, I'm going to Vegas. It'll take three days to get there, but it'll seem like a lifetime since I'm traveling with a busload of seventeen softball teammates who, collectively, are experiencing a synchronized mid-life crisis. They call themselves the Aging Bulls, and they're heading to a tournament. (Who out there likes beer league softball? Anyone? Anyone? Bueller?) Once we reach Las Vegas, I'll wait for the team to lose the first two games in their initial best-of-three series, then I'll return to New York and get on with my life. Forgive me if I sound less than excited, and I'll forgive you if you don't read the rest of this story.

Today I interviewed fifty-eight-year-old Leo Tarriso, a part-time first baseman and public defendant who, prior to our chat, was relieved of his driving duties after a mishap involving wild boar, sleet, and the state of Ohio. We spoke on the bus while waiting for his teammates to repair the damage.

Me: Interesting way to kick things off, Mr. Tarriso.

Leo: Okay, listen, I admit the accident was my fault. Everyone was counting on me to keep them safe, and I should not have gotten distracted. I take full responsibility. That said, I did not hit anything, technically, except corn. And who ever heard of a horde of wild boar running toward a moving vehicle during a sleet storm in June? In Toledo, for God's sake!

Me: You mean a "singular."

Leo: Huh?

Me: A group of boar is called a "singular of boar."

Leo: Hmm. Makes it sound like one of them is the same as the whole group.

Me: That was a brave maneuver, swerving into the cornfield to avoid a total catastrophe.

Leo: Not as brave as you were signing up for this trip.

Me: I don't think "brave" is the word I'd use.

Leo: Well, it takes a courageous person to plow into the unknown, whether it's a cornfield or a cross-country trip with the Aging Bulls.

Me: So, how did the Bulls qualify for this tournament?

Leo: Oh, it was hilarious. Sal heard about a senior softball tournament happening in early April in Asbury Park. Nine teams, two days, single elimination, with a trip to Vegas on the line. He signed us up on a lark, just to get us a little practice before our regular season. Only ten of us could make it that weekend, but we played out of our minds, winning all eight of our games. Vinnie Shalers pitched his heart out. Slate Hetan hit like Aaron Judge. Benny Eggan made a few ridiculous diving catches. It was like we actually knew what we were doing.

Me: Were the other teams any good?

Leo: They were awesome! We didn't stand a chance against any of them, but our catcher, Rocco Rupacava, noticed that seven of the other eight teams were using illegal bats. When he alerted the tournament brass, they disqualified those teams and gave us all seven wins. So we only had to *really* beat one team. And those guys were all in their early eighties, former high school teammates celebrating the anniversary of their 1955 state baseball title. Guess they just wanted to get together one more time before, you know, they got called up to the big club in the sky. But what a sweet group of men they were. It was really touching to see the love they had for each other.

Me: How'd the game go?

Leo: Oh, we crushed 'em. Couldn't pass up an excuse to go to Vegas.

Me: What's it like to be a member of the Aging Bulls?

Leo: Well, I've been lucky in my life to have a great group of friends from my hometown and another group from college, guys who'd give you the shirts off their backs, although no one would want to see any of them shirtless. Unfortunately, because of time and distance, we don't get together much anymore. But the Bulls have filled that void for me. The guys on this team really support one another. It's the kind of support that often takes the form of psychological warfare and aggravated assault, but that's beside the point. Mostly though, we offer a sense of belonging, a feeling that we're part of something. When you get to be our age, Isabel, you learn to appreciate friendships like these. You must have a group of folks you're close with, right?

Me: Sure.

Leo: Okay, good. Cherish those people. Because not everyone has that.

Me: Really? Not everyone has a support group of middle-aged, beer-swilling besties?

Leo: Exactly.

Me: What's your role on the team?

Leo: On the field, I share first base duties with Darryl Shonjon and several other Bulls who don't move too well anymore, which works out great for Darryl and me because neither of us minds taking a healthy scratch now and then. Off the field, I fill a more important role. Out of all of us, I'm generally considered the most responsible. So, I'm the guy who all the Bulls tell their wives they're out with at night. It's a blessing and a curse.

Me: So, the most responsible man here is the one who crashed the bus?

Leo: Hey, we went over this already. Boar. Sleet. Toledo. Cut me some slack.

Me: What are the chances the Aging Bulls can win this tournament?

Leo: I'd say about the same chances the 1980 Olympic hockey team had against the Russians. Wait, maybe Al Michaels will announce our championship game. Do you believe in miracles, Isabel Dominguez?

Me: No.

Leo: Well, when the Bulls win it all, I'll look just like Jim Craig celebrating with the American flag wrapped around my shoulders.

Me: Who?

Leo: Jim Craig, the goalie for the hockey team that won gold in Lake Placid. That was only like, what, seventeen years before you were born?

Me: Okay, Boomer.

Leo: Esiason? Love that guy, former Terp. On another note, are you in the market for a boyfriend? A few of us have sons around your age. I could give you their contact info.

Me: Um, I'm good.

I stop the recording and thank Leo, who shakes my hand and gallops away to sniff out a Yuengling. After bringing the bus back to life, Bo Loth buckles up in the driver's seat, steers the vehicle out of the cornfield, and gets us back onto the highway. Clouds thicken, and the interior of the bus grows darker. From what I can tell, Bo is one of the quieter Bulls. I pull my hoodie over my head and curl up in my seat, knowing he won't bother me.

Ten miles outside of South Bend, the team stops at a burger joint to pick up dinner. Pretending to sleep, I stay on board and ignore whoever's tapping on my shoulder and whispering my name. Fifteen minutes later, I open my eyes. On the seat next to me: a paper bag containing a bacon cheeseburger, a veggie burger, onion rings, and sweet potato fries. In a cardboard cup-holder next to the bag: a water and a Coke.

The bus rolls again.

As I wolf down the cheeseburger, I think back on my inter-view with Leo, who was open and genuine, and for lack of a more fitting description, "grandfatherly." He seems comfortable with his place on the Bulls, confident with his place in life, and I can't imagine anyone less like him than me.

It's past eleven when we arrive at our motel in a Chicago suburb, and frustration is the only thing keeping me awake. Sal checks the team in and hands out keys. After checking myself in, I lug my suitcase to my room and flop onto the bed, my chest tight, my cheeks heated. I want to go back home, which is crazy, because for the longest time, I just wanted out.

I think back to my First Holy Communion when I was seven. It was cold in Our Lady of Mercy that day. The heat wasn't working, someone had said. The music was pretty, the candles were nice, the incense stunk. I fidgeted in a frilly dress, wriggled in tight shoes. My hair had been blown out to crucify the curls. A lacey veil irritated the back of my neck, its ugly headband digging into my scalp. I felt like a young bride being given away to a ghost. I waited for the Eucharist, held out my hands like a beggar before Father Antonio, in his white robe, placed the papery wafer on my tongue. I hated the texture, the blandness, the taste of nothing, while Mami fingered her rosaries and hated that I wasn't a believer. Back home on Barker Avenue, the old folks outside our building celebrated my arrival. In our apartment, pink and white decorations hung on the walls. "Ava Maria" played on the stereo. Mami hummed along while arranging platters of rice and beans, plantains, and tamales on the table. I was mad at her (and her big, fat belly) for making a huge deal out of the day and hoped her new baby would steal the spotlight from me soon. I sat in the living room where Papi told his friends how far I could throw, how fast I could run. I sat in the kitchen where Mami told her cousins that my hair was too curly, that my manners were shit. God, how I wanted to be somewhere else, someplace where I could just be myself.

DAY TWO

MY PHONE ALARM, "Blue World" by Mac Miller, goes off at 6 a.m. Eyes still shut, I roll onto my back and wonder where I am. Then I remember and yank the covers over my head. When I emerge again, I check to see if Kay or my mom has texted or called, but the only text I have is from the Aging Bulls group chat.

Sal: Wheels up for Nebraska at 7 sharp.

The motel room smells like mildew and gloom. I make some coffee and reach into my backpack for my journal, which I haven't opened since starting at *Mature Living* over a year ago. I want to write about Mami's sickness, or what happened at the truck stop, but as usual, I'd rather do anything than spill out my feelings.

Three months after Papi died, Mami's best friend, Senora Rojas, suggested I keep a journal. She lived a few apartment doors down from us. For my twelfth birthday, she gave me a bag of school supplies and a thick, leather-bound book full of blank pages; she said writing about my feelings might help me deal with my loss. She told me keeping a journal had gotten her through years of sorrow. I stuffed her gift into my closet and didn't think about it again until winter break, two days before Christmas. My first entry wasn't exactly full of deep thoughts.

...I hope Mami gets me everything on my list this year, especially an iPod since she didn't get one for me last year. It's the least she can do for all the times I translate things for her and help her spell English words... Sixth grade is so easy. I'm getting A's in every subject except science which I'm getting an A+ in because it's even easier than everything else. My math teacher is Mr. Waxman and he's so mean. He tries to catch me making mistakes, but he can't because I never do. I'm probably smarter than him anyway... My winter training coach is weird and annoying. His name is Mr. Roberts and he's always trying to get me to join his club team. The boy who helps him is Francisco. He's really, really cute. I think he's in high school...

I pack my stuff and meet the team in the motel parking lot, where they're standing around the Anonybus, scratching their heads and mumbling like kindergarteners trying to solve a trigonometry equation.

"What's the problem?" I ask.

The answer: we won't be hitting the road anytime soon due to a flat front tire. The culprit: a shard of boar tusk. (Webb Ucho discovered the flat at dawn when he heard hissing coming from the bus while massaging his calves with a foam roller on the sidewalk after his daily five-mile run.) Bo Loth has contacted several local tire shops, but they don't have bus tires in stock, and getting one will take twenty-four hours. Rodney Pittbase consoles Leo Tarriso, who weeps openly upon hearing that, presumably, he killed one of the boar. And the miserable twelve-hour day ahead of me has just become more miserable.

On the hunt for supplies to repair the bus, Bo sets off for

a Home Depot a quarter mile away. Clete Shuheg tags along. Benny calls a deli across the road and places an order for eighteen egg sandwiches. As he and Rodney skitter off to pick them up, I go back to my room to work on my Bulls story, but my heart isn't in it. Other than almost dying on the bus yesterday, this whole experience has been a "wild bore." I'd rather watch a race between drying paint and growing grass. I never hang out with guys thirty years older than me, and if they utter one more corny dad joke, I never will again. There's not a generation gap between us, there's a generation crater. I'm pissed that this meaningless story, if ever published, will forever bear my byline, and I hope I'm able to get a new job before anyone sees it. I've already started looking, though I haven't told Kay.

Benny bangs on my door and tells me breakfast has arrived. I leave my room and find a bocce game has broken out on the motel grass: Nick and Harold vs. Sal and Darryl. The rest of the Bulls recline in beach chairs on the lawn, eating and cursing and cheering like Romans at a gladiator fight. Irritated motel guests awaken and leer out their windows as the heckling escalates to an alarming level. My head aching, I find an extra chair and sit down with my sandwich and the coffee Rodney bought me.

The motel manager, a twig of a man wearing a turtleneck and a porkpie hat, storms out of his office. "Ahh, hello, pardon me," he says. "What do you fellas think you're doing?"

"Kicking their asses," Darryl shouts, pointing at Nick and Harold. "My man Sal's a ringer. In bocce, I team up with an Italian dude every time." Then Darryl looks around and adds, "Sorry, Leo, wherever you are."

The Bulls explode with laughter while Leo Tarriso, on a beach chair next to me, frowns and wipes his eyes, still upset about the boar.

"That's it," says the manager, pulling out his phone. "I'm calling the cops."

Vinnie Shalers peacocks over and throws an arm around the manager. "Hold on, let's act like civilized human beings here," he says, slipping the guy a fifty. "Here you go, tiger, keep it fair."

The manager glances at the bill and slides it into his pocket. "All right," he says, "but keep the noise down to a low roar."

"Of course, one hundred percent." Vinnie shakes the man's hand. "We've got nothing but respect for this, um, motor inn? Lodge?"

As the manager shuffles off, Benny jabs Vinnie in the ribs. "Fast money, fast friends, right, Vin?"

"First thing my dad ever taught me," Vinnie says, holding up his sunglasses to the sunlight, checking for smudges.

I re-wrap my half-eaten egg sandwich, place it on the ground, and fiddle with my ponytail, trying to remember the first thing my dad taught me. Was it how to grip a softball, four fingers across the seams, some space between the ball and my palm, allowing for a strong wrist snap? Was it how to sprint to first base, in a straight line on the balls of my feet, arms pumping tight to my sides? Was it how to field a groundball, gliding in with my glove down and timing my steps: right, left, catch, right, left, throw? Or was it that no matter how much I practiced, I'd never be perfect?

Bo and Clete return from the hardware store with two bags of supplies. The Bulls admire Bo as he MacGyvers the tire, filing down the boar tusk, slathering rubber sealant over the compromised area, and using an air compressor to inflate the tube. In less than an hour, the Anonybus is good as new.

"You're a genius, Loth," Bryson says before plucking his guitar and crooning Journey's "Wheel in the Sky."

"Yeah, you can't hit for shit," Slate adds. "But it's nice to know you're good for something."

Clete saunters over and inspects the tire. "Looks okay to me," he says, petting his goatee. "And I got us a discount with my Home Depot credit card." He rubs his beer belly. "No hurry, but you guys owe me $8.40 each. I'll text you my Venmo."

We climb onto the bus, and I take my seat in the front. I tug at the neckline of my Nike sweatshirt, dreading another long drive, wondering how Mami and Ava are faring without me at home, hoping my sister's sugar levels are steady and my mother's keeping track of her doctor appointments. Checking email on my phone, I find a reply from the *Poughkeepsie Journal* in response to a job application I sent them last week. They say there are no openings at the paper now, but they'd like to set up an introductory phone call with me after Labor Day. Their timeline doesn't align with my urgency, but I accept.

Meanwhile, the Bulls have settled in, and we're ready to go. Behind the wheel, Benny adjusts his seat and the mirrors. I sit back and pull my Yankees cap over my eyes.

"Everyone good?" Benny yells as the engine revs.

"Hold on a sec," someone says. "Where's Hank?"

"Jesus Christ," Slate says. "Sornecki's the worst."

I lift my cap. Leo strolls up the aisle, stops next to me, and addresses the team: "I'll check Hank's room. What number was it?"

"We were in 105," Benny says. "I heard puking last night, but I thought it was part of a dream where I drank a whole bottle of Casamigos."

"That wasn't a dream," Nick yells from the back. The Bulls laugh, and Leo skips off the bus.

"Speaking of Casamigos," Rocco shouts, "who's ready?" The catcher pops open a fresh bottle.

Five minutes later, Leo staggers onto the bus, propping up a sickly Hank Sornecki, who pinballs halfway down the aisle before crumbling onto one of the couches.

"What the fuck happened, Hank?" Slate says.

Flat on his back, a hairy forearm draped over his eyes, Hank mumbles something about pepperoni nachos. Then he rolls onto his side and yacks into Rocco's batting helmet.

After a cleanup, we hit the highway, the open windows

doing little to eliminate the lingering funk of Hank's vomit. My head throbs as Bryson conducts a singalong, warbling through Led Zeppelin's entire catalog by the time we hit Iowa. In the backseat, Rocco and Biff bicker about Walnut Gap's commercial real estate market. As I root through my bag looking for Advil, someone smacks me on the shoulder.

"Ouch." I look up at Slate Hetan clutching a can of PBR.

He takes a swig and belches. "What's your problem, Dominguez?" He wipes his mouth with the back of his hand. "You've been in a pissy mood since we left."

"Excuse me?" I say.

"You're like a little black cloud in a baseball hat," he says. "Gonna have any fun or just cry the whole time?"

"I'm not crying," I say. "This just isn't my idea of a good time."

"Maybe not, but why drag the rest of us down?"

I turn toward the window. "Whatever."

"You think you're better than us just because you were a college softball star?"

"Star?" I say under my breath. "Hardly."

Five hours into the drive, we stop at a tourist trap in Des Moines called Apocalypse Pizza. Shivering in the fetal position, Hank stays on the bus, his arms wrapped around Rocco's helmet, while the rest of us march inside the restaurant. Heavy metal music jars my bones as we sit around a skull-shaped table featuring a two-foot-tall volcano centerpiece sculpted out of burnt pizza crust and oozing blood-red mozzarella cheese. I find a spot next to Bo and scan the menu on my placemat.

"Anything look good?" he shouts over Black Sabbath's "Children of the Grave" blaring out of the ceiling speakers.

"Not really," I yell. "Who picked this spot anyway?"

"Harold did," Bo says, leaning into my ear. "He keeps an alphabetical list of U.S. attractions and tries to visit at least one per year. He told me Apocalypse Pizza is second on the list, right after Aardvark Adventureland in Boca Raton."

The lighting in the place is drab, and I have to squint to see the decor. The walls are decorated with glowing neon murals depicting natural disasters. The college-aged waitstaff—two guys and two girls with their noses in their phones—slouch against a painted scene of a tsunami. They wear different-colored hats shaped like horses' heads and carry plastic weaponry on their belts.

One of the girls trots over to our table. "Welcome to the apocalypse. I'm Tiffany, the Horseman of Famine, and I'll be your server today. Can I start you off with some drinks?"

Sal looks up from his menu. "I'll make this easy on you, Tiff," he says. "We'll take six pitchers of Bud Light and five pies: the Doomsday, the End Times, the Prophecy, the Armageddon, and um, let's see, what do you think? The Nuclear or the Wildfire?"

The Horseman of Famine puts her pen to her lip. "The Nuclear is good," she says, "but if you like really, *really* spicy, I'd go with the Wildfire."

"Done," Sal says. "And throw in a few Day of Reckoning salads."

"Okay, just to let you know," Tiffany says, "the End Times and Armageddon take a little longer to cook, but I'll bring each pie out when it's ready. My co-worker, the Horseman of Conquest, will be right over with your beer."

I tap Bo on the elbow. "Wanna talk while we wait for the world to end?"

"Sure," he says, and we move to a rickety, earthquake-themed table nearby.

June 24 notes:

So far today, the Bulls bribed a motel manager into letting them play a noisy game of bocce; they paid less than nine dollars apiece to patch a flat tire; and one player threw up pepperoni nachos, which might've tasted better coming up than going down.

The subject of today's interview is Bo Loth, one of the team's outfielders, originally from Virginia, quiet and country-strong. He's a forty-nine-year-old stay-at-home dad and handyman extraordinaire who fixed the flat. He's not one to ratchet up the excitement, but compared to the other guys, he has the fewest screws loose.

I caught up with him—which was easy since his name rhymes with "slow sloth"—when we stopped at a pizza place in Iowa, halfway to Las Vegas. He wore construction boots, jeans, a white T-shirt, and a half-smile. With a *Rainman*-ish look in his eyes, Bo noted our wobbly table, produced a large Swiss Army knife, and sawed down two of the table legs till he was satisfied.

Me: How difficult was fixing that tire this morning?

Bo: Not too bad. I've never seen a boar tusk stuck in a tire before, but you gotta be prepared for anything. I used a strong sealant, so it should hold for a few days.

Me: Where'd you learn your DIY skills?

Bo: Mostly from my dad, who learned a lot growing up in rural Alabama without electricity, plumbing, or telephone service.

Me: You do a lot for the Bulls off the field, but what about on the field? And what do they do for you?

Bo: I give them an occasional big hit and some solid outfield play. I'm not a great player, but I try to help however I can, and they give me a chance to socialize on my own terms. I like being by myself but hanging with these guys once a week in the summer is fun.

Me: You seem like a low-key guy, not as immature as the rest. Am I off base there, or have you noticed that too?

Bo: I notice.

Me: Got any kids? You get them starter toolbelts yet?

Bo: Yeah, I have two kids, a boy and a girl. I try to teach them how to fix stuff, but they don't seem too interested. I was probably like that too when I was their age. My daughter is patient and confident and likes to figure things out. She doesn't love going with me to the hardware store, but at least she's learning it's not just for boys.

Me: That's cool, you're showing her she's equal.

Bo: I'm not a caveman.

Me: Maybe not in that respect, but where my parents grew up, girls weren't taught the same stuff as boys, and men treated women as inferiors. In Latin America, it's called "machismo."

Bo: Did your dad raise you that way?

Me: No, he didn't believe in that. He wanted me to be confident and tough, and I was like that when I played softball, but off the field, I'm definitely an in-the-background kind of person.

Bo: You seem confident and tough to me. And you're smart and funny too.

Me: I'm smart compared to the Aging Bulls. But funny? No one's laughed at anything I've said this whole trip.

Bo: You haven't really said anything though.

Me: I was kidding.

Bo: Sorry, sarcasm goes right over my head. But I think you've got the whole package, Isabel, and not to be creepy, but you're pretty too.

Me: Pretty? I don't think so. The best compliment I ever got was in high school, when our star quarterback called me a "less-hot Selena Gomez." Then he asked me to the prom.

Bo: Really? Did you go?

Me: That's not the point, but yeah, I did. And the next day, he ghosted me.

Bo: He what?

Me: Never mind.

After Bo's offhand comment, I'm even more self-conscious than usual, and I make a mental note not to talk about my looks with old married white dudes. In my home country, a girl's appearance is held to an Everest-high standard; Venezuela is a breeding ground for Miss Universe contestants. If I had a buck for every time my own mother got mistaken for J-Lo, I'd shop at Urban Outfitters instead of Marshalls. I've always been bitter about the beauty Mami didn't pass down to me, ashamed of my wide shoulders, pointy chin, big nose. Being around the Bulls doesn't help, because even though they're older and respectful, they're still guys, applying their own standards of beauty to me. For the remainder of the trip, I'll be happy to hide under my Yankees cap and baggy sweatshirt.

On the road after lunch, I scroll through glossy Instagram posts from two of my former college softball teammates vacationing in Cabo. I unclench my jaw and Google articles about the saturated journalism job market, the dying print media industry, and Latinas in the workplace. Then I go down a rabbit hole and land on a column called "The Impact of Structural Racism in Employment and Wages on Minority Women's Health." I copy the link and paste it into my Notes app.

In the back of the bus, Hank convulses with dry heaves, as the other Bulls drink and laugh while re-watching *Bull Slurham* for the third time since we left Chicago. Somewhere outside of Omaha, I doze off and sleep most of the five remaining hours to Big Springs. We pull into a Red Roof Inn, gather our luggage, and step into the cold Nebraska night. Slate stretches his inked-up arms toward the stars. He's wearing the same white T-shirt, black shorts, and grubby Maryland Terrapins cap that he's worn since I met him.

"This place has *good enough for me* written all over it," he says with more heartfelt satisfaction than anyone has ever expressed for a Red Roof Inn.

We huddle in the motel office, and I check in first. After checking in the Bulls, Sal hands out keys. "There's an all-night diner next door if anyone's hungry," he says. "What do you guys think? Meet up in ten minutes?"

The Bulls agree, split into pairs, and strut away to drop off their things. I sling my backpack over my shoulder and begin to walk to my room.

"How about you, Dominguez?" Slate says. "Feel like joining us?"

I keep walking. "Thanks, but I've had enough of you for the day."

DAY THREE

WHEN I WAKE in my dingy motel room, a small piece of me wishes I'd gone to dinner with the guys, but whatever. I'm more concerned about the weather alert on my phone: tornado warnings from Nebraska to Colorado. *Great,* I think, *our morning route will be littered with twisters.*

I consider going for a quick jog before we leave, but the sky looks angry. I haven't run in months, expending all my energy working at the office, searching for a job, and filling in at Café Isabel. I want to get in a workout, but the closest thing to gym equipment at the motel is a light fixture made out of a bicycle rim hanging in the main office. Although this assignment is an exercise in futility, it won't make me break a sweat. I resort to a superset of jumping jacks and sit-ups while watching *Good Morning, America.* The thin carpet is prickly on my back, and I find myself remembering the itchy dress I wore to my father's funeral—that and the fact that there were more people at the church than all the fans at all the games I'd ever played. Seemed like the entire Bronx shut down just for him. My cousin told me it was because Papi had been a famous baseball player, a legend back in Caracas, and sure enough, two rows of pews were roped off and reserved for members of the Yankees. Even a guy who

38

played for the Red Sox showed up, a tall man with long dark hair and intense green eyes. Later at the cemetery, he crouched in front of me, said he was sorry, and told me he'd spent two winters playing against Papi in Venezuela. He said "El Toro" was the best hitter he'd ever seen, and a talented catcher too. They were rivals back then, but they had respect for each other. "Your father was good enough to make the majors," he said, lowering his head, "but the injury was too much. I wish things had been different, wish he got to live his dream." When the player stood, his joints crackled and popped like the bowl of Rice Krispies I'd barely touched at breakfast.

I was glad to learn more about my father's baseball career, but I already knew how it ended: While Edgar "El Toro" Dominguez recovered from a knee injury, his wife, Magdalena, had a baby girl. When Edgar's knee got worse, and his six-month rehab became two years, he and "Maggy" moved their young family to New York, rented a two-bedroom apartment on the top floor of a six-story walkup, and called that place home. Edgar gave up the game, became a U.S. citizen, and opened Café Isabel on Jerome Avenue.

As soon as I could throw a ball, Papi would come home from work at four in the afternoon, seven days a week, and hurry with me to Reiss Field, a dusty diamond two blocks from our apartment. He'd pitch to me, hit me grounders and fly balls, and chase me around the bases till dinner time. I'd get so mad because he never let me beat him to home plate. I remember carrying my black Mizuno glove and yellow Easton bat down the sidewalk, back and forth every day, to and from that field, all year long, in rain and cold and brutal heat.

"No complaining, it's all part of the game," my father would tell me. "You might play for a championship in bad weather someday, might as well get used to it."

But it's hard not to complain on a morning like this. In the shower after my workout, I cut my leg shaving thirty seconds before the hot water runs out. I soap up and rinse off while a trickle of blood freezes halfway down my shin. Teeth chattering, I get dressed, pack, and drop off my key at the motel office. My hair frizzing from a drizzle, I stuff the rat's nest under my baseball cap. As I slough through the muddy lot with my suitcase in tow, Benny zips past me and splatters mud on the Air Jordans I had to save up for.

"Oh, shoot," he says. "Sorry, Iz."

"Sure you are," I mutter, and a new angle for the Bulls story occurs to me: an exposé of upper-class men blind to their own privilege, men who have no idea how much more they have than most other people.

On board, I borrow a tube of Clorox Handi-Wipes from Bo and try to clean off my sneakers, avoiding eye contact with the other Bulls as they parade onto the bus and track mud on the purple carpeting.

Nick Chinsola settles into the driver's seat. "Good morning, Isabel," he says, stiff and cheery. "Sleep okay?"

"Fine," I say, still focused on my ruined Jordans.

By 8 a.m., all of the Bulls are accounted for in the bus except one. Outside, Hank is alone in the parking lot, doubled over, rain dripping off his head as he ejects more pepperoni nachos from his gut. When he stumbles into his seat, the team gives him a standing ovation, and we're on our way. The plan: get to Las Vegas before midnight.

I spend the next hour scanning LinkedIn job postings, listening to music, and picking at a stale whole wheat bagel Wink brought me from the diner. Even with AirPods in, I can hear Rodney and Harold tracking the tornadoes, comparing Doppler radar updates on competing weather apps. The sky grows darker, and the trees along the highway sway as the Bulls drink Bloody Marys and rehash the highlights of their team's seven-year existence. The talk gets heated when it comes to the pitching staff, mainly Vinnie Shalers and Clete Shuheg. And tensions rise when some argue that Rocco, who'd performed well in the circle in emergency situations, is equal among the other hurlers.

"Although he's our catcher, I think Rocco's one of our best pitchers," Bryson says, cradling his guitar like a baby. "No offense to Vinnie or Clete, because those guys are great pitchers as well."

"Nah, I'm just a backup," Rocco says with a brashness that suggests he wants to be more than a backup. "I don't belong in the same conversation as our two studs."

Vinnie stands in the aisle. "I wholeheartedly agree with Bryson," he says, untangling the three gold chains around his neck. "Rocco, to his credit, has pitched great recently, as good as Clete, if not better."

"Well, I disagree," Clete says, picking bagel crumbs out of his goatee. "I've checked the scorebooks for the past five years, Shalers, and my ERA is at least a run less than yours, so if Rocco's better than anyone, it's you."

"Oh yeah, that's right, Clete," Vinnie says, adjusting his sunglasses. "And who keeps those stats? Oh, I forgot, you do, and you're not exactly Switzerland."

"But his gut's as big as Switzerland," Webb cracks.

Above me, a disco ball swings in circles as the wind wiggles the bus.

"Hey guys, can we stop fighting?" Rodney interrupts in his island accent. "We've got some serious weather heading our way, man."

Slate jumps in. "Relax, Rodney, and make yourself a drink."

"This is n-n-no joke, Slate," Harold adds.

Slate pulls back the drapes, peers at the coal-black clouds and tilting trees. "So it's a little windy," he says. "You pussies are killing my buzz."

Just then I get a text from my mother.

Mami: Chemo starts tomorrow.

Me: I thought it started next week.

Mami: The doctor suggested a change.

Me: Do you want me to come home?

Mami: No, I'll be fine.

Her response doesn't surprise me; my mother rarely shows her emotions. She kept her feelings under wraps while raising two kids and helping my father run the restaurant, and after he died, she shut them down for good. She used to let loose only when pushing me to improve my grades or work harder in softball. Still, most of the time I tune her out because I put more pressure on myself than she ever could.

The bus rocks as the bluster gains strength, inside and out. Vinnie and Clete continue their spat, teetering in the aisle, facing one another while holding onto swivel chairs.

"You can ask any of our pals back in Staten Island," Clete says, "and none of them will say you're better than me, Shalers."

"And you can ask any hitter in our league," Vinnie says, "and all of them will say they'd rather bat against you than me."

Rodney leaps to his feet and holds his phone in the air. "Guys, please stop!" he shouts. "The radar says there's a major tornado heading our way."

I look at Nick sitting rigid as a metal girder at the wheel, locked in on the road. Sensing my stare, he turns to me and arches an eyebrow. As I fumble with my phone to check the forecast, another text comes through from my mother.

Mami: Ava is staying at a friend's tonight. Please check on her tomorrow while I'm at the hospital.

Me: Of course. Are you sure I shouldn't come home? I could get a flight tonight from Denver.

Mami: No, Isabel. I'm fine.

Me: You don't have to do this alone.

Mami: Just check on your sister please.

Me: Promise you'll tell me if you need me.

While I wait for her reply, I think of the bind we're in. My mom and sister don't have health insurance. And unless I find a new job, we won't be able to afford Mami's chemotherapy or Ava's insulin, even with Medicaid. Also we'll lose our restaurant.

Rain breaks through the black sky and covers the windshield in a watery cloak. Nick flips the wipers on high speed. Meanwhile, Vinnie and Clete have inched closer to each other and now stand nose-to-nose, red-faced and shouting.

"Tell me to my mug that you're better than me," Clete growls, beating his belly like a war drum.

"Not only am I better than you," Vinnie says, poking a finger into his rival's chest, "but I'm the only one, other than Rocco perhaps, who should pitch in Las Vegas."

"Oh yeah?" Clete says.

"Yeah!" Vinnie says.

The rain comes down in buckets. Nick swerves into the slow lane as the Anonybus rocks out of control like a rodeo bull. Vinnie and Clete sneer and snort, bracing themselves between the spinning chairs. Someone wails in the backseat, and we all stand and look.

"Everyone sit down!" Nick shouts. "This thing could tip any second."

"My bad," Hank groans from the backseat. "And sorry about the smell."

Everyone sits except for Vinnie and Clete, still stuck in their stalemate.

"Look! It's r-r-right there!" Harold yells, pointing out the window at a giant twister chugging across the Colorado plains. "Speed up, Nick!"

The bus lurches forward. Hanging onto the swivel chairs, Vinnie and Clete fight to keep their balance. I look out the window at the tornado as my phone buzzes; it's my mother calling. I stuff the phone into my pocket.

Balling up his fist, Clete screams in Vinnie's face. "I'm gonna shut you up once and for all, you no good weasel."

Rodney cries out, "Guys, please!"

Clete cocks his arm. But before his fist flies, Vinnie crouches low and digs his fingers into Clete's stomach. "You ticklish, motherfucker?" he says, bobbing and kneading. "Huh? You ticklish?"

The adversaries giggle. The twister passes. Five minutes later, the weather clears. I look around the bus at the cast of characters and consider the craziness. It's like I'm being punked, and everyone else is in on the joke.

Rodney minds the wheel while an exhausted Nick sits across from me. He dials his phone and bends over, his head resting on his hand. I assume he's calling his wife and kids to tell them about our brush with death. Then I hear him whisper, "Yes, I took care of that. I told you yesterday." Behind us, a clatter builds. Nick speaks louder and plugs a finger in his ear. "I know, I know. I will," he huffs. "We don't have to talk about this now."

Hank groans. "Oh, god, here it comes again." And he lets loose something that sounds like a dying goat.

"C'mon, Hank!" blares Benny.

"Goddammit!" shouts Slate.

"Holy Christ!" Rocco roars. "Are you still using my helmet?"

As Hank chucks it up, the Bulls yuk it up—all except for

Nick, who presses his phone to his chest, whips his head around, and yells, "Can you guys shut up back there?"

The bus quiets for a moment, and when Nick hangs up, Leo slinks into the seat behind him and puts a hand on his shoulder. "Everything okay?"

"Yeah, fine," Nick says. "Just some family stuff."

As Leo returns to the back, Nick locks his fingers atop his Jake Gyllenhaal hairdo and looks across the aisle at me. "Sorry about that."

"You're fine," I say, knowing I need another interview with a Bull at some point and figure a conversation with an irritated Nick will be quick, if not painless. "Think I could ask you a few questions?"

He sucks his bottom lip, shakes his head. "Now's not a good time."

"Cool." I pop in my AirPods and fish out my book, *All That You Had*, from my backpack. If I had to guess, I'd say Nick's having marriage problems. Either that or his kids aren't speaking to him because he's a hothead who can't relate to them, probably never takes the time to try. I pull my shirt up over my nose. The stink of Hank's vomit has taken over the bus. Poking my head into the aisle, I steal a look at the ill man lying in the back, pale faced and groaning, holding his stomach.

Noting Hank's torment in the rearview mirror, Rodney parks the bus at a scenic overlook. "Okay, guys," the Trinidadian says. "We can get out here and stretch, and there's a food truck if anyone's hungry."

"Great idea," says Biff, who's been asleep the entire day.

I get off the bus and hike toward the edge of a massive gorge called Devil's Canyon. According to Google maps, we're off Route 70 in Utah, just south of Moab. A few of the Aging Bulls snap pics of the gorge. Some make calls to their wives. Most assemble around the food truck, which specializes in grilled cheese sandwiches and sports a sign: *Grate Expectations!*

Staggering away from the rest of the herd, Hank flumps onto a picnic table bench. He drops his head, gags and coughs. When his tremors subside, he leans back and closes his eyes. Baking in the summer sun, he wipes off the sweat puddled in his fuzzy eyebrows and takes several deep breaths while I sit perched on a guardrail nearby.

"Hey, great trip, huh?" he says in my direction.

"Yeah, awesome."

"You wouldn't happen to have any water in your backpack, would you?"

"It's half empty and a day old," I say, "but it's all yours if you want it." I pluck the warm bottle out of my pack and walk it over to Hank, who guzzles the contents.

"Thanks," he says wiping his mouth. "You're a lifesaver."

"Want to repay the favor and give me an interview?"

"Sure," he says with a smirk. "But if I were you, I'd keep a splatter-proof distance."

I sit across the picnic table. Hank's face is white as a sheet, but he shows signs of life. His gray T-shirt (with a picture of a tank on the front) is soaked in sweat, and a tumbleweed of chest hair pushes out from the neckline. I set the voice recorder on my phone and admire Devil's Canyon, an expanse like nothing I've seen growing up in New York, beautiful and terrifying. Its sparse terrain, plateaus, and rock formations belong on another planet. The sun beats down. A buzzard circles overhead.

June 25 notes:

Except for Slate Hetan, the Bulls have been pretty nice to me so far, which I sort of don't get, because I haven't gone out of my way to be nice to them. I'm beginning to think that it's all an act, that they just want me to make them look good in the story. I can't help but wonder what they're like when there's not a reporter around, especially a young, brown female reporter.

My interview today is with Henry "Hank" Sornecki, the youngest Bull (at 46). From what I hear, he's an "unexpectedly competent" outfielder, and "massively overrated" hitter from Sculville, NJ, a town that sounds as scary as what's happening in Hank's intestines. He reminds me of an amusement park caricature, resembling a real person the way Lego Han Solo resembles Harrison Ford. His teammates say Hank looks like Gru from *Despicable Me*, but I don't see it. Gru's head shape, nose, and eyebrows are far less cartoonish. For our conversation, we sat on a picnic table bench on the edge of Devil's Canyon, at a rest stop off a Utah highway. Hank's the player who's been laid up with food poisoning, but considering how awful he feels, he's polite as can be, which leads me to believe it's all part of his shtick.

Me: So, you've been pretty sick the past couple of days, huh?

Hank: Ugh, yeah. Remind me to lay off the pepperoni nachos next time we hit a truck stop.

Me: Other than the throwing up part, has the road trip gone as expected?

Hank: Well, the bus accident and tornado threw a monkey wrench into the operation, so there was that. Hmm, I wonder if Bo carries a monkey wrench in his toolbox.

Me: What do you love most about being on the Bulls?

Hank: For me, other than hanging out with the guys, it's a tension release. I got four kids under twenty years old and a business that doesn't run very smoothly, mostly because I'm the boss. Thank god for my wife. I don't know how I've fooled her this long.

Me: What about on the field?

Hank: Obviously, it's not the winning that I love. We don't do a ton of that around here. But I'm used to losing, played four years of high school tennis, never won a match. And it's not the competition that I love, unless you count how hard I try to be noncompetitive. So, there's really no on-the-field reason I love this team. Guess it's just the drinking.

Me: The Aging Bulls could be on this trip for three weeks. How can you take so much time off from work?

Hank: Some of us can work remotely, but most guys probably only took a week, since we'd need to win a couple of games to stay longer, and that's not going to happen. What do your parents do?

Me: My mom runs a restaurant in the Bronx that she and my dad started, but he died a long time ago.

Hank: Oh, I'm sorry. Next time I go to a Yankees game, I'll stop by the restaurant. What's the name?

Me: Café Isabel.

Hank: That's cool. But probably seems weird, right? Like you're carrying your family on your shoulders. My kids should open a restaurant someday and call it Hank's Hash House.

Me: Wow, hashtag squad goals.

Hank: So, I'll bet you're pumped to write a story about us, huh?

Me: And I'll bet your house that no one will read it.

Hank: You're on, but if you win, you have to take my kids too.

Me: Ha.

Hank: You never know, Izzy; your story might win a Pulitzer. Stranger things have happened. Look at the Bulls; we're on our way to friggin' Vegas to play for a world championship. Who ever thought that'd be possible?

Me: That's some low-key flex.

Hank: Wait, I've heard my daughter say that. Isn't it like when you're bragging but trying to seem like you're not?

Me: Yup.

It's midnight when we arrive in Las Vegas and pull in front of our hotel, a run-down relic on the north end of the strip. I rub my eyes and look out the window. The place is huge but not fancy, weathered and dusty, green with gold trimmings, like a Middle Eastern palace disguised as a Wild West saloon. Arched above the main entrance, fourteen neon-green letters glitter in the darkness: *Emerald Outpost*.

I topple out of the bus, groggy and grimy, and stand behind a wall of Aging Bulls. Emerging from the hotel, a large man plods toward us wearing a periwinkle leisure suit and a green necktie dotted with dollar signs. "Great to meet you all, I'm Stu Rucosa, Sal's second cousin and owner of this fine establishment." Cousin Stu's natural hair color is surely gray, like Sal's, but he's opted for an orange comb-over. His scent, a funky fusion of Alberto VO5 and snake oil, slithers through the humidity. While he speaks, his arms flitter and jangle, as if he's controlled by a puppeteer. "Welcome to the Emerald Outpost, Sin City's most sinful hotel," he announces, tugging at his collar. "But don't tell your wives, that'll be our little secret."

"Hey, Stu, thanks for the family discount," Sal says after sucking in a yawn. "We appreciate the help, and by the way, the place looks great."

Stu faces his pride and joy. "We're certainly proud of her," he says, beaming. "It's a six-story hotel, but there are three sides to every story: your side, my side, and the truth." Stu turns and winks at his cousin. "What happens at the EO stays at the EO, if you catch my drift."

Harold raises his hand. "What's the history b-b-behind this place?"

"This brilliant edifice, my friend, was constructed in 1958 by my father, Sal's Uncle Silvio." Hands in his pockets, Stu jingles loose change while reciting his spiel. "Over the years, it's been home to all the great entertainers, everyone from Yakov Smirnoff to Bobby Sherman to the masked theatre troupe Mummenschanz."

"Sweet," says Bryson. "Did Thin Lizzy or Little Feat ever play here?"

"I'm afraid not," Stu says. "But a fabulous AM Gold tribute band called the One Hit Blunders plays every night at our Ruby Slipper Lounge, and an Italian reggae band called the Pastafarians has a residency here also. As you can see, we only book top-of-the-line acts."

"Sounds like it," says Benny. "I bet those bands really bring the house down at the Ruby Slipper." Only Hank laughs.

Vinnie shakes Stu's hand. "It's an honor to meet you, sir. May I ask about your gambling facilities and various recreational activities?"

"Well," Stu says, "we have a casino in the lobby with dozens of slots as well as multiple tables for craps, blackjack, poker, and roulette. There's a hot spot called Skat's Bar & Grill where we serve our signature drink, the Razzamatazz, but they also mix a mean Rusty Nail. And there's the lounge, as mentioned. Oh, and we also feature an all-you-can-eat buffet restaurant called Stuffy's 24/7. For a fine dining experience, we have Chachi Hibachi, owned and operated by Scott Baio's sister-in-law's nephew. It's very popular. And out back, we have two swimming pools and a lazy river."

"It sounds awesome," Sal says. "We're all pretty beat. Can you check us in?"

"Of course," Stu says, leading us inside the EO. "I have ten rooms reserved. Sixteen of you will double up. Cousin Sal gets a room for himself, and we have a single for the lady as well."

Stu gives Sal and me our keys while the Bulls pick out room-mates: Slate and Benny; Darryl and Webb; Bryson and Bo; Wink and Rodney; Hank and Leo; Clete and Vinnie; Nick and Harold; Biff and Rocco.

We take the elevator to the third floor, and I shuffle to my room like a zombie. The card key works on the fifth try, and I open the door. After crossing the threshold, I stop in my tracks. Looking around, I suddenly miss the Red Roof Inn. The psyche-delic paint colors and late-60s décor in the room remind me of old-school reruns I'd watch with my dad; I feel like I'm on the set of *The Mod Squad*.

I fling my suitcase and backpack onto the shag carpet, plunk on the edge of the bed, and stare out the window at the skyline. I snatch a pillow and punch it, wishing I hadn't accepted this assignment, wondering again if I should call Kay and quit.

It's 1 a.m. when I turn on the shower. Waiting for the water to warm up, I sit on the bathmat, pull my knees to my chest, and watch the spray hit the wall. Droplets splatter onto my cheeks and take me back to my very first memory. I was three years old, kneeling on blue shag carpeting in our family bathroom, trying not to cry. I'd locked the door and was running water in the tub, making it as loud as I could, hoping to drown out my parents screaming at each other in the hall. They were arguing about me, a fight that had started at the jewelry store. Mami wanted my ears pierced; Papi didn't. She said it was part of our culture, to show off my femininity. That's why she'd taken earrings to the hospital when I was born; she wanted the nurses to do it, but Papi had said no then too. "You should be proud of your daughter," she yelled over the sound of the water. That's when I remember ripping out my new earrings, throwing them in the toilet, and sobbing on that blue carpeting, thinking my father wanted a son instead of me.

DAY FOUR

I ROLL OUT OF bed and open the curtains, revealing a dull morning light. I clump to the bathroom and splash cold water on my puffy eyes. There's no towel on the rack, so I use tissues to dry off. I slip into a pair of black shorts and pull on my gray Tupac T-shirt. I tie my hair back with a scrunchie, step into my flip-flops, and text Ava, like my mother asked me to do.

Me: All good?

Ava: yup why?

Me: Mami told me to check on you.

Ava: she's standing right here

Me: What? She said her treatments were starting today.

Ava: they changed it, something was wrong

Me: Oye, tell her to call me please.

Sitting on the bed, I write in my journal about how Mami and I always get our wires crossed, how we have trouble seeing eye to eye, how Papi and I rarely had that problem. I'm only a few lines in when I realize where this is headed. I drop the pen and close the book. Even though Senora Rojas gave me the journal so I could write about my dad's death, I'm still not ready to go there. Avoiding the topic has become a habit of mine.

Halfway through seventh grade, I'd written in my journal only a dozen times since receiving it eighteen months earlier. I was too busy, overscheduled with softball lessons, tutoring, working at Café Isabel, and violin, Mami's new obsession for me. Even if I'd thought about my feelings, I wouldn't have had five minutes to write them down. But when spring softball season started, Mami let me drop the violin, and I picked up my journal again, tried to use it at least once a week, mostly to complain.

> ... Today was the first day of middle school practice and my team is terrible. The girl who plays first base can't catch, and the girl who plays third can't reach her anyway. I should ask Coach Xavier if I can play the whole left side of the infield by myself. It's so frustrating. We probably won't win a game all year... It's a good thing Mami doesn't come to my games. She would probably yell at me from the stands if I ever struck out. She drives me crazy and makes me do so many things I don't want to do and expects me to smile through it all. Sometimes I hate her so much...

I take the elevator downstairs to meet the Bulls for breakfast. In the lobby, I bump into Nick and Harold, who are heading in the opposite direction.

"Hey there," Nick says. "Coming to breakfast?"

"Yeah," I say. "Isn't it at the restaurant, Stuffy's, or whatever?"

"Nope," says Harold. "Sal's cousin reserved a b-b-ballroom for our m-m-meals and meetings, sort of like a h-h-home base."

"Cool," I say, noticing Harold's stutter for the first time.

"And you'll love the name of the ballroom," said Nick. "The Taj Meh Hall. Get it?"

I offer an eye roll. "Yes, I get it."

When we enter the ballroom, I realize the terrible pun is the best thing about the place. The Emerald Outpost's signature room, a replica of the famed mausoleum, as tacky as the real Taj Mahal is classy, boasts a design that would get any interior decorator fired: a trompe-l'oeil ceiling giving the optical illusion of a dome; foam arches and spires above the entrance and around the perimeter; and wall-to-wall carpeting with a reflecting pool design. All that's missing is an animatronic Shah Jahan.

By the time we get there, most other Bulls have already filled their plates, all except Bo, who's taken the Anonybus to a repair shop for a replacement tire. The breakfast buffet includes pancakes, sausage, scrambled eggs, toast, hash browns, granola, and raspberry Danishes. Standing in line behind Slate, I watch as he seizes the last pancake, the last sausage, and the last Danish. He turns to me. "Want one of these?"

"No thanks," I say and drop two slices of burnt toast onto my plate, followed by a scoop of runny eggs. My phone buzzes, and I read the text.

Kay: Come back to NY, corporate is freezing our expense account, just use the notes you have so far if we end up needing your story.

Me: Sounds good.

Before I can add the perfect emoji to describe my excitement, my mother calls. I put my plate down, leave the ballroom, and answer the phone. Mami is speaking Spanish, her fallback when she's nervous, same as me.

Mami: Mi tratamiento fue cancelado hoy. (My treatment was canceled today.)

Me: ¿Por que? (Why?)

Mami: Habia algo mal con mi analisis de sangre. (There was something wrong with my blood test.)

Me: Tomare un vuelo esta noche. (I'll catch a flight tonight.)

Mami: No vuelvas solo por me. Tienes un trabajo que hacer. Cerrare el café por un tiempo. (Don't come back just for me. You have a job to do. I'll close the café for a while.)

Me: No podemos permitirnos cerrarlo ahora. (We can't afford to close it now.)

Mami: Esta bien. Tengo una renunion con un agente de bienes raices mañana. Venderemos en unas semanas. (It's okay. I have a meeting with a realtor tomorrow. We'll be selling in a few weeks.)

Me: Mi jefe me enviara a casa de todos modos. Te vere pronto. (My boss is sending me home anyway. I'll see you soon.)

As I hang up, a woman pushing a poodle in a stroller stops a few feet away. The dog growls, and the woman says, "That's right, Ivanka, that girl should learn to speak English or go back to Mexico."

I clench my fists and bite my lip. As I wheel around to head back into the ballroom, Slate blocks my path. "What was that all about?"

"Nothing," I say. "Just an ugly dog with a Karen for an owner."

"How do you know that lady's name?"

"Forget it," I say.

"Who were you on the phone with?"

"TBH, none of your business."

"Hey, lose the slang," he snaps. "My daughters talk that way, and it drives me nuts. I can barely understand people when they talk normal."

"Don't get so salty," I say. "That was my mom on the phone. She's not feeling well, but she doesn't want me to worry. I told her my boss is sending me home, so I'll see her soon."

"You're leaving?" Slate says. "That's bullshit. Who's gonna write our story?"

"Who cares? There probably won't be one anyway. The magazine can't afford to keep me here. Besides, my mom needs help. We own a restaurant, and she can't run it while she's sick."

I return to the ballroom—back to my plate of sad eggs and burnt toast—and sit alone in the corner.

"Okay, we've got an off day today," Sal announces to the team. "Do whatever you want, just don't break too many laws." He looks at Rocco before continuing. "Tomorrow, we start our first round series against West Virginia, so we need everyone ready and available."

I suck down my orange juice, put my dirty dishes in the cleanup bin, and slog toward the door.

Slate yells, "Where are you going, ding dong?"

"To pack," I yell back.

Back in my room, I load up my suitcase. While praying my corporate card doesn't get declined, I book an 8 p.m. flight. With seven hours before I have to leave for the airport, I lower the volume on the TV and try to nap. Ninety sleepless minutes later, a group text comes through.

Slate: Mandatory bonding session at Bellagio Hotel water fountains. That means you too, Dumingez.

I scoff at the misspelling and hot-foot a quarter mile down the Las Vegas strip in hopes that this so-called "bonding session" will provide a morsel of material for whatever skimpy story I might have to write. When I show up at the Bellagio, my sweaty shirt sticks to my skin. Lined along the fountain wall, the Bulls chill in their swimsuits. It's mid-afternoon. The place is crawling with tourists, and two burly security guards lurk nearby.

Slate gathers everyone together and lays out a ridiculous plan: Leo and Vinnie will stand near the hotel entrance, fifty yards from the fountain, and distract the guards with a fake fight about Shalers counting cards at a blackjack table—purportedly cheating Leo out of a thousand bucks. Then, Slate tells the guys, when the guards leave to break up the spat, the Bulls will jump into the water.

I move to the side as Leo and Vinnie assume their positions, begin shouting, and attract a crowd. The guards abandon their posts, and fifteen Bulls rip off their shirts and plunge into the fountain pool.

"C'mon, Dominguez, get in here!" Slate whisper-shouts while treading water. "We've got thirty seconds."

I take a giant step back. "Are you crazy? Not a chance."

He splashes me. I leap to the side, dodging the water. The Bulls scramble out of the fountain and dry off with their shirts. The security guards return to their posts. Leo and Vinnie join their soaked teammates and get high-fives all around.

I sit on the fountain wall away from the fray and check my phone. I still have four hours before I have to leave for the airport.

Slate sidles next to me. "Should've jumped," he says. "Missing all the fun, kid."

I look out at the water. "My loss."

The other Bulls head back to the Emerald Outpost, and Slate waves them on. "We'll catch up."

"What?" I say, slumped on the damp concrete.

"I gotta talk to you." He sounds serious for a change. "About going home to help out your mom—"

I stare straight ahead. "Yeah?"

"Well, I beat you to it."

"What are you talking about?"

"I spoke with your mother."

"You what?" I whack him on the shoulder.

"Calm down," he says. "I called her this afternoon and told her I'd help staff Café Isabel for a few weeks till she feels better. I own a small chain of restaurants. One of my GMs will be there tomorrow with two of my cooks."

I glare at him. "How could you do that without asking me?"

"Better to apologize than ask permission," Slate says. "I got my suppliers on it too. They'll deliver ten food pallets in the next two days. The place will be fully stocked. You got nothing to worry about till the tournament's done."

"I told you," I say. "The magazine is ending my assignment. I'll be home tomorrow, so tell your people we won't need their help."

"Too late," he says as the sun glows over his shoulder. "And hey, you could probably use another interview, right?"

June 26 notes:

During their first full day in Vegas, the Bulls have done nothing of note except illegally swim in the fountains at the Bellagio Hotel. I wonder how they'll spend the final two days of their trip. Wait, I already know: getting trounced on the softball field. Good thing I'm leaving tonight.

My final interview is with the team's most unlikeable player: Slate Hetan, a swashbuckling troglodyte who I can imagine pillaging the town of Walnut Gap with a knife between his teeth. He's a fifty-two-year-old third baseman from New City, NY, who idolizes Daniel Craig and Morris Buttermaker, the kind of person who ponders life's three essential questions: Does pineapple belong on pizza? Should a hot dog be considered a sandwich? And when's last call?

For our talk, we sat by the Bellagio fountains. Slate wore a white T-shirt and a tight pair of short shorts that he either stole from a costume closet on the set of *Casino Royale* or from John Stockton's locker back in 1985. When he spoke, he took his time, choosing his words carefully, as if he had a lot to choose from.

Me: I don't have any questions, and I doubt our readership will care about your escapades, and there's no real story here, and I'm leaving soon anyway so—

Slate: There's always a story. You just gotta look a little harder. But if you're gonna tell it, you'll have to stay.

Me: Well, I'm not staying.

Slate: Hey, I know people, and I sense you got hidden talent. If you stick with us, you'll write the best story your magazine's ever seen. I got a special feeling about this tournament.

Me: How do you know what makes for a good story?

Slate: Because I've lived one. As a kid, I rode the short bus all through school. No one believed in me. After five years of college, I tried to be an actor but couldn't remember my lines—turns out that's kind of important. Who knew? Anyway, I opened a coffee shop because my girlfriend thought it'd be cool, and because I didn't know how to do anything else. That was twenty-five years ago, and that little shop became a career. Sometimes you just gotta say, "What the fuck."

Me: Is that quote from *Risky Business*?

Slate: Beats me, I only watch Bond movies.

Me: What's your point?

Slate: My point, Dominguez, is that I tried, and I gave that coffee shop all I had. You gotta do what you do best. For me, it's making lemonade out of chicken shit, or however that saying goes. For you, that's something you need to figure out.

Me: Speaking of chicken shit, how did the Bulls get their start?

Slate: Benny and I used to play on a team called the Squids. At the same time, we were coaching our daughters in weekend softball tournaments with a bunch of other dads, really good friends. We loved hanging out with those guys, but every Sunday we'd have to leave them for our games with the Squids. We hated doing that, so we formed the Bulls. We knew none of our friends were any good, but it didn't matter because we just wanted to be together.

Me: You said you coached your daughter?

Slate: Yep, both of them, two pitchers. For fifteen years, I plopped my ass on a plastic bucket and caught for them while they practiced. Still got bruises on my shins. Now my favorite memories are of sitting on that bucket.

Me: What do the Bulls mean to you?

Slate: Just like those days with my girls, I'm gonna treasure every day I got left with my boys.

Me: What's your role on the team?

Slate: On the Bulls, I'm the horns. I like to gore people as much as I can.

Me: Why so many tattoos on your arms?

Slate: Most of them are of talking animals. I love talking animals. Probably because I didn't have a lot of friends growing up, and I wished my dog could talk to me. Actually, I think he did a couple of times. Maybe I was drunk. What's that tattoo on your wrist? "El Toro"?

Me: Oh, nothing.

Slate: But why'd you get it?

Me: No reason. Just a drunk night in college.

Slate: I'm not a language guy, but doesn't that mean "The Bull" in Spanish? Must be a sign from above.

Me: You own a restaurant called Blue Moose, right? What's the story behind that name?

Slate: It's for the dog I told you about, my best friend for fifteen years; his name was "Moose." When he died, I was crushed, couldn't shake the blues. When I opened my coffee shop, the name seemed obvious.

Me: Which leads me to my last question: how'd you get the name Slate?

Slate: Like I said, I'm a big James Bond guy, but my favorite movie is *True Romance.* Love the character Clarence, played by Christian Slater. When I turned eighteen, I legally changed my name to Slate, short for Slater.

Me: What's your real name?

Slate: It's Clarence, but Slate's way cooler, don't you think?

At the Emerald Outpost before my flight, I sit on the edge of my bed and stare at my phone; every minute lasts an hour. I drag my bags outside and wait for my taxi. Just as it pulls up, my phone rings.

Me: Hello?

Slate: Dominguez, it's Slate, where are you right now?

Me: Three seconds away from getting into a cab and never seeing you again.

Slate: Don't go anywhere. Stay right there for one minute.

Me: Clock's ticking.

Fifty-five seconds later, Slate shows up with Vinnie in tow, smirks on their faces. Vinnie jogs to the driver's side of the cab and hands the guy ten bucks. "Give us a few, will ya, chief?"

Slate turns to me. "You said your magazine can't pay for you to stay, right?"

"Right."

"Well," says Slate, "what if the Aging Bulls pay your expenses?"

"I'm not a charity case."

"No one said anything about charity, Isabel." Vinnie puts an arm around me. "But how do you feel about luxury?"

"Huh?"

The scrappy Staten Islander hands me a gold key card. "I fell into some luck at the poker table," Vinnie says, "and the EO wanted to comp me. So I arranged for you, my friend, to stay in a penthouse suite, drinks and meals included, for a total of two weeks, which happens to extend through the duration of the tournament."

"Sorry," I say. "My boss is expecting me back tomorrow."

"Yeah, about that," Slate says.

The cabbie sticks his head out the window. "Hey, sweetheart, let's go."

I grab the handle of my suitcase. "Yep, coming."

Slate moves in front of me. "I called your boss."

"You didn't," I say letting go of the handle. "Unbelievable." I step away and hit Kay on speed dial.

Kay: Hey, Dominguez, I thought you might call.

Me: What's going on here, Kay? I thought my assignment was canceled.

Kay: No, I said I couldn't pay for you to stay. And since I don't have to now, you can keep working on this story.

Me: There is no story!

Kay: Well, find one. And take plenty of pictures while you're at it. I obviously can't afford a photographer for this.

I hang up, apologize to the cab driver, and leave Hetan and Shalers there at the entrance. In the elevator, I bang on the button for the sixth floor and frown at the key card Vinnie gave me, gold plated with the words *Funnymoon Suite* etched on the face. The elevator's lazy door opens. In front of me on the wall are two arrows pointing to opposite ends of the hallway. To the right: The Repenthouse Suite. To the left: The Funnymoon Suite.

Turning left past the ice machine, I totter to the end of the hall. Plastered onto the door of the suite is a caricature of Yakov Smirnoff's smiling face. A speech balloon above his head captures his catchphrase: "What a country!"

I enter the room as if I'm tiptoeing onto the auditorium stage at Northwestern where I gave my final oral presentation on the Ten Elements of Journalism. On the back of the door hangs a framed quote from an old-time actress my dad used to love: *I'm not funny. What I am is brave. – Lucille Ball*

The place is huge: a kitchenette, a sitting area, a bathroom as big as my family's apartment, an enormous oak desk, a fireplace, a king-sized bed, a wall of windows at the back of the room with sliders to a balcony overlooking the Las Vegas strip. I slide open the door to the balcony, step outside, and then retreat from the desert heat.

The suite is staged with props from famous comedians: Gallagher's sledgehammer, Steve Martin's arrow headband, and Sam Kinison's beret. Edgar Bergen's puppets, Charlie McCarthy and Mortimer Snerd sit on the fireplace mantle. It's like the whole room's laughing at me. I throw my suitcase on the floor next to the bed while grumbling about the Bulls going behind my back and making me stay, keeping me from what's really important at home. At the desk by the window, I set up my laptop and type an email to Kay.

> If you want me to stay, I'll stay. But I doubt I'll find a
> legit angle for this story, and I don't know if I have it in
> me to keep looking. The Bulls are like every other group
> of men I've ever met. They're entitled and ignorant and
> tone deaf. They act nice at times, but their courtesy and
> concern come across as phony. They think they can do
> whatever they want, especially Slate Hetan, no matter
> the consequence. If you let me tell our readers who these
> guys really are and why I'll be rooting against them in this
> tournament, then I can deliver a worthwhile story. Let me
> know.

I decide not to send the email yet and file it in my drafts folder. After closing my computer, I curl up in bed with *All That You Had*. I open the novel and pull out the laminated bookmark, a keepsake from my father's funeral. On the front, the words *Edgar Dominguez, July 4, 1976 - July 10, 2008,* rest under a glossy photo: my favorite shot of Papi at eighteen, playing for the Venezuelan national team, his chest out, showing off his yellow, red, and blue jersey, his fresh face bragging of youth, his bright eyes harboring a faraway dream. On the back of the bookmark: Psalm 23, "The Lord Is My Shepherd," written in full under an image of an araguaney tree, reminding me how much Papi shined.

I set the marker on the nightstand and begin reading where I left off, at the end of the first act, where bitterness and anger propel the main character to search for her missing father, the part where she's not in a good place, but she's moving forward.

DAY FIVE

*I*M UP EARLY to work on my Bulls story, sitting in bed with my laptop, a fresh cup of coffee on the nightstand. After four aggravating days with the team, I'm thinking I might need therapy. But I've been to only one therapist in my life, a grief counselor when I was in college, and I still don't totally under-stand her analysis. She told me I was too young when my father died to realize the permanence of death, that I couldn't grasp what losing him meant, that he left me with an "abandonment wound," that my mother had one of her own. She said I followed a simple plan during my childhood, a paint-by-numbers manual to secure a college scholarship and the love of my father; for both goals, my instructions were the same and easy to follow. But I wasn't a little girl anymore, the therapist said, and I needed a new plan for my journey into womanhood. I would need to dig deep and take inventory of my problems in order to fix them. If I slept through those problems, she said life would wake me up, and that wouldn't be pleasant.

I take a sip of coffee and start typing, writing about the Bulls' apparent inability to accept the next stage in their lives, about adult men who refuse to grow up, intent on acting like little boys, doing little boy things, while people like me are forced to leave our childhoods behind.

Till I lost him, my dad coached all my teams, never missed a game or a practice. Mami managed the restaurant and juggled childcare for Ava, while Papi and I took trains all over the city. Those train rides to softball games were my favorite thing in the world. Just me and him, talking, mostly about baseball and his other true love: American pop culture from the '70s and '80s. The man was obsessed, and he knew his stuff. Through osmosis and constant quizzing, I knew my stuff too, including the important questions: Where's the beef? Who framed Roger Rabbit? What's so funny about peace, love, and understanding? By third grade, when kids at school stole first kisses and paired off holding hands, I cared more about *Mork & Mindy* and *When Harry Met Sally*.

When I was nine, my father bought a beat-up livery van, painted *Bombers* on the side, and drove our club team to tournaments as far away as DC. Sometimes I thought he wanted to win those tournaments more than I did. Sometimes he got so mad at an ump or opposing coach that I wanted to disappear, and when he got mad at me for not hustling, I did disappear. On those days, he'd lecture me on the ride home. "We can't win unless you put your whole heart into every game, every inning, every pitch. Todo tu corazón."

After he died, all joy in our family vanished. The energy we once felt at home was gone. Our apartment was just a shell, a place to eat and sleep. Mami ran the restaurant, and I kept playing ball. I had talent, worked hard, and tried to be a good teammate. But my "whole heart" wasn't in it.

Some days I'd stay home from school, pretending to be sick, and lie on the couch, reading, scribbling in a notebook, dreaming up stories about girls who lived fairy tale lives. Girls who dotted the *i*'s in their names with tiny hearts. Girls who had money and light skin and small noses and freedom and fathers. I'd immerse myself in other places, other times, other people. I fantasized about writing the Great American Novel when I grew up, but that was before I realized I had nothing to say and no one who'd listen even if I did—a lesson my life continues to reinforce.

As I schlep down the hall to breakfast, a teenaged boy in a backwards Astros cap and Hawaiian shirt stops me and asks if I can bring more towels to his room.

"Find someone who works here," I say.

In the lobby, a group of men and women with heads hung lower than mine stand apart from each other along the wall like evenly-spaced pylons on a highway shoulder. They all wear plastic nametags, muted clothing, and dour expressions. I walk past them, toward the Taj Meh Hall, scanning faces that belong in a wax museum.

Sal's cousin Stu makes a beeline toward me. "Good morning, Ms. Dominguez," he says. "I trust you had a restful sleep."

"Yes, it was great," I lie. "Who are all these people?"

"The EO is hosting back-to-back-to-back conventions in the next nine days," he says. "This one's for NATBO: the National Association of Toll Booth Operators. They're here every summer, not the most enthusiastic gang, keep to themselves mostly, but nice to have around when you need change for the vending machines."

Somehow, the breakfast buffet is more unappetizing than yesterday's. With a greasy set of tongs, I drop an ice-cold pancake and two shriveled sausage links onto my plate. Bo Loth sits across from me. We eat in silence. At the table next to us, Bryson and Rocco admit to English professor Wink that they skipped more college classes than they attended before grilling him on the proper use of a semicolon. Over the ballroom speakers, a Muzak version of 50 Cent's "In Da Club" sets a bizarre mood.

After the Bulls finish eating, Sal holds a team meeting. "Okay, boys, the East semifinals begin today," he says. "We've got West Virginia at 3:00, bus leaves at 1:40 to get us there an hour before first pitch. They're a good team, got a bunch of thumpers. First baseman's named Hans Groone, supposed to be a real jerk, like the Ty Cobb of the tourney, the kind of guy who'd plunk Mother Teresa in the ass just to set up a force at any base. Their pitching is average, so we should be able to put up some runs. The game isn't for another five hours. Until then, take a nap, hang by the pool, gamble away your life's savings. I don't care as long as you're on that bus."

Half of the Bulls hit the pool; the other half hurry to the casino. Slouching in my chair, checking my phone, I open the email I drafted for Kay and reread it. Realizing it wasn't me, but spite, who wrote the part about the guys being ignorant and how I'll be rooting against them, I hit delete. Just then someone sneaks behind me, and I jump.

"Oh, hey Isabel," says Harold. "Didn't mean to s-s-surprise you, just f-f-forgot my hat, sorry."

"No problem," I say.

"Hey, I'm going to t-t-try my luck on the slot machines," he says. "Care to j-j-join me?"

"Thanks, but I should do some work."

"Maybe next time," he says. "See you later on the b-b-bus."

"Oh hey," I say, catching him before he ambles off. "If you see a waitress, can you send her in here? I could use a drink."

"Isn't it a l-l-little early?"

"You know what they say, Harold, it's five o'clock somewhere."

I spend the next three hours in the ballroom ordering Irish coffees and updating my resume, wishing my portfolio had more to offer than the handful of articles I've written for *Mature Living*, which no one considers the gold standard, or even the tin standard, of publications. When I search "journalism jobs" online, I find that *Viacom, The Daily Beast, New York Public Radio,* and *Telemundo* are looking for reporters; I'll make the switch from print to multimedia if I have to.

At 1:40 p.m., the Bulls and I file onto the Anonybus, and we head ten miles north to the Big League Dreams softball facility. Along the way, the guys are quieter than normal. Other than Benny, who's driving and singing along with the radio, the only noise comes from the speakers on the mounted TV playing a DVD of *Bad News Bears: Breaking Training.* I sit alone again, ignore a text from Kay asking how things are going, and focus on the desert rushing past me outside the window.

Twenty minutes later, Benny pulls into the facility's parking lot. Surrounding the lot are four replica Major League fields: Dodger Stadium, Wrigley Field, Fenway Park, and Yankee Stadium.

"Where are we playing today, Skip?" Benny asks.

Sal checks his phone for an update from the tournament director. "Hang on one second," he says, scrolling through his emails. "Our series against West Virginia will be at, let me see here, Dodger Stadium."

Rocco springs out of his seat. "Just call me Mike Piazza today, brothers!"

"You've got the great hair and the questionable personal life," says Slate. "Now all you need is talent."

The guys unload their equipment and lug it toward the Dodger Stadium knockoff. The vast parking lot, burning under the Vegas sun, contains a smattering of cars and a fleet of buses, expensive, decked-out machines from all over the country with team names on the side panels. We walk past buses for the Lions from Astoria, Oregon; the Tigers from Okeechobee, Florida; and the Bears from Coalwood, West Virginia.

The Bulls trot into the stadium through a gate under the bleachers behind home plate, and I shuffle in after them. I've never been to Dodger Stadium, but I remember sitting on my dad's lap watching VHS recordings of World Series games between the Yankees and Dodgers from the late '70s as Papi pointed out the details of the Dodgers home field, the light stanchions rising above the bleachers, the scrubby pines on the hills beyond the outfield wall. This is a mini-version of that place I locked in my memory.

I rummage in my backpack for the reporter's notebook I've yet to crack open. Being on a ballfield again, for the first time in years, quickens my pulse, and I jot down some impressions: the banners and flags flying in centerfield; the bleachers running along both baselines and behind home plate; the desert stretching out for miles beyond the outfield wall; the bases spray-painted ghost-white; the infield grass perfectly manicured, not a blade out of place; the baseline dirt made of red clay—the kind of dirt any little girl would love to practice her slides on.

If I were still a girl, I'd love to play on this field. But I'm done with the game. And the game is done with me.

I stand behind the Bulls as they congregate in front of the first base dugout and meet with the tournament's director. He's a small man who speaks in a monotone voice as he goes over the tourney rules and procedures. His manner is precise and calculated, as official as the badge on the lanyard around his pipe-cleaner neck.

"Okay, Aging Bulls," the director says. "All contests will consist of seven innings with a two-hour time limit. You will have the 3 p.m. timeslot for each one of your games."

"Excuse me," says Webb, standing front and center. "What if we're tied after two hours?"

"Not to worry. I've heard about your team," the director says. "It's unlikely your scores will be that close, or your games will last that long."

After the meeting, the Bulls begin their pregame routines:

stretches and calisthenics and sprints. With temps over a hundred, these routines last all of ten minutes before the team retreats back into the dugout shade and cracks open beers. Across the field, along the third baseline, the Bears from West Virginia warm up in groups of five, hitting into a bow net, playing pepper, shagging flies, and stretching under the supervision of an athletic trainer. Each Bear is six-foot-two or taller, except for the stumpy Hans Groone. Every player is tidy in his full uniform, a crimson *WV* stitched on his black hat, a bloody bear claw emblazoned across his chest.

In the Bulls dugout, Clete Shuheg and Vinnie Shalers toss a coin to decide which pitcher will start the game. When the quarter turns up tails, Clete lets out an "Awwright!" Vinnie demands a redo, on account of a faulty flip, but Sal shoots down the request and relegates Shalers to rightfield. The other outfielders—after hearing Clete will man the hill—hustle out of the dugout to limber up some more.

Just before game time, Sal gathers the team together. "The rules say we can bat our roster," he announces, "and no one came this far to sit on the bench, so all seventeen of us will hit. That means some of us might only get a couple at-bats per game. But it's not like we're gonna win this tournament anyway."

I flip a page in my notebook and scratch out the lineup as Sal rattles it off: "Leading off, Webb Ucho in right centerfield; batting second, Vinnie Shalers in right; batting third, Benny Eggan in left center; batting fourth, Slate Hetan at third base; batting fifth, Nick Chinsola at second base; batting sixth, Sal Rucosa playing wherever; batting seventh, Bryson Lowdan in leftfield; batting eighth, Hank Sornecki switching off with Bryson; batting ninth, Rocco Rupacava behind the plate; batting tenth, Clete Shuheg pitching; batting eleventh, Bo Loth switching off with Vinnie in right; batting twelfth, Leo Tarriso at first base; batting lucky thirteenth, Darryl Shonjon switching off with Leo;

batting fourteenth, Biff Nerby at short; batting fifteenth, Wink Sillano switching off with Nick at second; and batting sixteenth and seventeenth, Harold Hapnets and Rodney Pittbase; you two figure out how to get yourselves in somewhere."

The Walnut Gap saps jog onto the field. Compared to the well-dressed West Virginians, the Bulls are slobs, who'd feel right at home with Chico's Bail Bonds as a sponsor. Their untucked short-sleeved jerseys are royal blue with white stripes running down the sides. Across the chest, in orange block lettering, is the word *Bulls*. Most of the guys wear gym shorts. Some wear baseball pants. A few wear cutoff sweats. Harold wears cargo shorts. All of them wear cleats except for Rodney, who wears Skechers. Judged on optics alone, the team's odds for success are lower than Slate's IQ. The umpire yells, "Play ball!"

Leading off for the Bears is Hans "Chopper" Groone, a muscular gnome whose reputation precedes him in the order, who's earned his nickname by sliding into bases with one purpose: chopping down infielders like so much timber. The stadium is only half full, and no one's standing or cheering, but they all know the mean and mustachioed Groone is a decent hitter (who'd be the first to tell you), a dirty player (who sharpens his rubber spikes), and a sore loser (who pees into the Gatorade of any teammate whose average dips below the Mendoza Line).

But on this day, West Virginia's game against the Aging Bulls doesn't go as Chopper—or anyone—expects. Slate slugs four extra-base hits. Biff turns in several spectacular plays at shortstop, looking like a capable replacement for missing stud Mac Lervacci. And Clete, his beady eyes laser focused behind wraparound Oakley's, pitches better than Vinnie had hoped, and he gets a couple of hits too. The Bears from Coalwood don't know what hit them, except for Groone's smacks to the backs of their heads, and the Bulls, to everyone's surprise, win 8-3. As the players line up to shake hands, I have two thoughts: the team I'm assigned to cover is better than I gave them credit for, and my stay in Vegas has just gotten longer by at least a day.

Afterwards, the celebration in the parking lot lives up to its billing, with tons of laughter and drinking, me checking the time on my phone every two minutes, and more drinking and laughter. The Bulls have pulled off an unlikely upset, but Vinnie is cranky about Clete's success in the circle, and he makes it no secret.

"Those chumps stunk," Shalers says. "We play better teams back in Walnut Gap."

"No way, those Bears got some bangers," Rocco says before chugging a yellowish liquid from a Poland Springs bottle. "Clete just shut 'em down, starting with that cocky son-of-a-bitch Groone."

As Clete fondles his gray goatee, Webb Ucho puts his arm around him. "I bet the Bears were starstruck," the outfielder says. "They couldn't believe they were hitting against the guy who played Kenickie in *Grease*."

Eventually the Bulls split into smaller groups, rehash the game, and make fun of each other. Off to the side, with his back to the team, Nick is checking his phone.

"Hey, Chinsola, what the fuck?" Slate yells. "Get the pole out of your ass and come over here. You part of this team or what?"

Nick swings around and slips the phone into his pocket. "Sorry, Hetan," he says. "I was just Googling the number of people in human history born without a brain. Funny, only your name came up." Nick reaches into a cooler, presents a bottle of Lambrusco, uncorks a wellspring of forgettable insults, and sprays them at Slate.

I sip on a beer, keeping my distance from the idiocy. The Bulls try to rope me in, but I want no part of them. My feet ache, but I refuse to sit when offered a chair. A passenger plane zooms overhead, flying low above the parking lot, off to somewhere else. My chest feels heavy.

"Okay, who's with me?" yells Rocco. "I've got eight tickets to—"

"I'm out," Darryl says.

"But I haven't even—"

"I'm still out."

The Bulls all laugh.

After some cajoling, Rocco manages to wrangle four guys to go with him to see David Copperfield at The Mirage. The takers: Rodney, Biff, Bo, and Clete.

As the team packs up to leave, Vinnie gets a call. "Hey, Shuheg. It's your wife. She needs to talk to you."

"About what?"

"Probably wants to know why you don't pick up when she calls," Vinnie says, holding out the phone. "Put down your husband-of-the-year trophy and find out. She says it's something about one of your daughters."

"Gimme that," Clete says, grabbing Vinnie's cell. As he listens to his wife talk, his face contorts, and his eyes bulge. "Don't put that booze away yet, Bulls," he announces after he hangs up. "We've got some more celebrating to do. My oldest daughter just got engaged!"

A roar goes up, filling the air as Clete's teammates mob him with high-fives, hugs, and a shower of beer. Clete smiles through it all, his joy on display for all the world to see. I shove my notebook into my backpack and take my seat on the bus.

Back at the hotel, Clete approaches as I wait for the elevator. He stands close to me, smelling like stale Yuengling, dried sweat, and fabric softener, wearing the same smile he sported in the parking lot. I slide a half step away. "Congrats on your daughter's engagement."

"Thank you, Isabel, it's a great day," he says. "My girl's a sweetheart, and she's marrying a good guy. I can't complain."

"Great."

"You know, you should get my interview before I leave."

"You're leaving?"

"Yup. We're throwing a party for the kids tomorrow in Walnut Gap," he says. "Catching a redeye in a couple of hours. Just broke it to the Bulls that I have to miss the rest of the tournament."

"Hmm." I stare at the elevator door then turn to Clete. "Why don't we get your interview at the airport?"

"You're going home too?" he asks.

"Yeah, I let the guys know already," I lie. "*Mature Living* is going out of business, and my boss wants me to come back. Your interview will be my last." I scan Clete's eyes for suspicion, but it's clear no one's filled him in on what's happening.

Up in my room, knowing I can't use my frozen expense account, I test my Discover card's credit limit and book a $410 flight leaving that night. Without telling anyone, I pack and share a cab with Clete to McCarran Airport. We have separate flights, forty minutes apart, but I'm ready to go. I don't want to be with the Bulls any longer, don't want to "find the story," don't care if Kay *and* my mother both want me to stay. I'm wasting too much time in Las Vegas. I need to take care of my family and find another job, can't let my mother sell the restaurant.

Waiting for our redeyes, I sit with Clete at his gate—my backpack and book on the seat between us—while we eat chicken sandwiches and cheese fries from Shake Shack. He wears a blue New York Mets hat and a bright orange Mets T-shirt that stretches over his big belly; I feel like a character in *It's the Great Shuheg, Charlie Brown*. He's nice to talk to, friendlier than I expected, and I'm already used to his squawky voice.

When we finish eating, I throw our trash away and settle in, ready to start the interview. "All set to give me the final word, Clete?"

"I am, but are you certain you want to leave?"

I check my phone, making sure it has enough life for the recording. "Yep, got my marching orders, and my bags are packed." Then, to distract him, I add, "And without their stud pitcher, soon the other Bulls will be packing their bags too."

"You make a good point there, Isabel." Clete brushes a colony of crumbs off his shirt. "Should I get closer so you can hear me better?" he asks, a smudge of honey mustard coloring his chin whiskers.

"Sure."

He grabs my stuff from the seat between us and puts it on the other side of him. "All right," he says with a gap-toothed smile. "Let's do this."

June 27 notes:

Today the Aging Bulls kicked off the tournament by winning their first game against West Virginia, and some guy named "Hans." Afterward, they celebrated in the parking lot of a softball facility called Big League Dreams before some of them went to a magic show. And now, one of the team's better players is about to disappear, so their chances of winning another game are slim, and their stay in Las Vegas won't be much longer than mine.

My no-doubt-about-it final interview is with Clete Shuheg, the self-proclaimed "best pitcher" on the Bulls, who's going back to Walnut Gap, bailing on his team to attend his daughter's engagement party. Clete's a fifty-nine-year-old Staten Islander, thick and stout like a Guinness, confident and secure (especially for a Mets fan). He's feisty, fearsome, and oddly entertaining, a cross between a badger and an orangutan. But for some reason, I like him.

Me: You must be excited to be going home.

Clete: I don't really want to leave, but I have to. No one's more loyal to the Bulls than me, but no one's more loyal to his family either.

Me: And your daughter's getting married. That's exciting.

Clete: I've got two beautiful daughters. Other than my wife, those girls are the apples of my eye. We've always been close, and we always will be. But this is a bittersweet moment. That's what it's all about though, isn't it? Kids grow up, fall in love, move away. Life goes on.

Me: Are you upset you'll miss the rest of the tournament?

Clete: Of course, but not as much as the Bulls will miss me. Besides, I'm on another team in Walnut Gap called the Gym Rats, so I'll still get to play, and those guys are psyched I'm coming home.

Me: Were you surprised the Bulls won today?

Clete: Not really. When I won the coin toss and got the start over Shalers, I knew we had a good shot. I gave up three runs, but only one was earned. The official scorer counted the ball over Sornecki's head as a two-run double, but I would've made that catch if I were in left. Unfortunately for the Bulls, Clete Shuheg can't be everywhere at once.

Me: What kind of name is Shuheg anyway?

Clete: My ancestors were Nordic. There's actually a Scandinavian legend that the first Shuheg male was created as a love toy by Freyja, the Norse goddess of sex.

Me: What do you love most about being on the Bulls?

Clete: The competition. The camaraderie. The beer.

Me: What about Vinnie Shalers and Slate Hetan? You seem to have contentious relationships with those two.

Clete: Vinnie and I go back a long way, been rivals since our Staten Island days. But we don't have a real rivalry. Just like a hammer and a nail don't have a rivalry, and I'll give you one guess who's the hammer. Then there's Slate Hetan, the guy who abuses everyone and calls it "love." He's the worst part about being on the Bulls, but he's also the best part.

Me: Aren't you the oldest player on the team?

Clete: I sure am, almost sixty, and proud of it too. I think playing with younger guys keeps me young, and they appreciate my wisdom. I've been around, Isabel, and I've seen some things. I was alive when JFK got shot, when MLK delivered his "I Have a Dream" speech, when *Petticoat Junction* was must-see TV. And I still got a lot to offer. When you love the game as much as I do, you don't just give it up.

Me: You don't look terrible for sixty, other than your thinning hair and thickening waist.

Clete: I can drop a few pounds whenever I want, and I'm not going bald like those other guys. I just have a low face.

Me: How will the Bulls fare without you?

Clete: They're gonna have a problem. They're losing a great pitcher, and expectations are lower now than ever. But I'm sure someone will step up. It probably won't be Shalers, but Rocco's a semi-capable pitcher. Who knows? Maybe that magician he's seeing tonight will turn him into Jenny Finch, and the Bulls will win it all.

Me: So losing you could work in their favor?

Clete: It's unlikely, but it's not impossible. Without me, this would be a true Cinderella story.

Me: That would be unbelievable.

Clete: Yeah, and you shouldn't miss it, Isabel.

When Clete's flight begins boarding, he gathers his things and gives me a fist bump. "I don't know when we'll see each other again," he says, "but good luck with everything."

"Thanks, you too. Have fun at the party."

"Oh, I will." He beams and shakes his head. "Still can't believe my little girl's getting hitched. One of these days, your father will say the same thing."

"I bet."

Clete waves goodbye and gets in line with his fellow passengers. After he scans his ticket, he looks back at me and gives me a thumbs up. When he's gone, I collect my things and move to a seat by the window, watch his plane roll out onto the runway and take off. The sky is clear, a perfect night for flying, a perfect night for leaving. I stroll through the terminal and settle at my gate fifteen minutes before boarding.

As I concoct a text for Kay about needing to come home for a family emergency, a PA announcement cuts through the calm: "Attention ladies and gentlemen, due to technical issues, JetBlue Flight 442 departing at 11:40 p.m. into LaGuardia will be delayed approximately forty-five minutes. We're sorry for any inconvenience."

An hour later, a chunky woman arrives at the gate, introduces herself as an airport rep, and breaks the news to me and fifty other exasperated travelers that McCarran is experiencing a "mainframe computer system shutdown."

"What does that mean, exactly?" I ask.

The woman snaps her gum. "It means we're evacuating the airport and cancelling all flights for twenty-four hours—"

"What?"

"Minimum."

With no choice, I get a cab and return to the hotel. Back at the Emerald Outpost, I pass by the Ruby Slipper Lounge where The One Hit Blunders are singing "Alone Again, Naturally" by Gilbert O'Sullivan. On the lookout to avoid any Aging Bulls, I take the elevator back up to the sixth floor.

Inside the Funnymoon Suite, I open my suitcase, drop my socks into the top dresser drawer, and feel jealous of Clete's daughter. I stuff my shirts into the middle drawer and think that, if I ever get married, my father won't walk me down the aisle. I dump everything else into the bottom drawer and hate that Papi won't be there to dance with me.

After a shower, I down two nips of Bacardi from the minibar fridge. I grab my phone and scroll through my saved voicemails, landing on a message my dad left me a month before he died. For the past thirteen years, whenever I upgraded to a new phone, the first thing I'd do is make sure that recording transfers.

Hola, mi corazón, it's Papi. Ready for our tournament? I'm parked across the street from the school, behind a green truck with a dog hanging out the back window, barking like crazy. Sounds like Mami when I get home too late. Call back if you can't find me. Oh, wait, there you are, Izzy. I see you now, my love.

To keep from crying, I throw back two nips of Grey Goose. When I slam the minibar door closed, a framed quote falls to the floor. I look at it through the fractured glass. *A day without laughter is a day wasted. – Charlie Chaplin*

nd I think of all the days I've wasted, how I spent an entire
er not laughing when I was ten years old. Mami had

returned to work fulltime at Café Isabel. Ava was two, and I had to babysit her all summer long. Had to feed her breakfast, read to her, give her lunch, try to get her to nap. I'd hear my friends laughing outside on the sidewalk and watch them through the window, but I could never play with them. At four o'clock, when my father came home to take me to Reiss Field, we had to bring Ava too. On the way, he told me jokes and stories, tried to make me laugh, tried to make me smile. At the diamond, my sister sat in her stroller near home plate, sipping on a juice box, while Papi hit me grounders and flyballs. After I finished batting practice, he'd unbuckle Ava, and she'd totter around helping us collect the balls in the outfield. Then he'd chase me around the bases, with Ava in his arms, before taking us back to Barker Avenue, where I was back on babysitter duty. And I wouldn't come close to smiling till my father came home the next day.

DAY SIX

*W*HEN I AWAKE, there's a jackhammer in my head. I roll over in bed and paw around for my phone. It's not there. I rub my eyes and get up, sidestepping empty liquor bottles and pieces of glass from the broken picture frame. I look in the bathroom, on the desk, under the dresser. I hurry back to the bed, rip off the comforter and sheets, launch the pillows onto the floor, and finally find my cell on the mattress by the headboard. Dead.

I plug it into a charger and wait. Finally the thing gets some juice, and I see the time, 7:07 a.m., just past ten back home. I dial my mother, but the call goes straight to voicemail. So I shoot her a text.

Me: Mami, when is your new chemo appointment?

Me: Mami??

I brush the knots out of my hair and get dressed. With two hours before breakfast, I decide to read a few chapters of my book, but like a bad joke, it's lost too. Not on the nightstand, not on the desk, not in my backpack. *It's got to be somewhere!*

My heart races and I wring my hands. I could buy another copy, but I could never replace the bookmark. Eventually I give up the search, distraught, and try to reach Mami again. When she doesn't reply, I open up my journal, wondering how else the day could go wrong and why everyone, and everything, is hiding from me. Don't they know that hiding is *my* specialty?

The summer before I turned fourteen, I revealed secrets in my diary that I'd never tell anyone. That leather-bound book found new life during those hot months, and I ensured no one else would lay eyes on it by keeping it where I knew Ava or Mami would never look: buried at the bottom of a softball equipment bin I kept in the corner of my closet. (Papi had given me the blue and white plastic bin, with *Yankees* written on the side, for my tenth birthday, and I stored everything I needed in there: mitt, cleats, bats, helmet, wristbands, batting gloves, elbow pad, sunglasses, eye black stickers, headbands, athletic tape, Band-Aids, bubble gum, and sunflower seeds.) My journal was the only item in the bin having nothing to do with softball. But that summer before ninth grade—when my body and my feelings about boys didn't belong to a little girl anymore—my diary was priceless. And I was the dragon guarding the gold.

… Mariel Moreno had a party at her apartment last night because her mom went to visit her grandmother in the DR. I told Mami I was going to see Toy Story 3 with Sara… I told Sara not to let me drink too much at the party, but she left me to hook up with Steven. I didn't want to stay but I promised I'd walk home with her, so I waited… When "Soulja Boy" came on, Jacob pulled me off the couch and started dancing with me. Then he got a bottle of Smirnoff and took me into Mariel's bedroom. He kissed me and felt me up under my shirt. I wanted to do more, but I had to be home by eleven. He told me to text him, but Mami won't let me text boys…

At breakfast—as Leo forks food into his mouth and tells me a joke he told me yesterday—he gets a call, and the smile slips off his face. The conversation is so quick that when Leo hangs up, his mouth is still full of hash browns. He stands in the center of the Taj Meh Hall, finishes chewing, and addresses his teammates: "I know this is going to be hard for some of you to believe, but Rocco's in jail."

"What'd he do this time?" the team asks in unison, using body language alone.

Leo scans the room for Rodney, Biff, and Bo. "You three went with him to that magic show last night. It was your turn to watch him. What happened?"

"We don't know, man," Rodney says, his diamond earrings twinkling in the ballroom light. "We never went to the show. Rocco was supposed to meet us with the tickets outside the theatre, but he never showed up."

Relaxing in his seat, Biff stretches his arms, rocks back in his chair, and catches himself before tipping. "Whoa! Yeah, we waited for a while then went to The Naughty Nighty gentleman's club instead." He lowers his sunglasses and looks at Bo. "Isn't that what we did?"

Bo shrugs.

"Well, he's in jail now," Leo says, shaking his head. "And I was his one phone call. God, being a lawyer sucks."

"Did he say why he was arrested?" asks Bryson, looking more and more like Rob Lowe every day.

Leo shifts from side to side, gathering his thoughts. "He told me he went to the show by himself and claims a security guard nabbed him for storming the stage."

"Why?" asks Bryson.

"He said he was saving someone's life. Copperfield asked a volunteer to come onstage to help with a trick. The woman got into a box with only her head sticking out. Copperfield began sawing her in half, and that's when Rocco rushed up to save her."

"You're shitting us," says Slate.

"I wish I were," Leo says, "because then I wouldn't have to go to the station and talk the LVPD into releasing a man on the brink of insanity."

"Hey, Izzy." Vinnie is leaning against the wall in the back of the room. "Yo, what do you call that vampire dog in Hispanic folklore? You know, the thing that drinks the blood of cows and sheep and stuff like that?"

"El Chupacabra."

"Yeah, yeah," Vinnie says. "Well, we've got our own legendary creature called El Rupacava, and when he's not here, it sucks the life out of the Bulls. If we're gonna win, we need Rocco. You know what I'm saying?"

After breakfast, I search my room again, but I still can't find my book. I grab a cab to the airport, bum rush the customer service counter, and ask the clerk if anyone found a book at my gate the night before.

"No ma'am," he says, poking around his desk. "Haven't seen any books here in, oh, I don't know, maybe two or three days."

"What about a lost-and-found box?" I ask, my cheeks overheating. "There has to be one somewhere. Can you please check?"

The clerk steps into a back room and returns in less than a minute. "Sorry, ma'am, we've got nothing here." Then he slides a piece of paper across the counter. "But you just fill out this form, and we'll keep an eye out."

I go back to the hotel, a mess.

At 2 p.m., the Bulls and I are at Big League Dreams, back at the fake Dodger Stadium. This time, they're without their starting catcher (the incarcerated Rocco Rupacava); their part-time first baseman (Rocco's legal counsel, Leo Tarriso); and their ace pitcher from the day before (father-in-law-to-be Clete Shuheg).

Shutting down the vengeful West Virginian sluggers will be the responsibility of Vinnie Shalers. Since arriving in this inferno called Las Vegas, Vinnie has been the most popular Bull; it seems like everyone wants to hang out with him, probably because he's the shadiest thing around.

Trying to put my lost book out of my mind, I lean against the fence along the rightfield line to watch Shalers, a crafty lefty, warm up in the bullpen with his new catcher, Rodney Pittbase— who doesn't have Rocco's knowhow or skill behind the plate but makes up for it with his congeniality, willful spirit, and joy of the experience. Plus he smells a lot better, and the scent of his cologne finds my nose before his words find my ears.

"Hello, Isabel. Don't make too much fun of me, okay?" Rodney says, waving to me. "I never played softball growing up in Trinidad, man. This game is a lot more different than cricket."

"Don't worry," I say. "I've seen much worse players." And I consider for a moment whether or not I have.

Once the game starts, Rodney forgets everything he never knew about softball and plays like a gregarious Thurman Munson, calming the sometimes-skittish Shalers with his smile and taming the sluggers of West Virginia with his friendly banter. Even the evil Chopper Groone falls under Rodney's spell, striking out in his first two plate appearances. After his second K, he hurls his helmet and complains to the ump that Rodney's niceness and sportsmanship isn't allowed in softball.

Through four innings, the contest remains close until Sal and Bryson each crush two-run homers to break the game open. Biff and Wink contribute three hits apiece while, in the pitcher's circle, Vinnie holds onto a three-run lead. And the Bulls shock the men's senior softball world with a 12-9 victory and a series sweep of the Bears from Coalwood.

The postgame celebration rivals the previous day's, with the Bulls cheering and making speeches and handing out game balls to the heroes of the battle. After those formalities, the parking lot turns into a daycare center: Benny ducks behind teammates and spits streams of beer at Webb's crotch from ten feet away; Hank and Nick toss sunflower seeds into Bo's ear, convincing him that a moth is trying to break into his brain; Sal and Darryl organize empty cans on the ground to spell out various parts of the female anatomy.

Meanwhile, Slate stands to the side with Biff and Wink and a bottle of tequila. He takes a swig and inserts himself between the two men, slinging his arms around them while Biff prattles on about the game. During a rare pause in Biff's story, Slate jumps in. "Nerby, you did good today, you really did," he says, trying not to slur. "But when you go over every stupid detail of every stupid play, I wanna put a gun in my mouth. And you look like a Muppet. And you run like you have four knees."

"Ha-ha-ha-ha-ha-ha-ha," Biff responds. "Good one, Slate."

Then Slate zeroes in on his next target. "Wink Sillano, dude, I'm so proud of you," says the insult machine. "Before today, you hadn't gotten a hit since 2017. Fuck, this must be the greatest moment of your life. I love you, man." And he hugs Wink, if only to keep from falling.

The party spills over from the lot to the bus to the hotel lounge, the Ruby Slipper, where the Pastafarians are in the middle of their set. Their reggae cover tunes, with an Italian twist, create a frightening score for the scene as I sit among the sweaty, dirty Bulls, who've taken over four tables in front of the stage. Still upset over my lost book, I order a Tito's and tonic while the guys gloat over their win, bellowing at the top of their lungs. Only Rodney seems focused on the music.

"Hey, Sal, who's our next victim?" shouts Hank.

"We're in the East Finals against the winner of Florida and Georgia."

"What are we doing tomorrow?" asks Benny.

"Whatever we want," Sal says. "We have an off day!"

The Bulls cheer as I stab at my ice cubes with a straw.

After arguing their case all day at the Vegas police precinct, Leo and Rocco stroll into the lounge to the beat of "I Shot the Sheriff," prompting a standing ovation from the team and hugs all around. Leo guzzles the closest drink he can find while Rocco high-fives the whole crew, soaking in the attention. "You guys ain't gonna believe what happened," he says with the throaty bombast of a Tony Soprano sidekick.

"What happened in your mind," Leo butts in, "or what *really* happened?"

"Hey, come on, Tarriso," Rocco says, "even the sarge at the station bought my story."

"No, he bought himself some peace and quiet after listening to you whine for twenty-four hours. That's the only reason you're out of that cell."

"Look, whatever," Rocco says, motioning for a waitress to come over. "All I know is some woman's still in one piece because of me."

"That's weird," Webb says, "since women usually end up broke because of you."

"Man, if I were her and saw you running at me," says Benny, "I'd *beg* for someone to cut me in half."

During the ribbing, no one else notices Rodney heading for the stage. I flick Nick on the shoulder and point to the Bulls backup catcher, who is now jamming on the steel drums with the Pastafarians.

Nick laughs and leaps out of his seat. "Hey, Bulls! Check out the drummer."

But everyone is too busy harassing Rocco to notice.

I reach over and tap Vinnie on the forearm. Like a whip he spins and faces me, fists up and ready. "What?! You wanna go?" he snarls with a Scottish brogue, his brow furrowed, his lips pursed.

"Hey, easy!" I say.

Vinnie drops his fists, glances over both shoulders, and bops in his chair. "Oh, oh, sorry, my bad. What's up?"

I point at the stage. "Look."

"Yo! That's insane," Vinnie says, standing and flailing his arms. He performs some sort of jig, cups his hands around his mouth, and shouts, "Go, Pittbase! Go, Pittbase!"

The rest of the Bulls jump up and dance.

For the next ten minutes, I watch in amazement as Rodney Pittbase, with no wild pitches or passed balls or basic softball skills to worry about, puts on a show—brushing, striking, tapping, flicking, or doing whatever one does on the steel drums—while his brothers cheer on the man who normally does all the cheering. I take out my phone and snap a few photos.

After the set, the Bulls congratulate Rodney with hugs and backslaps, then they leave to shower and change; half have plans to hit the casino, the other half are late for a Bruno Mars concert at the MGM. The Ruby Slipper is empty. Rodney and I stand alone in front of four tables that look like frat party wreckage. He finds a clean napkin and wipes the sweat off his shaved head. "So what did you think, Isabel? Be honest with me. Did you enjoy the music?"

"I did," I say. "You were really good." And I mean every syllable of it.

He laughs and dabs his cheeks with the napkin. "I have an idea," he says. "Maybe I can give you my interview now. It will be like a *Rolling Stone* profile, man. Maybe someone will discover me, and it will be my big break, all because of you."

His smile enlightens the room. He's still wearing his Bulls jersey, the decal letters peeling off the front, the #1 on his back already gone, leaving behind a ghostly outline. His diamond earrings dazzle. Vitality emanates from his pores, and I can't help but forget my troubles. Just being near Rodney makes me feel better.

"Come meet the band," he says, and I follow him to the stage.

He introduces me to the Pastafarians—three guys named Vito wearing dreads and gold chains—who are packing up their instruments. One of them hands us a couple of beers and says, "Hey, Rod, you can sit in with us anytime. You got good energy, bro. Much love and respect."

After the Vitos excuse themselves, Rodney and I sit on the edge of the stage, feet dangling. We raise our bottles and tap them together. *Clink*.

"Here's to you, Mr. Pittbase," I say. "You're an amazing talent."

"No, no. I'm a little rusty," he says with a laugh. "But thank you, that was a lot of fun, man. Those pasta guys are a really, really tight band." He sips his beer and looks at me. "So, what should we talk about, Isabel Dominguez?"

June 28 notes:

The Bulls will be staying in town a while, having beaten West Virginia to wrap their first-round series two games to none. I can't believe what's going on, can't believe the Bulls won, can't believe Leo got Rocco out of jail. Part of me looks forward to seeing what happens in the tournament. The other part wants to hitch a ride on the next hay wagon out of town.

My interview today is with Rodney Pittbase. He's a fifty-three-year-old outfielder and backup catcher who filled in for Rocco this afternoon. He lives in Walnut Gap but is originally from Trinidad. His accent is disarming. His charm is bewitching. Of all the Bulls, Rodney looks the most like a bull, strong and squat, impressive, but with earrings instead of a nose ring. We sat on the edge of the stage at our hotel's lounge where Rodney had just played the steel drums with the house reggae band. He looked comfortable on the stage, just as he'd looked on the field. He's not an expert softball player or musician, and he shouldn't feel safe in either place, but after speaking with him, I learned he feels safe being himself. And so he feels safe everywhere.

Me: Where'd you learn how to play the steel drums?

Rodney: Back home in Trinidad. I'm not that good if I don't practice, but I love it, man. After I moved to the States, I played with the Pan Jersey Steel Orchestra doing gigs all over the Northeast. That was a really fun time.

Me: You caught a great game earlier today. Did you surprise yourself?

Rodney: Every time I do something good on the field I surprise myself. I grew up playing cricket, so softball is still new to me. Cricket is a really different sport than softball. But I go out there and I get my hits and I make my throws. And I get a lot of exercise.

Me: Are you enjoying the trip so far?

Rodney: Oh yeah, man. Las Vegas is a crazy place. But I love being around all the guys, drinking some beers while they talk a lot of shit. The Aging Bulls is a special team, and it's a real nice cultural thing.

Me: What's a nice guy like you doing on this team?

Rodney: The Bulls are my brothers, man. They're my friends, and they make me laugh. They make me happy.

Me: What's your role on the field?

Rodney: I bring a lot of energy to the team. Sometimes I play, and sometimes I don't. But it doesn't matter. I try to help out however I can.

Me: Being from Trinidad, did you ever feel like an outsider?

Rodney: I was twenty-six when I left the island, but I blended in good here, never felt like an outsider because I was mostly around with the Trinidadian community that lived in New Jersey. I was born someplace else, but I see myself as American too. Some people might hear me talk and not accept me because of my accent, but that's okay. My home is where my family is. Where are you from, Isabel?

Me: My parents brought me to New York from Venezuela when I was a baby. I only went back once, when I was seven, to visit my grandfather in Macuro.

Rodney: No way! Macuro is right near Trinidad, man. I used to take a boat there with my brother. That's a beautiful place. Do you remember it?

Me: I was only there for a week, but I remember everything. The fishing boats floating on the bay. The sea turtle eggs hatching on the beach. The cacao trees blowing in the wind behind my grandfather's house. The baseball glove my cousin made for me out of a milk carton. The song I heard in every voice.

Rodney: Those are good memories, Isabel. Hold tight to those.

Me: Why are you so positive, Rodney?

Rodney: Maybe because I didn't have a lot growing up. Now I'm grateful for everything. My friends, my family, my house, my job. And especially my brothers here, the Aging Bulls.

Me: What's the secret to having an outlook like yours?

Rodney: I just try to be myself and try not to care what anyone thinks. But I try to be nice to other people, and I always felt comfortable around different people of different races and cultures. And I don't get depressed or nothing because I always do what makes me happy.

Me: I can't remember the last time I was really happy.

Rodney: We bring happiness to each other, I think. It's all around us, and we're all worthy. We just have to love everyone and open our eyes.

Me: You and I are different people though. I've never been comfortable in my own skin. It's hard to love everyone else if you don't even like yourself.

Rodney: We're not so different, Isabel, and there's so much to like about you.

Me: You're nice to say that.

I've known only one other person with Rodney's bulletproof attitude about life: a boy from the Bronx named Lucas, a boy I once loved. We met at a coffee shop the week after I graduated from Northwestern. He was a senior at Columbia University, a history major, a reader like me. We dated for two months, took a break during the summer, and hooked up again in the fall. But his relaxed demeanor miffed me. Stress breezed right through him. Nothing rattled him. We never fought or even disagreed. He said his name meant "bright" and "shining," joked that his laid-back disposition was a gift from God, told me he was lucky, that other Black men had heavier crosses to bear. We said we loved each other on a warm Sunday in September. We broke up in the rain two weeks later. It was probably my fault.

When I get back to my room, it's midnight, and my eyes are heavy. After brushing my teeth, I notice the message light blinking on the suite phone. It's the front desk, saying they have a FedEx package for me. Down in the lobby, a clerk hands me a small envelope sent from Walnut Gap. I tear it open to find my copy of *All That You Had*, with a handwritten note included.

Sorry, Izzy, I took your book by mistake before boarding my flight last night. (Big fan of that author, by the way.) When I heard you stayed in Vegas, I asked a friend at FedEx to rush this out. Also, if you need more quotes for your story, my cell is (917) 555-1053.

Your pal & ace pitcher,

Clete Shuheg

PS: Tell the Bulls I said good luck without me. They're gonna need it!

DAY SEVEN

*B*EFORE I SHOWED an ounce of talent as a kid, a softball scholarship was the key to my future, what Papi wanted for me. After he was gone, my mother hijacked his dream and flew it like a madwoman. She'd never seen me play, was always too busy at the restaurant and taking care of Ava, but she knew that a scholarship was the only way she could send me to college. My first recruitment letter arrived the day before I stopped wearing a training bra.

I attended an elite private high school on the Hudson, one that waived my tuition, presumably in exchange for the banners I'd help raise in their gym rafters. Code-switching back and forth—between my neighborhood, the classroom, and the diamond—I was a triple threat. I started every game at shortstop, wore number six like my dad, made only four errors my whole high school career. My team won three conference championships, and I earned all-state honors four consecutive years, hit .535 overall. But no matter how many hits I got, or how many plays I made, or how many banners I raised, it would never be enough once I stepped off the field. My name was still Isabel Dominguez, and a name like that comes with limitations.

I accumulated so many trophies that we had to store half

of them at the restaurant. Mami was on a first-name basis with sports reporters from the *Times*, *News*, and *Post*. My picture was in *USA Today*. Ohio State wanted me. So did Arizona, Alabama, USC, and Villanova. We kept my offer letters, over forty of them, in a nightstand drawer next to my parents' bed, on Papi's side. When signing day came, I chose to attend Northwestern. Chicago was only a twelve-hour bus ride from New York, and the Wildcat coaching staff promised I'd start right away. But mostly, I wanted to go there because of Will Peterson, a Northwestern alum and author of my favorite novel, *All That You Had*. Silly reason, I know.

But not as silly as the guys I'm covering on this trip. Having swept the team from West Virginia, the Bulls have a free day before their next series. That means a free day for me as well, but there are a thousand other ways I'd rather spend it than in a fake town with fake people. And it hits me that four days in Vegas is three days too long. With no plan other than eating breakfast and going over my notes, I throw on sweats and pull my hair back in a ponytail. As I grab my room key off the dresser, another framed quote stares at me: *Aim high, and you won't shoot your foot off. – Phyllis Diller*

Down in the ballroom, our buffet table boasts a host of new options: organic granola, challah French toast, sliced cantaloupe, and cheesy grits. After I fill my plate and sit down, Sal clinks a fork against his glass of cranberry juice. "Good morning, everyone," he says. "Can I have your attention, please? Since we'll be here for at least another three days, I need to confirm that everyone took the extra time off from work. I don't need any of you losers calling me an hour before tomorrow's game saying you gotta go home. We all good?"

Just then, Biff walks into the room. "Sorry, I just heard something about work and losers, but I can stay as long as you need me since I'm sort of between jobs right now."

Webb chuckles. "Man, that's like a Neanderthal saying he's sort of between ice ages."

A spoon falls to the floor. Someone coughs.

Benny taps me on the elbow. "Hey Iz, feel free to use that quote. It might be the funniest thing Webb will ever say."

Vinnie raises his hand, gets up from his chair, and rubs the ginger scruff on his chin. "I'd just like to say that I have, indeed, alerted my employer of the situation, but I can neither confirm nor deny their approval." Before Sal can interject, Vinnie raises his hand again. "That said, I will not pull a Shuheg and desert you. I will stay for the duration of this tournament, however long that might be."

"Good to hear," says Sal.

"I might have an issue," says Nick, rocking in his chair, cracking his knuckles. "There's a chance I'll have to leave at some point in the next few days, but don't worry, I'll let you guys know as soon as possible."

"Leave me off that text chain," says Slate at the buffet table, spooning grits into a bowl.

After breakfast, I decide to hang by the pool but need to go back to my room and change. On the way to the elevator, I cut through the casino along a yellow path that winds around the gaming tables. When I see Rodney fist bumping a cigar-smoking Colonel Sanders lookalike, I can't help but laugh. Passing a school of sharks playing high-stakes poker, I brush shoulders with the front desk clerk who gave me the FedEx package from Clete last night. We look back at each other and wave.

On the outskirts of the casino floor, near the elevator, Harold sits at a slot, talking and laughing with an elderly woman who's banging on the side of an adjacent machine. I smile at them and keep walking. Two seconds later, I hear, "Hey, Isabel!"

I stop and pivot.

"Have you tried the slots yet? They're r-r-really fun," Harold says as I inch toward him. "I've played each day s-s-since we got here. This hotel has the highest slot machine winning percentage in Las Vegas. I looked it up online."

"Wow, that's great," I say and tilt my head to get a better look at him in his chair. He reminds me of a cool nerd, like he could be Michael Cera's dad, or a secret millionaire who's invented something obscure like the paperclip or the Chia Pet. He's wearing cargo shorts and a blue *Life Is Good* T-shirt with a picture of a stick figure sleeping in a hammock. A stainless-steel beer growler sits on a table next to him.

A young waitress in a green miniskirt steals behind Harold's seat and puts a hand on his shoulder. "Hello, Mr. Hapnets. We've got a full-bodied blond IPA on tap today. Can I grab your growler and give you a taste?"

He whips around. "Er, um, y-y-yes please. Thank you, Penny."

"Someone's thirsty," I say under my breath as the waitress sashays away. Then I turn to Harold with an arched brow and a smirk. "You're quite a celebrity around here, aren't you?"

"Only because I'm up a f-f-few hundred bucks. Hey, let me introduce you to someone." He spins his swivel chair to face the old woman at the machine next to him. She yanks on the lever and claps before looking up at me. "This is Dottie Willoughby," Harold says.

My jaw drops and I hurry to her side. "My god, Dottie. It's me, Isabel Dominguez, the reporter who wrote the story about you and your rutabagas last year. It's so good to see you."

"Oh, yes, Isabel," says Dottie, her eyes lighting up. "My dear, how are you?" She rises from her seat and hugs me tight.

"I'm okay, I guess. What are you doing here?"

"Well, my husband and I used to come to the Emerald Outpost every June since our honeymoon in 1959. This was our special place." The smile falls from her face. "Alan passed in

March, but he made me promise to come back here one more time. So I could say goodbye for both of us, I suppose."

"I'm so sorry," I say.

"Thank you, sweetie," Dottie says, and her smile finds its way back. "But guess what? I still have my rutabagas to keep me company."

"Do you still have the one that looks like Debbie Harry?"

She grimaces. "I do, but it's not aging well."

We laugh and I drape my arm over her shoulder. "I'm so glad you're here," I say. "What a crazy coincidence."

She reaches up and pats my hand. "The universe always gives us the seeds we need, but we can't hold onto them, Isabel. We have to plant them, or nothing will grow." She winks at me and—

Quack. Quack. Quack.

While waiting to hear from my mom, I'd taken my phone off vibrate and accidentally activated the duck ringtone. Now I pull it out of my pocket and press it to my chest, then I touch Dottie's arm. "Sorry, I have to take this. It's my boss." Stepping away from the clattering slots, I answer the call.

Me: Hey.

Kay: Izzy, I'm hearing rumors that corporate might not shut us down after all.

Me: No, really?

Kay: Yes, really. If we survive—and that's a monumental if—it wouldn't hurt to have a killer piece about the Bulls. Our next issue has to shine.

Me: I was afraid you'd say that.

Kay: What's the big deal? It's a routine human-interest story. Plus, you played the sport; you should have some insight.

Me: I know, but there's something I can't explain about this team.

Kay: Well, you better find a way.

I stuff my phone into my back pocket and rejoin Harold and Dottie by the slot machines. While I apologize for taking the call, Hank trudges over from the roulette wheel, apparently having lost his shirt. (Fortunately for him, he wears a sweater of human hair under all his shirts.) Head hanging low, he grumbles and scuffs at the floor. Looks like it'll take a heroic effort to drag Hank out of his funk; only the giant Bloody Mary he holds seems up to the task.

Harold takes a gulp from his newly-filled growler of beer and says, "C'mon, Hank. It c-c-can't be that bad."

"I dunno," says Hank, nailing an impression of Eeyore. "This hasn't been my day. Or week. Or month. Or year."

"Well, I have an idea that m-m-might cheer you up," Harold says. "Let's hit the b-b-buffet. I'll buy you and Dottie lunch."

"Okay." Hank turns to me. "You hungry, Izzy?"

Before I can answer, Harold says, "I'm sure Izzy's got b-b-better things to do." Then, as the three of them head off, Harold babbles something about *hacking into databases* or *snacking in potato faces,* one or the other.

On my way back up to my room, surprised that Harold didn't want me to join them, I wander through the casino toward Nick yelling into his phone under a marble statue of Emerald Outpost founder Silvio Rucosa. When he sees me, Nick hangs up and says, "You okay?"

"Yeah, you?"

"Yeah."

"Great," I say. And I wait. And I wait.

"Okay, see ya," he says.

At a craps table, Vinnie Shalers entertains a group of very large men wearing United Steelworkers T-shirts. I stop to watch. He tosses four hundred bucks at the dealer, rakes in his chips, and rolls sevens and elevens six consecutive times. "Yo, look at that," he shouts. "Some guys have all the luck, huh?" The union workers keep putting money down and keep winning. Awash in the love of laborers, Vinnie bounces on his toes, trying to stay steady while withstanding backslaps that would knock over a forklift. He notices me standing off to the side and points. "Hey Izzy, come on over and help me out."

I shake my head.

Vinnie signals for a timeout and boogies over to me.

"What?" I ask.

He holds out his hand, offers a pair of dice. "Here you go, kid. Roll one, will ya."

As the workers circle around, I focus on Vinnie. "No thanks," I say.

"Roll the dice," booms the largest of the men.

Vinnie slides in close. "Yo, listen, Izzy, my homeboys here ain't the type who take no for an answer. Know what I'm saying? Do us both a favor here and give it a roll."

I snatch the dice and fire them onto the board: snake eyes.

"Hey, no problem," Vinnie blurts. "You can't win 'em all, right fellas?"

Back in my room, I change into my one-piece swimsuit and cover up with a pair of jean shorts and a knockoff Derek Jeter jersey Ava bought me for Christmas. I tie back my hair, throw on my Yankees hat, grab my sunglasses and backpack, and make my way to the pool. Under my seared feet, the patio is a bed of coals.

I pass Sal, Leo, Darryl, Slate, and Benny sitting under a cabana sipping on frozen drinks. Leo spots me and says, "Hey Isabel, you like pina coladas?"

"And getting caught in the rain?" Benny adds.

I cringe and stop. "No, but if you see Rupert Holmes, tell him I'd love to escape."

"Nice!" Benny says, raising both arms in triumph. "I respect the Yacht Rock knowledge."

On the other side of the pool area, I stretch out on a chaise. A DJ shouts out a bachelorette party before pumping EDM remixes into the air. Sorority girls in string bikinis giggle and splash during a game of water volleyball. Lubed-up bros with eight packs pound beers in the shallow end. A small school of preteens play Marco Polo while their parents sit poolside, catching rays and drinking Mai Tais. I close my eyes and take in the sounds: inane conversations, slurred flirtations, mindless chatter, all set to a monotonous, pulsating beat.

"Hey, Jeter, you from New York?"

I open my eyes. Three flabby men in their early thirties stand over me. I slide my sunglasses to the end of my nose. "Yup."

"That's dope, us too," says one of the guys. He's sporting a Post Malone concert tee and a camouflage bathing suit. "We run a hedge fund on Wall Street."

I fold my arms across my chest. "Cool," I say as another man, pasty-faced with a black goatee, leers at me and fiddles with the paper umbrella sticking out of his drink.

The third guy squats next to my chair and jerks a thumb toward his buddy in the concert tee. "Hey, this stud here is getting married next week. Before he takes the plunge, he'd love one night with you. We can make it worth your while if you know what I mean."

As I reach for my bag to leave, I feel his finger on my back, tracing the curves of the #2 on my jersey. I twist around and knock his hand away. "What the hell!"

"Excuse me," says someone in a deeper voice. I glance over my shoulder at a tall, sinewy guy around my age. Loose, dark curls adorn his head. Small silver hoops, one in each ear, twinkle in the afternoon sun. His perfect smile brags of the braces I'm sure he once wore. His complexion: a beautiful mix of Black and white, tanned to perfection. Wearing khaki shorts and a white linen shirt, the guy holds two giant cups of purple slush with spiral straws. He cuts in front of the three cretins, sits at the foot of my chair, and hands me a drink. "Hey, babe, here's your Razzamatazz. They're super sugary, and the bartender says they'll kick your butt if you're not careful."

I question the stranger with my eyes. "Thanks."

The dirtbags slink away.

Once they're out of earshot, I offer up the cup. "I appreciate the gesture," I tell the guy, "but I don't need your help."

He refuses to take it back. "Do me a favor. Hold onto the drink and hang out here for a minute. We don't have to talk. Let's just make sure those dudes get the point." He sips the purple concoction and contorts his face. "Man, I forgot how sweet these things are."

"Why'd you order them?"

He wipes the corner of his mouth with his thumb. "I didn't order them," he says. "I made them." He puts his drink down and holds out his hand. "My name's Russell. I'm a bartender here. Normally, I work nights at Skat's, but I pick up extra shifts when I can."

I wait a beat and put my hand in his. "Hi, I'm Isabel."

"Nice to meet you, Isabel." Russell takes another sip of his drink. "You gotta try this. It's actually not terrible, tastes like a SweeTarts-flavored Slurpee."

I stir my drink with the spiral straw and take a sip. The coldness shoots against the back of my throat and freezes my brain. "Wow," I say shaking my head, unpuckering my lips. "That was not what I expected."

Russell touches my heated arm and laughs, his dimples like

quotation marks around a smile sweeter than any Razzamatazz. "So," he says, "how long are you—"

"Ouch, ouch… oh my gosh, Izzy," cries Leo, waddling toward my chair, his arms stiff at his sides, terror baked onto his burnt face. "I don't mean to bother you… ouch, ouch… but I could really… ouch, ouch… use your help."

I put my drink down and spring to my feet. "What's wrong?"

"I fell asleep on the lazy river and… ouch, ouch… got a crazy sunburn." He can barely move, the front of his blistered body a boiled-lobster red. Beads of sweat race down his forehead. "The other guys left," Leo says, wincing. "Please, can you bring my stuff inside and… ouch, ouch… help me find some aloe?"

"Sure." I look at Russell. "I gotta go."

"Yeah, of course." He hands me my backpack. "Maybe I'll see you at Skat's sometime."

"Thank you," I say. "I hope so."

I gather Leo's things from the cabana and walk with him into the Emerald Outpost. Before we reach the gift shop, he looks around and says, "Okay, I think we're clear of that jerk who was pestering you."

"You mean the guy I was sitting with?"

"Lucky I saw you when I did," he says. "I almost left without you."

"You're joking, right?" I say and wonder if Leo has ever let his daughter out of the house after dinnertime. "I don't need saving, and I was actually into that guy."

"No, really? Geez, I'm sorry."

I head back to the pool, but Russell is gone, and he's not inside at the bar either. While deciding if I should text Leo and rip him for ruining my day, a reminder I'd set on my phone pops up: *check airport situation and JetBlue credit.* I Google news about McCarran's recent computer issue, find that their system is back up and running. But now there's a glitch in *my* system, and I'm no longer desperate to leave.

I enter the lobby, where members of the toll booth convention cause a backup, halting all who pass, chatting with them, and waving them on when the next person stops by. It takes me five minutes to move thirty yards. As I near the elevator bank, on my way back up to my room, I spot Biff Nerby leaning against a wall snacking on a bag of candy. Scarecrow skinny with a billboard grin, he wears long basketball shorts and an oversized Yo La Tengo T-shirt. His glazed-over eyes are visible only when he removes his sunglasses and wipes them on his shirt.

"What's up, Biff?"

After he finishes chewing, he beams. "Hey, Isabel. Or should I call you Izzy? Some people don't like nicknames, and some do, so I don't know what to call people sometimes. You know what I mean? So which do you prefer?"

"Doesn't matter."

"Okay, cool," says Biff, combining three syllables into one. "Hey, I'm going on a desert hike. Wanna join me?"

"That's nice of you," I say. "But that's the last thing I want to do. Wait, I take that back, it doesn't even make the list of the things I want to do."

"Ha-ha-ha-ha-ha-ha-ha-ha-ha-ha. That's funny." His laugh is soft and hypnotic, like a miniature lawn mower stuck in low gear. "Wanna try a gummy?"

I stare at the bag in his hand. "Those don't look like Gummy Bears," I say as Biff gives me two.

"They're not from the vending machine, Isabel," he says. "They're THC edibles and might affect you in a strange way. Everyone reacts differently."

"First time for everything, right?"

"But only eat one per day," he says. "Don't overdo it, and be careful, they'll totally change the way you see things."

"Might be just what I need." I examine the edibles. I've never done drugs of any kind before, never wanted to feel out of control, but I'm starting to wonder if that's part of my problem. I pop a gummy into my mouth.

While I chew, Biff explains that he's heading into the desert to search for peyote cactus plants. "And Black Rock City is only four hundred miles north of here. That's where the Burning Man Festival is," he says. "It'd be pretty cool to catch some of that, don't you think?"

"Seriously?" I ask.

"Sort of kidding about Burning Man," he says. "Dead serious about the peyote. Ha-ha-ha-ha-ha-ha-ha-ha-ha."

"I'll pass on the hike," I say. "But can I get an interview before you leave?"

He contemplates the question as if I've asked him to explain Zeno's dichotomy paradox. I'm still waiting when my knees go weak, and I give my second gummy back to Biff.

June 29 notes:

Something is totally "off" about this off day. The weirdness began earlier at the pool, where I got harassed by three Wall Street sewer rats. Then a cute guy appeared out of nowhere and chased away the rats. Then overprotective Leo needed "help" with his sunburn and sabotaged my conversation with the cute guy. Then I left Leo and ended up in the hotel lobby with Biff Nerby and his incredible edibles, unquestionably the weirdest part of all the weirdness.

Biff and I sat on a plush green couch, which changed colors on me three times in the course of our five-minute interview. The son of Walnut Gap's mayor, Ed Nerby, Biff is a fifty-one-year-old infielder filling in admirably at shortstop for the absent Mac Lervacci. For our talk, Biff wore a too-big Yo La Tengo T-shirt and baggy shorts, an outfit that swallowed up his lean six-foot frame. His orange and cream Aging Bulls trucker hat sat atop a patch of brown straw. Dark sunglasses disguised his soul.

While we spoke, members of a toll booth operators convention clogged the Emerald Outpost lobby, and the warbling mass of automatons played tricks on my foggy brain, moving in slow motion, as my view of the world skewed. In front of me on the couch, bespectacled Biff ballyhooed about perfection, fatherhood, and Mets old-timer Richie Ashburn.

Me: So, you're going on a desert hike in killer heat to look for peyote?

Biff: Yeah, it comes from a certain kind of cactus that grows around limestone. I heard it grows wild in Nevada, but I also heard it doesn't. It's supposed to be illegal to take the plants out of their natural habitat, but I'm not taking the whole cactus, and the buttons will grow back if harvested correctly. I'm not sure if I'll find any, but you never know. The desert holds many secrets. Oh, and can we keep the gummy and peyote stuff out of your article? I'm starting a new job soon.

Me: Of course. You gonna rock that fit in the desert?

Biff: Oh, my outfit? Yeah, it's kind of the only thing I brought out here other than my uniform. Are you a YLT fan?

Me: I never heard of the band Yo La Tengo. But you know that means "I have it" in Spanish, right?

Biff: Yeah, funny story behind that. In 1962, the Mets had a shortstop from Venezuela named Elio Chacón who didn't speak English and would collide on popups with centerfielder Richie Ashburn because Richie would yell "I got it! I got it!" but Elio only understood Spanish. So Richie learned to say, "Yo la tengo!" to avoid those collisions. Isn't that really interesting?

Me: Fascinating. What do you think about the tournament so far?

Biff: It's been really fun. I mean we're doing better than anyone thought we would, so that's kinda cool. Was that a good enough answer? I don't know what you want me to say.

Me: It's fine, Biff. What does being on the Bulls mean to you?

Biff: I don't know. I guess it means that I have to remember to be somewhere every Sunday afternoon. Ha-ha-ha-ha-ha-ha-ha. But seriously, it's important to me because these guys are all my friends, and I like being with my friends.

Me: What's your role on the team?

Biff: Well, I was the starting shortstop for a long time, but this year Slate recruited Mac Lervacci, who's really good, probably better than me. So, now I play second sometimes or short when Mac's not around. I used to be a lot better than I am now, but I guess that's what happens. Nothing ever stays the same.

Me: Are you happy with the way you've been playing?

Biff: Me personally? I think so. Can I play better? Probably not. Can I play worse? Maybe. But I have gotten a few hits so far, and I've made a few good plays in the field. That's more than anyone expected.

Me: What's your life like away from softball?

Biff: It's all about my two daughters. They're the loves of my life. I coached them both when they were young. All of us guys coached our daughters together, and now we're playing together, and getting old together, and having a lot of fun doing it. For me, the Bulls remind me of the great moments I had on the field with my kids, just teaching them stuff about life. We told all the girls we coached that softball's like life. Nobody's perfect, but that's okay. The best hitters fail seven out of ten times. And everyone makes errors.

Me: But shouldn't we try to be perfect? Isn't that the goal?

Biff: Perfection is a myth, Isabel. I told my girls, "Just do your best and see what happens." Like my best friend Steve Quigley always says, "We were born to be real, not to be perfect."

Me: What about your dad? Isn't he the mayor of Walnut Gap? Did he demand a lot from you growing up in the public eye?

Biff: My dad's a great guy, and a great father. He never pressured me to be anything important. He just wanted me to be me. What about your dad? He was a really good player, right? I remember reading about that guy, Edgar Dominguez, in *Baseball Digest* back in '94 or something. He was on a list of best prospects after the Yankees signed him when he was eighteen, I think. Wasn't he a catcher? Am I getting any of this right?

Me: You might know more about him than I do. But yeah, he played, and he loved baseball, talked about it all the time. We live near Yankee Stadium, and he'd take me to one game every year. One of my earliest memories is going to Game 1 of the Subway Series when I was three. My dad pulled some strings and, somehow, got me an autographed baseball from Jorge Posada. I still have it in my closet back home. Funny, what I remember most about that night is getting cotton candy stuck in my hair and my dad helping me get it out, how patient he was with me. I don't really remember the game, but he used to brag that I stayed awake for all twelve innings and high-fived the fans in our section when Jose Vizcaino won it with a walk-off single.

Biff: He sounds like an amazing father. You must've learned a lot from him.

Me: He was amazing. And he tried to teach me, but I don't know how much I learned.

Two hours later, I'm still feeling loopy when I meet the Aging Bulls downstairs at Chachi Hibachi for "a fine dining experience," as Cousin Stu had suggested. The only one missing at dinner is Biff.

I need to sit down and when I do, the restaurant becomes a Tilt-A-Whirl, and the air gets thick. My mouth is dry, and I want to barf. Trying to focus, I guzzle a glass of water while the guys recall their daughters' travel softball tournaments. They talk about coaching their girls on a team called The Villagers. They reminisce about long car rides, and hotels with pools, and going out to eat together. They gush about how talented their kids were and how hard they competed. I'm trying to take mental notes for my story, but the room is rotating, and I'm having trouble staying upright in my chair. Then a short man in a chef's hat grabs a plastic squeeze bottle and squirts sake into Slate's mouth from ten yards away, and I know I'm hallucinating. I throw my head back and close my eyes.

Next thing I know, I'm in an elevator with Rodney. My arms

and legs are noodles, and I can see out of only one eye. When we get to the top floor, Rodney helps me to my suite and leaves before I can thank him. I slump in a chair by the window and squint at the skyline. The lights are fuzzy, like everything else. Muffled noises creep into my ears; music plays low somewhere. My eyelids sag, then close like curtains falling in a theatre, and I see my parents again. Summertime. The day my team won the city championship. I was eleven. Papi had said goodnight to me hours earlier. I'd been asleep but woke to the sound of my father singing Mami's favorite song, from the Enrique Iglesias CD he'd given her for her birthday. I remember rolling out of bed and tiptoeing past my MVP trophy and into the hall, peeking around the corner into the living room where my parents were dancing, wrapped in each other's arms. I watched as Papi crooned, "I can be your hero, baby. I can kiss away the pain." He saw me and smiled, waved for me to come closer. When I did, he lifted me up, and I joined my parents in the dance, laughing and singing as the song played again.

DAY EIGHT

I'S NOON, AND I'm still dazed. Dragging myself out of bed is like moving a bill through Congress. The gummy Biff gave me kicked my ass. (He warned me, so why didn't I listen to him? Maybe because nobody else has all week.)

A heaviness builds up in my lungs; it's like someone has mixed molasses into the air. Trying to piece together what happened last night, I scroll through my texts and reply to one I received from Biff, at 8:31 p.m., which includes a selfie of his darkened face in front of an orange haze.

> Biff: You should've come hiking, Isabel. Desert sunsets are bananas! Actually more like tangerines. Hahaha... FYI, I can't find what I'm looking for, so I'm giving up.
>
> Me: Hey, I still feel weird after that gummy. Any trick to recovering?
>
> Me: Pls hit me back.
>
> Me: asap

The inside of my mouth feels like The Sahara, and my stomach is in shreds, but I'm starving and dial room service. On the other end of the line, a soft-spoken woman tells me my oat-meal, toast, and coffee will be ready in thirty minutes or less. Expecting a call back from Biff, I place my phone on the bath-mat and jump into the shower, trying to hold myself together. The water pounds on my shoulders but feels like feathers on my skin. I hold a tiny bar of soap in front of my face and wonder if it has a soul. I lather up a body that isn't my own and think about all the times I wished that were true. Fifteen minutes later there's a knock on my door. "Room service."

Still soapy, I turn off the shower and snag a green terry cloth bathrobe—with an embroidered EO monogram—off the door rack. I shove my arms into the sleeves, knot the belt, and scram-ble out of the bathroom. "Just a minute," I call.

My hair dripping wet, I unlatch the chain and open the door just wide enough to peek out. A short, broad-faced, middle-aged Hispanic woman forces a smile. "Hello," she says. "You ordered breakfast?"

I look down to make sure my robe is closed. "Yes, thank you," I say. "Sorry about the wait. Come on in."

With small steps, the woman dodders in, pushing a metal cart with three covered silver platters. She wears black slacks, a black suit vest, and a white blouse. Her straight black hair is tied back tight; a wispy strand of gray hangs in front of her forehead. Her skin is darker than mine. A silver crucifix dangles on a dainty chain around her neck. Her nametag reads *Maria*. She stops in front of the bed and looks around, everywhere but at me. "Where would you like this, miss?" Her Castilian accent and Mayan eyes tell me she's Guatemalan.

I wipe my hands on my robe. "Um, that's fine right there, I guess."

The woman takes the lids off the platters, places them on the cart, and backs away. I step farther into the room, closer to her. She covers her right wrist with her left hand. A dull gold wedding band strangles her plump ring finger. Her gaze trained on the food, she nods and says, "Okay, miss, I have your oatmeal with raisins and walnuts on the side, an order of dry wheat toast, and a carafe of coffee for one." She looks at me for the first time since I opened the door. "Does everything look satisfactory?"

"Yes, thank you," I say. "It all looks great. I appreciate it very much."

She nods again and hands me the check. "Well, I'll just ask you to sign this then."

Remembering that my meals are on the house, I calculate a forty percent tip and tally up the bill. As I scribble my name, a droplet of water falls from my hair and smudges my signature. I close the booklet. "Here you go. All set."

Toying with her necklace, the woman smiles and walks away from me with her head down. "When you're finished," she says without turning around, "please leave the cart in the hall. I'll remove it later. Enjoy your day."

As she opens the door, I step toward her and say, "Muchas gracias, Maria."

She stops and looks back at me. "You're welcome, miss." And she leaves.

After eating, I pass out on the couch and wake up in a panic. I have ten minutes to catch the bus. I look in the mirror. My hair's a mess, my curls more unruly than usual. (What did Mami always tell me when I was little? "Fix your hair, Isabel." That was code for, "Straighten it, look whiter.")

I comb out my Latina locks, pull on my Yankees cap, and burst out of the room with my notebook and backpack. In the lobby, a group of cheery-cheeked people wearing smiley-faced nametags prance about, bustling in conversation. It's another convention, for sure, but an opposite vibe from the Toll Booth Collectors of America. Hustling past the front desk, I run into a girl my age and nearly knock off her toothy grin.

"Don't you just love this?" the girl says, straightening the pleats on the poodle skirt she might've borrowed from Laverne DeFazio. "Gosh, these are my favorite three days of the year. My name's Shania. Hey, are you going to the seminar this afternoon? It sounds incredible. The keynote speaker is a famous occupational sociologist, Dr. Joshua Christopher Joy. Have you heard of him? He'll be talking about why vet assistants are the happiest people on earth."

Shania the speed talker finally pauses, and I follow up. "You're all veterinarians?"

"No, silly," she says. "Well, that's the ultimate goal, of course. But even if I don't make it to the mountaintop, I'm satisfied doing what I'm doing. Feel like I'm making the world a better place for all our fur babies, you know?"

"Uh-huh," I say, suddenly feeling guilty for flushing Ava's goldfish down the toilet when she was five, after she cut the fingers off my batting gloves.

"What about you?" Shania asks. "Why are you here?"

"Good question."

Before the Bulls and I leave for the game, we wait on the bus for Biff, who hasn't responded to our group text chain all day. "Whatever," Sal finally says, standing next to me. "If he doesn't show, we'll figure it out."

I turn to Sal. "I interviewed Biff yesterday afternoon, before he went on a hike in the desert. He texted me at sunset but didn't reply when I texted him back this morning."

"I wouldn't worry, Izzy," the Bulls manager says. "This isn't the first time Nerby's gone AWOL. Even if he's in the desert, you shouldn't sweat it." Sal smiles at me and waits a beat. "Get it? Desert, sweat it?"

I raise my eyebrows.

"Forget it," he says.

During the bus ride, concern about Biff gives way to

excitement and nervousness about the game against Florida. When I see Leo, Bo, and Hank sitting together, I leave my seat up front and move to the middle, settling in a swivel chair across from them.

"Well, look who's joining us in the cheap seats," says Leo.

My chair moves on its own, spinning slowly, turning me to face the men for a few seconds, then turning me away. I wait till they can't see my eyes and say, "Hey, I want to apologize."

"For what?" Hank asks.

My chair spins me to face them. "For being so rude to everyone at the start of this trip," I say. "I was upset about stuff happening at home, and I treated you all like crap."

"Actually, I may have deserved it," says Leo. "I mowed down those hogs."

"And I almost threw up on you," adds Hank.

My chair spins me toward the rear of the bus, and then back to face the guys just in time to catch Bo's reaction. "I accept your apology," Mr. Fix-It says, forearms folded in front of his pecs like fallen tree trunks, a goofy smile on his grill. "I wouldn't say you were rude though. Irritable, maybe, but not rude."

I laugh as Leo leans in and says, "Izzy, imagine how upset you'd be if Bo hadn't fixed the bus, and we were still in Toledo."

"I would've walked home," I say. "Trust me."

We arrive at Big League Dreams, and chatter among the players grows louder. But when we step off the bus and parade through the lot, the Vegas heat is intense, hot enough to melt Slate Hetan's heart, and the chatter dies down.

The series pitting the Bulls from New Jersey against the Tigers from Florida will take place at a replica of Chicago's Wrigley Field, complete with ivy crawling on the outfield walls and a promised recording of Harry Carey's "Take Me Out to the Ball Game" during the seventh inning stretch.

While the Bulls unload their equipment in the dugout, the

Tigers finish batting practice. All eyes are glued to Florida's best player, ace pitcher and super slugger Valentino Timms. In his tight orange uniform with black stripes, with his flowing blond locks and the physique of a Disney prince, he mesmerizes the crowd. I'm wowed and can't stop taking photos of him. If we were in Chicago, the BP moonshots Valentino launches over the leftfield wall would land beyond the Waveland Avenue rooftops.

"Any word from Biff?" Benny asks Sal.

"Nope," Sal says. "He probably went to the real Wrigley."

The game is over before it starts. Without Biff or Mac, Slate fills in at short while Sal takes over at third. After the first three innings, the left side of the Bulls' infield has muffed five grounders, and the Tigers go up 6-0. In the midst of the beating, a pissed-off Rocco barrels into the dugout and bashes a Gatorade cooler to bits with his catcher's mask. But Bo picks up the plastic pieces, finds a roll of duct tape in his bag, and patches up the jug like nothing ever happened. Due to Leo's debilitating sunburn, Darryl plays the whole game and keeps the score close, scooping two low throws from "Alligator Arms" Hetan in the fourth. But in the fifth, Darryl transforms into a croquet wicket and lets two routine rollers mosey through his legs.

The Aging Bulls play true to their name in the sixth; Vinnie's fastball flattens out, losing what little pop it had, and the Tigers lace lasers all over the park, including a check-swing dinger by Timms. Left centerfielder Benny Eggan doesn't help matters, misjudging three flyballs: the first, when he uses his knees as skis and fumbles a basket catch, turning Shalers into a basket case; the second, when he cuts in front of Webb in right center, stumbles, and bungles a low liner; and the third, when he breaks in on a ball twenty feet over his head and plays a can of corn into a bases-clearing double. Final score: Tigers 10, Aging Bulls 3.

In the postgame parking lot, a familiar scene plays out, having nothing to do with the outcome of the game. Rocco challenges Bryson to a chugging contest and beats him by a gulp. Wink and Harold engage in a hot debate about which of them should hit last in the lineup. Nick orders four dozen wings from a nearby Hooters—and gets ridiculed by his teammates for giving the Door Dash driver a one-star rating because he forgot the celery. No one seems affected by the loss except Darryl, who looks extremely pale for a Black man and must feel terrible because he doesn't have a beer in his hand.

Like he's wearing an inflatable Sumo suit, a bright-red Leo flounders over to his fellow first baseman and says, "Don't tell me you're mad about those errors you made."

Darryl wipes his head with a towel and coughs. "If committing errors made me mad," he says, "I'd be angry all the time." And he coughs again.

"I'd give you a hug," Leo says, "if it weren't for my third-degree burns and whatever disease you have."

Meanwhile, off to the side, a storm brews between the team's two best athletes. "Seriously dude," Webb says to Benny, "you need to get your eyes checked. Might be time for glasses, old man."

Benny scratches the back of his neck and finishes his Miller Lite. "I know, I know," he says. "I'll make an appointment when we get home." He drops the can, squashes it with his Adidas slides, and kicks it at Webb.

Before Benny gets another beer, Slate puts his arm around his friend. "I've never agreed with Ucho about anything, but he's right," he says. "You're the best outfielder I've ever seen, Ben, but your best days are behind you."

Webb rides the momentum. "And it's not just your eyesight, Eggan," he says. "It's your speed. Admit it, you've lost a few steps. Or twelve."

Since the beginning of the trip, I've only seen Benny smile and laugh, but I can tell he's losing patience. "Yo, I'm fifty-four-years-old. What do you expect?" His voice is louder now, and the lot falls silent, as if E.F. Hutton is offering financial advice. With all eyes locked on him, Benny says, "Everyone slows down eventually."

"True," says Slate. "But till now, you weren't like everyone."

Benny leaves Slate's side. "I'm getting more wings," he says. "Want any?"

"Nope," says Slate as his buddy walks away. "I just want my left centerfielder back."

I follow Benny to the backside of the bus where a large tin, formerly filled with wings, balances atop a canvas bat bag. He grabs two paper plates from a stack on the ground. There are six drumsticks left in the tin; we each take three. I pull two Brooklyn Summers from a cooler.

"Wanna talk?" I ask.

"Sure," he says.

I hold our plates and beers while he picks up two folding chairs, and we relocate to the opposite side of the bus, away from the seven o'clock sun. We sit facing each other, eating our chicken, drinking our beer, and I see him like I haven't before. Previously, his youthful attitude and slim build fooled me. Now, up close, his small face appears older, age spots and skin tags showing themselves for the first time. Under the tattered brim of his cap, the laugh lines on his cheeks and crow's feet by his eyes dig in deep. The soul patch under his bottom lip is mostly gray. Still, Benny is physically fit for fifty-four, seems to occupy the same body he had in college, and the same mind he had in grammar school. By the way he moves in the field, I can tell he's still as good as he used to be but was never as good as he thought. And as we talk, he sounds like someone who doesn't want things to change.

June 30 notes:

Today, a stacked Florida team beat the Aging Bulls in Game 1 of the East Finals. The score was 10-3, but it wasn't that close. To put it bluntly, the Bulls stunk, and Timms the Tiger was GR-R-REAT! To be fair though, the hacks from Walnut Gap were down another key player, starting shortstop Biff Nerby, who mysteriously missed the game. His teammates don't seem concerned, but I smell something fishy about his absence.

That smell might be Benny Eggan's uniform. After the game, I hung out with the Bulls' left centerfielder (and his stinky jersey, which might not have been washed since Obama left the White House). Benny's a really good outfielder who had a really bad game, dropping three fly balls he'd normally catch in his sleep. He's a children's book illustrator from a small town in Western Massachusetts, and he's worn the same gray cutoff sweats for a week now. He's got a little face and a big heart, seems open and honest, like he has nothing to hide, a book for all to read.

Beside the team bus, Benny and I sat in beach chairs drinking beers, eating chicken wings. I was comfortable talking with him. He was loose and bendable, like the perfectly broken-in Celtics hat he never takes off. It's clear that the man loves softball as much, if not more, than any other Bull, and I know he feels a bone-deep connection to the game. I know because it's the same connection I felt a long time ago. Players like us can spot one another a mile away.

Me: You guys are strange. Even when you lose, you still have fun.

Benny: We're not good, and we know that, but we have a blast playing with each other. Slate and I weren't super-close with the guys on the team we used to play for. I mean, they were good dudes, but it wasn't a barrel of laughs. So we got all our best friends together and formed the Bulls, and it's perfect. We'd rather lose together than win alone.

Me: Speaking of losing, you had a tough time in the outfield today. What happened?

Benny: One of those games, I guess.

Me: How did missing Biff affect the outcome?

Benny: It messed up our infield defense, but Slate and Sal will be the first guys to tell you they shouldn't have made all those errors. Now that I think of it, they might be the only guys to tell you that.

Me: What does being on the Bulls mean to you?

Benny: It means everything. For me, playing ball with my friends turns the clock back forty years every Sunday. But I'm not completely naïve, contrary to public opinion, and I know every season could be our last, so I'm savoring every moment. Because being fourteen once a week is kind of awesome.

Me: What's your role on the Bulls?

Benny: Just to go as hard as I can, use whatever athleticism I still have, get on base, make the plays I'm supposed to make. Webb and I are the only guys on this team who can still run, other than Shalers who's got a little life left in his legs. But my eyes are going, and I'm slowing down. I'm getting old all at once and, honestly, it feels like a punch in the face. But I've never been in a fight in my life, so how would I know?

Me: Some Bulls describe your gratuitous dives in the outfield as a little "extra." Actually, I think the word they used was "ridiculous."

Benny: I only know one way to play, and my argument for flying around is that I'm better in the air than on my feet. Plus, I like to entertain the fans. Not that we ever have any fans, but you know what I mean.

Me: Do you wear number six for a reason?

Benny: It's been my number since high school and for four years when I played with a semi-pro team in my hometown. Those were some of the best years of my life, and I identify those good feelings with the number six. Whenever I put on my jersey, it reminds me how much I love the game.

Me: That was my dad's number when he played, so I wore it too. My grandfather was a big Yankees fan back in Venezuela, and leftfielder Roy White, who wore number six, was his favorite player.

Benny: I loved those Yankee teams too. I didn't get it from my dad though. He didn't know a lot about sports. But he never missed any of my games. He and my mom were my biggest fans.

Me: So I heard that you're the one who wrote and produced the *Bull Slurham* mockumentary. Why?

Benny: Because this doesn't happen to everyone. Having this much fun with so many friends, who you really care about, is kind of amazing. I wanted to immortalize that feeling, document it before it was too late. When we stop playing, I don't want any of us to forget what we had.

Me: Seems like getting old really bothers you.

Benny: I think about mortality all the time, ever since my parents died, almost twenty years ago now. Things change, I know that, and I'm an expert at moving on, but it's hard sometimes. So I try to live in the moment, and I don't look back, and I don't look too far ahead, and by doing that, everything stays the same.

Me: What's life like off the field for Benny Eggan?

Benny: I've got a great family and a great job. I love drawing pictures for kids, and my stuff is pretty good. I don't make much money, but that was never the goal. I just do it for myself, and I don't care what anyone thinks. The way I look at it, all you have is who you are, so you owe it to yourself to make that person proud. If you mess up, just forget about it and move on.

Me: You understand a lot of people can't afford to mess up, right?

Easy for Benny to go all out, to dive without fear, to move on after making a mistake. Life builds safety nets for people like him, strung up and ready long before they're born. But I need to play steady and cautious, and I never forget my mistakes.

Like junior year of high school when I committed the worst error of my career. Last game of the year, we were up by one in the bottom of the seventh, runners on second and third, their catcher was at the plate, no wheels at all. She hit a routine grounder to me at short, and I lined up the candy hop. Right, left, catch, right, left, throw. Wide of first, two runs scored, game over. End of season, thirteen wins, one loss. *I had so much time. Why did I rush?*

Before we leave the lot that night, Sal asks the Bulls if anyone has heard from Biff; no one has. "Okay, I need a consensus," he says to the team. "Is it time to start worrying?"

"Who gives a shit?" Slate says.

"We should care a little," says Leo before he dips his hands into a cooler of ice water, places them onto his crispy forehead, and admits what most of the Bulls are thinking: "I can't believe I'm saying this, but if we want to win, we need Biff."

Vinnie steps into the center of the group. "Who saw him last?" he demands, throwing his arms up. "Let's narrow this down right now."

Sal gives me a reassuring nod.

"I guess I did," I say and turn all of their heads. I tell them everything, starting with the interview and ending with Biff's text.

"What did it say?" asks Vinnie.

I pull my phone out of my pocket and check the text. "He just said he loved desert sunsets and that I should've come on the hike." Then my heart stops as I read the rest verbatim: "'FYI, can't find what I'm looking for, so I'm giving up.'"

"Damn," says Vinnie.

For a moment the Bulls fall silent, but then there's a collective shrug.

"He'll turn up," Sal says. "He always does. Anybody up for blackjack?"

The Bulls brighten, all at once, and hurry onto the bus.

DAY NINE

Y MAIN ISSUE with the Aging Bulls is that they're allowed to blow off reality and live in a fantasy world where everything's peachy, win or lose. But where I come from, losing isn't an option—not if you want to get into a good high school and go to college, not if softball is your only ticket. And then, even when you win, things might not be so peachy.

College was not what I expected. I breezed through high school with a 3.9 GPA, but classes at Northwestern were more challenging, and the homework was endless. Days whooshed by so fast, I couldn't get anything done. Softball ate up all of my time, between early morning workouts, practices, games, travel, team meals, film sessions, and meetings. By the end of freshman year, I had no friends other than a few teammates; I hadn't been on a date; my GPA was barely above 3.0; and I'd played in only fourteen of our sixty games, barely got a sniff of the infield grass.

But I didn't deserve to play, because as accomplished as I'd been back in New York, my accolades and skills—compared to the other girls—were nothing to write home about. That summer, after our coach left for a job at a more "successful" university, I gave up my scholarship and quit. And I never wanted to pick up a glove again.

Strange, I didn't miss playing at all, and my final three years of college were better than my first, aside from the boatload of student loan debt I incurred. In my free time, I got to know the campus, built relationships with professors, drastically improved my GPA, and made diverse friends who expanded my world, showed me there was more to life than softball.

To Mami's dismay, I transferred out of pre-med and into the Medill School of Journalism, and I worked my way to the top of my class. I wrote in my journal every day and even dated a few boys. My future seemed so full of promise then, but of course real life is never a fairy tale. It's a lesson the Bulls might finally learn if Biff turns up dead. As I take the elevator down to breakfast, I'm thinking my story might end up being less of a human-interest piece and more of a cautionary tale.

On my way to the ballroom, I sidestep vet assistant Shania and her chirpy friends outside the hotel gift shop fawning over someone's French bulldog. When I arrive at the Taj Meh Hall, I notice some of their cheer clinging to me, and I brush it off as the Bulls huddle around their manager.

"Okay, listen up," Sal says. "Biff's still missing. I checked with his people back home, but no one's heard from him. His buddy, Steve Quigley, did say that Biff mentioned starting a new job soon, but he didn't have any details. Anyway, I went to the police this morning and filed a missing person's report."

"Did you tell the cops that Biff has a habit of disappearing?" says Nick.

"Yes," says Sal.

"Did you tell them that since the inception of the Bulls, Biff's been late to every game?" says Hank.

"Yes," says Sal.

"Did you tell them I could care less," says Slate, "or couldn't care less, or whatever?"

"No," says Sal. "But they told me not to worry. They're going to search the desert. They don't want us taking matters into our own hands."

"Look," says Bo, "I don't consider myself a hero, on or off the field, but we should probably do something."

After a quick bite, the Bulls wrangle a plan to find Biff, and Vinnie barks out instructions. "Leo, Hank, and Bo, check the pool area. Slate, Rodney, and Benny, ask around in the lounge. Find out if those Pastafarians remember seeing our shortstop. Webb, Darryl, and Bryson, cruise the strip. Maybe Biff went back into that gentleman's club and lost track of time. Rocco, Sal, and Nick, you guys case the casino. Talk to the pit bosses and see if Cousin Stu can get security to help us. Harold, Wink, and I will hit up the patrons at the buffet. Maybe Harold's gal pal Dottie saw something."

"What about me?" I ask.

"Izzy, you'll be our point person," Vinnie says. "Post up in the lobby, and we'll all check in with you. Let's meet there in a couple of hours."

Within thirty minutes, Slate and his group join me in the lobby after striking out at the Ruby Slipper. I smell liquor on their breath, but Rodney assures me they looked high and low for their missing friend (between two rounds of Rusty Nails). Soon, the other groups return, coming up empty as well, and the Bulls exchange their sleuthing hats for softball caps.

Our trip to Big League Dreams is a sober affair. So miffed by Biff's disappearance, the team can finish only a twelve-pack of Corona during the twenty-minute drive. The AC on the bus is busted, and the afternoon is ablaze. Sweat shoots out of my pores, and I feel faint. Opening my window for some air, I see a funeral procession pull into a Dairy Queen on the other side of the street, and I don't know whether to cry or laugh. Adding to the greenhouse effect, Webb blows his stack when his copy of *Major League* melts in the DVD player right before Charlie Sheen throws a pitch "just a bit outside."

When we arrive at the phony Wrigley Field, the Florida Tigers are ready to pounce. A beleaguered herd of Aging Bulls will be a mere appetizer for the carnivores from Okeechobee who, with a win, will move on to the U.S. Finals. With a queasy stomach and a heavy heart, I take my seat near the dugout, prepared to witness the inevitable circle of life and sad demise of the team I'm now rooting for.

On the field in front of me, five minutes till game time, a fired-up Rocco brings his brethren together and squats before them. Shin guards strapped on, catcher's mask in hand, the Bulls' inspirational leader and resident philosopher does what he does best: motivates his team with a meandering, incoherent diatribe. As the players close in tight, I snap some pictures.

"Listen, no one's giving us a chance here. No one's ever given us a chance," Rocco shouts. "But if there's one thing I know, it's that the Bulls don't give up. We've been through too much together to back down now. Yeah, we got crushed by these guys yesterday. But today's another day. And tomorrow's another day. And the day after that is the day after that."

"Get to the point," Slate says, "before I strangle you with your jockstrap."

Rocco throws his head back, flinging strands of sweaty hair off his face. "The point is that life is short," he says. "And we've lost a brother. Biff is somewhere in that desert, all alone, maybe hurt. God, he might be dead for all we know. But you know what he'd say if he were here? He'd say, 'Yeah, I might be dead, but I ain't losing to these motherfuckers.' So let's go out there and play like we're dead! Let's go! Let's go! Let's go!"

No one moves.

"What? Too soon?" Rocco says.

When the contest begins, the Bulls wisely ignore Rocco's

advice and come out looking very much alive. In Biff's absence, Slate and Sal man the left side of the infield again, this time making all the plays. Still limited by his sunburn, Leo subs in at first base for Darryl, who's pulled himself out due to dizzy spells. Nick whacks a pair of doubles, and by the end of the fourth, the Bulls have a 4-1 lead. Bryson and Bo both drill dingers in the fifth, continuing their hot hitting, and the game looks like a lock at 7-2. After Harold and Wink rip back-to-back singles in the sixth, I make a note that the bottom of the lineup might be the key to the team's success.

Things get tense in the seventh, however, when the home plate ump ejects Shalers after Valentino Timms smashes a homer and Vinnie calls him a "knob goblin." But Rocco's a rock in relief, while Rodney fills in like a champ behind the dish, and the Bulls tame the Tigers, 7-6, to tie the series at one game apiece.

Later, in the parking lot, Sal lobs frosty brews at us and lifts his can for a toast. "Great team effort," he says. "Now guzzle those beers and let's get going."

"That's it? We're leaving?" I ask before taking a sip.

"Yeah," says Sal, "Cousin Stu hooked us up with seats to Cirque du Soleil, show starts in a few hours."

"You're seeing a show tonight?" I say. "Shouldn't we keep looking for Biff?"

Sal sucks down his beer. "The police say they'll find him. We can't do much else but wait," he says. "Besides, this is *The Beatles LOVE* we're talking about, Izzy. Tickets are impossible to get."

We take the Anonybus back to the Emerald Outpost. Most of the Bulls bolt to their rooms to shower and change, but Darryl stays on the bus, doubled over in his seat while Webb rubs his back.

"Is everything okay?" I ask.

Webb turns to me. "He's not feeling well, trouble breathing, slight fever, swelling in his hands and feet, some sort of virus. I'll get him settled in our room and look after him. Count us out for the show tonight."

"Shouldn't we call a doctor?" I ask.

"No, he'll be fine," he says. "I aced a course on infectious diseases in med school. The Bulls call me 'Webb MD.' I got this."

I skip the show too. After dining alone at Stuffy's, I poke my head into Skat's to see if Russell is bartending, but he's not. (Between Russell and Biff, I'm beginning to wonder why men have been vanishing immediately after speaking with me.) I wander the strip to clear my head. Just before 8 p.m., I get a text from Webb asking if I can pick up some ground cinnamon and a jar of honey at the Food Mart, says it's for Darryl.

I buy the stuff, return to the hotel, go to Room 321, and tap on the door. While I wait, soft cello music plays inside the room, accompanied by the serene sound of rolling waves. I lean in closer and hear voices, low and calm, but can't decipher the words. I knock again and Webb opens the door. He's in his bare feet, wears wire-framed glasses, tapered jogger pants, and a fitted white V-neck; looks like he could be on his way to either a Pilates class or a board meeting. His almond complexion, similar to mine, highlights his cheekbones. I'm taller than he is and notice his dark hair thinning on top.

"Hey, thanks for coming," he says.

"How's our patient doing?" I ask, switching the Food Mart bag to my other hand.

"He's pretty sick."

"Is he awake?" I say, wondering if I'd actually heard voices.

"No, he's been out the whole time. Needs his rest."

Standing in the doorway, I peek over Webb's shoulder. Darryl's in his uniform, lying still in a bed next to the window. The lights are low, but he doesn't look well from what I can tell. Webb opens the door wide and moves to the side, revealing a full view of the room. Stepping inside, I do a double take when

I spy an old Asian woman sitting in a chair next to Darryl's bed. Her hair's pulled up in a bun, and she's wearing a red kimono. Light from the nightstand lamp filters through her body and shines bright against the wall. I step farther into the room as the woman folds her hands and bows her head. In the window, I see only one reflection: my own.

I turn to Webb. "Is that a nurse?"

He smiles at me, and I follow his gaze back toward Darryl. The woman is gone.

I blink and shake my head. "Where'd she go?"

"Who?" he asks.

"Duh," I say. "The woman in the red dress, that's who."

Webb tilts his head. "The mind is a fickle tour guide, Izzy." He lets go of the door, and it closes behind me. "It lets us see what we want to see, but it stops us from seeing what we need to see."

Looking at him sideways, I hand him the bag. He leads me to the kitchenette and asks what I know about Traditional Chinese Medicine. Says he's preparing an herbal remedy called Gui Zhi Tang to reduce Darryl's chills, aches, and sweating. He pours some water into a small pot, mixes in the cinnamon and honey, then digs through a leather bag on the counter. "I always take this with me when I travel."

"What is it?" I ask as he places a few jars next to the stove.

"Fresh ginger, licorice root, and Chinese red dates called jujube. My grandfather was an expert at making potions," he says with a chuckle while parsing his ingredients. "Funny, I always called them potions, like he was a witchdoctor or something."

I settle onto a stool across from him at the counter as a cacophony of smells—sweet, bitter, and sour—collide in the air. Behind me, Darryl rolls over in bed, groaning. Webb dumps his herbal mixture into the pot and dials the stovetop burner to medium heat.

"When I was seven, my family and I spent three weeks in Hong Kong," he says while rummaging through the utensil drawer. "We went to visit my grandparents. My grandmother was my favorite person in the world. I called her 'Po-Po.' She always sent me gifts and letters, and we talked on the phone every Sunday."

"She sounds cool," I say.

"Yeah, she was the best," he says. "But when we got to their house, she was really sick. I wish I had known." Webb finds a wooden spoon and begins stirring. "A few hours after we arrived, my grandfather asked me to help make a special kind of tea for her. He said it was her medicine. We mixed together roots, flower petals, powders, and all kinds of things. I remember the bubbles popping in the pot and the steam swirling in the air, like a magic potion. My parents and brothers talked in the living room with some other relatives while my grandfather poured the medicine into a cup, and we brought it to her bedside. I asked him if the potion would make Po-Po feel better. He said it would. She looked so small in that bed, like she was about to vanish." Webb puts a finger to his chin and stirs faster. "The cup was really hot, so I held it for her as she drank. After her last sip, she patted the space next to her on the bed, motioned for me to come, and I fell asleep beside her."

"What happened?" I ask.

Webb stops stirring and stares at the stove, his lip curled, the wooden spoon loose in his hand. "The next morning, I woke up on the living room couch. My mom was sitting with me. She told me Po-Po was dead. I cried and ran to my grandfather. I remember screaming at him. 'You said the potion would make her feel better,' I yelled over and over. He told me the medicine took away my grandmother's pain, that now she was where she belonged, and that whenever I needed her, she'd be with me."

I shift on the stool; my eyes fixed on him. "What else did he say?"

"He quoted an old Chinese proverb." Webb adjusts his glasses and looks up at me. "All of life is a dream walking. All of death is a going home."

Webb strains the hot mixture into a porcelain cup. It looks like potpourri mixed with vegetable broth, smells like wisdom. He strolls across the room and eases into the same chair the phantom woman had occupied. He rubs his friend's shoulder and wakes him up. "Hey bud, here you go," Webb says. "Drink this. It'll make you feel better."

Darryl takes a few sips and gives the cup back. "Any vodka in that?" he murmurs before rolling over and falling asleep again.

"You sure he'll be okay?" I ask Webb, hoping his potion won't have the same effect on Sho-Sho as it did on Po-Po.

Webb places the cup on the nightstand. "As soon as his fever breaks, he'll be out of the woods. And you can quote me on that."

July 1 notes:

Today, the Aging Bulls beat Florida in Game 2 of the East Finals, knotting the series. All the guys played well, even those at the bottom of the lineup, the ones Slate makes fun of the most. The team lives on to fight another day, but Biff never showed, and no one's heard from him. On top of that, another Bull might be out of the tournament.

While Darryl lay sick in bed, I interviewed Webb in the kitchenette of the room they share. Webb is one of the team's best athletes, an outfielder with a medical background who always seems to be in control. He's forty-nine years old, small but strong, sleek and tireless, thin-skinned and toothless, like a baby shark. He grew up in Pennsylvania, just outside Philly, and went to Lower Marion High School, same as Kobe Bryant. After watching him play this week, I can tell Webb has Kobe's "Mamba Mentality," the ultimate mantra for his competitive spirit, a constant quest to be better every day.

Me: How sick is Darryl?

Webb: Pretty sick. His fever's dying down, but I'm keeping an eye on his vitals. He should be fine.

Me: The Bulls pulled off a great win today. What do you think of the tourney so far?

Webb: It's awesome. If Eggan can get his act together in the outfield, we might have a shot at the title.

Me: Are you concerned that Biff is still missing?

Webb: I am concerned. I've hung out with Nerby too many times, seen him "lose his bearings" on enough occasions to *not* be concerned. That said, we're probably a better team without his weak bat in the lineup.

Me: What's the best part about being on the Bulls?

Webb: It's the love, Izzy. It's the love.

Me: Speaking of love, your team went to see *The Beatles LOVE* tonight and skipped the parking lot hang. What's so special about the parking lot?

Webb: The parking lot? With Hetan or without Hetan? That's a big question. Because without Hetan, it's a communal, heartfelt place where we lift each other up in good spirits.

Me: What about with Hetan?

Webb: It's a fucking nest of vipers.

Me: Why are the Bulls important to you?

Webb: Because I could never beat my older brothers in sports, and I'm the youngest of four. They'd tease me and say I didn't try hard enough, and it pissed me off. I always second guessed myself, thought I'd never win. I got a great education and I'm successful, but I still doubt myself sometimes. The Bulls tease me a lot, but they make me feel like I'm good enough. Except for Slate. He sucks.

Me: Would you say you have a chip on your shoulder?

Webb: A chip? It's more like a whole canister of Pringles. But I didn't get it just from playing sports against my brothers, I got it from real life. I was a good athlete in high school, and it was easy to prove myself and fit in there. But outside of sports it was tougher, you know, being Asian in a white community, dealing with all the perceptions. That we're smarter, less emotional, more competitive. Those reminders that you're different, they're hard to ignore.

Me: Growing up, did you experience much racism?

Webb: My whole life, I've heard it all. Even when it goes unspoken, I hear it loud and clear, and when it happens, it hurts. You don't forget those moments because of the emotional responses they elicit. They stay with you like scars. I know you know what I mean. That's why I play so hard and won't ever stop, even as I get older. I don't want anyone thinking they can beat me, not even Father Time.

Me: Isn't it exhausting though?

Webb: Yeah, but it gives me the juice to keep going. What about your softball career? Do you still play?

Me: No. When my father died, I lost my love for the game. I quit playing in college, just didn't need it anymore.

Softball was our thing, his and mine. I never wanted it for myself.

Webb: I get it, Izzy. But wants and needs are two different things.

In the Funnymoon suite, I stand among the gags and props, away from the seriousness of real life. On a chair in the corner, a whoopee cushion lies deflated next to a bookcase stacked with the biographies of Pryor, Carlin, Rickles, Bruce, and Foxx, as well as the complete anthology of *Jester's Digest*. On the bottom shelf, a vintage snake-in-a-can, disguised as a container of mixed nuts, awaits its next victim. I pick up the can and shake it. I turn it over in my hands and examine it. I stretch my arms away from my body, crane my neck, and peel off the lid. Nothing springs out but Woody Woodpecker's annoying laugh.

I flip on ESPN; the Yankees and Angels are knotted in the ninth. Needing to check in back home, I sit on the couch, text "Feeling okay?" to Mami, and hit Send. *Swoosh.* Brett Gardner strikes out on a 3-2 slider in the dirt.

As Gary Sanchez moseys to the plate, I pry off my sneakers, text "You good, sis?" to Ava, and hit send. *Swoosh.* "The Kraken" pops to second.

Up next: My boss and Gleyber Torres. I haven't communicated with Kay since she told me the magazine might survive two days ago. Gleyber hasn't hit the ball out of the infield in over a week. I still have faith in both of them. I fiddle with my phone and lean back on the couch, text "Trip is getting interesting" to Kay, and hit send. *Swoosh.* Gleyber swings and—

The TV dies, and the room goes black. I look out the window; the Vegas lights are shining bright on the strip. Only the Emerald Outpost has lost power. I turn on my phone's flashlight and stumble around searching for switches on walls and lamps, flicking them on and off like a fool, hoping one might work. My heart pumping fast, I find my way back to the couch and sit still for a moment. And there, in the dark, I receive three texts:

Mami: Better every day.

Ava: yeppers!

Kay: Should make for a great story.

Then the room brightens, and the TV is back on. Gleyber's rounding the bases, and the announcers are raving about "exit velo." I get up and switch off all the lights except for the lamp by the couch. When I sit back down, the narrow beam shines on my face, and I recall a blackout in 2003. It was a Thursday; I was almost six. Papi and I had just come home from our work-out at Reiss Field. People on the street were talking about how the power in our apartment building had gone out after we left. The whole city had lost electricity, they told us. At dusk, Senora Rojas came over with her four-year-old daughter, Pia. We ate peanut butter sandwiches and watched the sun set from our terrace, hoping the lights would come back on, knowing they might not. When it got dark, the adults lit candles and drank plum wine in the kitchen while Pia and I played flashlight tag. I snuck around for hours that night, avoiding the light, knowing if it shined on me, I'd lose. There was only one spot in our whole apartment where I was safe; that was on the couch, under the picture of the araguaney tree. I called it "home base," the only place where the light couldn't get me.

DAY TEN

T 5:30 A.M., I spring out of bed and turn off my alarm before it can do its job. I check my phone for word on Biff, but there's no update, and for now, no news is bad news.

Tired from sitting around for the past ten days, I change into leggings and a T-shirt, brush my teeth, and text the Bulls to ask if anyone wants to join me for a workout. Hank, Bryson, and Webb agree to meet me at the hotel gym at seven. We hop on four treadmills facing the floor-to-ceiling window, running the length of the room, overlooking the Vegas strip. The day is bright. For the next forty minutes, the guys and I run and sweat to a string of '90s rap tunes pumping out of the gym's sound system.

Feeling good after my workout and a shower, I write in my journal about how things are turning around for me on this trip, how I'm closer with the team now. I mention the care Webb showed Darryl last night and try to make sense of the woman I thought I saw at his bedside. As I fill a whole page with ink, I can't help but think of the conversation I had with Webb, and our similar experiences with racism.

During my freshman year of high school, I had plenty to write about in my diary: how I was relieved whenever another person of color walked into one of my classrooms, how kids either hated me for my "free ride" or asked what kinds of drugs my dad sold to afford Long River Prep's $34,500 per year price tag. But softball still dominated my life and my thoughts, and I filled page after page of my journal with the good stuff, the bad stuff, and the worst stuff. One night that spring, following my first varsity game for the Chiefs, I came home, grabbed a pen, and divulged an ugly truth.

> *... Today there was a note in my locker that said, "Hey, Spic-abel, no one wants you at this school!" I don't know if I should take it to the principal or if I should tell Mami. Or if I should tell anyone... We won our game this afternoon 11-3, beat our rival for the first time in eight years. I got four hits and drove in six runs, but none of the girls wanted to sit with me on the bus... Coach Arsdale told me I played great, said he's thinking of moving me up in the order, maybe hit me third. But our centerfielder, Carli, is a senior and always hits third. Tomorrow, I'm going to tell Coach I want to stay in the five hole...*

In the ballroom after breakfast, the team and I stand in a circle discussing their rubber match with Florida, set for this afternoon, and the current situation regarding Biff. Most of the guys sound nervous when talking about the game. Some look scared. A few have probably already packed their bags. I stand quiet between Slate and Benny. When the nattering dies down, Sal says, "What do you think, Izzy, we got a shot against the Tigers?"

The Bulls stare at me and wait, like they have all the time in the world, like they want to hear my opinion. My focus on the floor, I clear my throat and put a finger to my lip. My shoulders loosen. I lift my gaze to meet Sal's. "You guys need to take the fight to them." The men nod in unison, and I add, "If you punch 'em in the mouth early, they'll be on their heels. Put up a crooked number in the first few innings, and they'll start to press."

"The kid's right for once," Slate says before kicking me in the calf. "We gotta jump on those bastards."

The team whoops and claps. Benny slaps me on the back. Vinnie musses my hair. Amid the commotion, Rodney darts into the middle of the circle. "But what about Biff? We can't keep playing and just forget all about him."

"I'm with Rodney," Wink says, projecting his voice for the first time I can recall. "We should keep looking."

Rocco adds, "I'm Facebook friends with Biff's dad, Mayor Ed. He's offering ten thousand bucks to anyone with info on his kid's whereabouts."

Slate steps forward. "Forget Nerby. Where's Darryl?"

"Still in bed," Webb says, "not fully recovered yet."

"Did he get any rest last night?" asks Bryson.

Webb yawns. "Tossed and turned for hours, talking in his sleep. Had fever dreams, screaming about rabbits or something."

Nick inserts himself into the conversation. "Rabbits?"

"Yep," says Webb. "He just kept yelling, 'I love bunnies!' again and again, whatever the hell that means."

"Did you wake him?" Nick asks.

"No, I just raised the volume on my white noise app and let him sweat it out."

"Okay, back to Biff," Leo says, cutting in front of Nick. "I'm concerned. We all know he's aloof and flighty and absent-minded."

"And aloof," says Bo.

"Correct," Leo replies with an eye roll. "But this is serious. I've put some more calls in with his family, but they still haven't heard from him, and I've contacted his friends."

"Which took about thirty seconds," Benny butts in and quickly adds, "I'm kidding, of course. C'mon, I love the guy."

"My point," Leo continues, "is that Biff hasn't been in touch with anyone since he went on that hike."

Wink scratches at his beard and drags out an idea. "Let's withdraw from the tournament and scour the desert," he says. "Who cares if the police told us to stay put? Izzy said he mentioned the Burning Man festival in Black Rock City. Maybe he's trying to hitch a ride there."

The suggestion elicits little reaction.

"Look," Wink says, "Biff's a dad like all of us. He's got daughters who are wondering where he's gone, how he could just disappear. We owe it to them to find him, or at least look."

Something about Wink's choice of words, his conviction in them, stirs a notion in my gut, and I want to follow him in the search.

"Gimme one s-s-second." Harold taps a calculation on his phone. "Black Rock City is four hundred sixty-five miles from Vegas," he says. "It'd take one hundred fifty hours to w-w-walk there. Biff's been missing for sixty-eight hours. Walking nonstop, assuming nobody p-p-picked him up, he'd cover forty-five percent of the total distance, which would p-p-put him in Goldfield, Nevada."

"And you all thought I was the one with wacked-out theories," says Rocco.

"It's 10:30 right now," Harold continues. "So, if we d-d-drove an average of seventy miles per hour, we could be there by 12:50."

"We're not going anywhere," Slate says. "I ain't giving up a chance to win a trophy for Shalers. The poor guy's never won a thing in his life."

Vinnie points at Slate and nods. "He's spot on, you know."

"Let's keep playing," says Webb. "Biff's smarter than we think."

"You won't be saying that when we ID his body at the morgue," Sal says. "Or maybe you will, I don't know."

"Why don't we vote on it?" Hank says, wiping sweat off his dome, looking surprised that he's contributed to the discussion. "Either we pull out of the tourney and form a search party, or we keep playing and hope for the best. We've got fourteen Bulls here without Clete, Biff, and Darryl. Majority rules, assuming there's no tie."

The team agrees to a secret ballot. Benny fetches fourteen plastic forks and spoons from the buffet table and gives one of each to every Bull. "When I count to three," he says, "throw a fork into the circle if you want to look for Biff. Throw a spoon if you want to finish the tournament. Ready? One... two..." Then Benny stops and looks at his utensils. "Wait, sorry, which one did I say means keep playing?"

"Spoon!" the entire team yells.

"Okay thanks," Benny says. "One... two... three!"

The votes are cast.

Leo rakes the ballots off the carpet and tallies them. He sighs and shakes his head. "How about that?" he says. "It's my dad's favorite cocktail: seven and seven. Who's the tiebreaker?" The room falls silent.

I walk into the circle. Leo hands me a fork and a spoon. I cast my vote.

"Well, Biff, wherever you are," Leo says as he picks up the spoon. "Hope you're comfortable, because the rest of us have a tournament to win."

Three hours later, the Bulls and I pack up the equipment and find our seats on the bus. Bo reclines behind the wheel, in no hurry to depart, a grin plastered on his face.

"What's the holdup, Loth?" Slate yells from the back while

ripping open a beer. "We didn't make you our designated driver to sit in the parking lot."

"Just waiting for a straggler," Bo replies, yanking the door release lever.

A voice booms, "Who you calling a straggler?"

The team turns to the front of the bus. Bo claps and stomps, displaying a high level of excitement, which for him constitutes anything above a pulse. The rest of us sit up tall in our seats and explode with cheers as Darryl swaggers onto the bus in full uniform. He raises both arms, nods and smiles, welcoming the praise like a returning war hero. After a full minute of applause, Slate says, "Hey, you're here."

Darryl shakes his head. "Brilliant observation. Someone get that guy a Rubik's Cube." And he strides down the aisle, hugging each teammate along the way, laughing his loud and joyful laugh, which is indeed, as Mac Lervacci had warned, highly contagious.

"How you feeling, big guy?" asks Benny.

"Like a hundred bucks, tax free," says Darryl. "Now let's kick some Tiger tail."

We arrive at Big League Dreams, back at the Wrigley replica, and I head for my spot in the stands. During previous games, I sat in the front row between the Bulls' dugout and home plate. For this game, I sit in a seat next to their dugout. The scoreboard thermometer reads 105, hot enough to make Jehovah's Witnesses take up telemarketing. As I root out my notebook from my backpack, the Bulls pair up and play catch. Along the leftfield line, the Florida Tigers sign autographs for a group of schoolboys and flirt with their moms.

Moments away from the first pitch, Slate jogs off the field after loosening up. When he reaches the dugout, I catch his eye and give him a nod. He nods back.

"Hey, go get 'em," I say.

"Shut up," he replies, and we both laugh.

My inspirational words have an obvious effect because Slate thumps two homers, the first in the opening frame with a runner on board, a straightaway rocket that leaves the park so fast the outfielders never take their hands off their knees. The second dinger comes in the fourth, after Webb and Benny walk and Valentino Timms tries to handcuff Slate with an inside fastball, which the Bull's cleanup hitter turns on like a mob rat, swinging his thirty-four ounce Miken Maniac with such force, his forearm tats have to hang on for dear life. On impact, the softball screams. The Tiger's third baseman leaps for the low laser, but it's already past him. The ball buzzes by the schoolboys sitting along the leftfield line—providing the first close shaves of their young lives—and clangs off the metal foul pole. From my seat, I can identify the dent. The Bulls from Walnut Gap have come to play.

But the Tigers from Okeechobee have done the same, despite a Koufaxian effort by Vinnie who, after six innings, has K'd six Floridians with a tricky assortment of windups, off-speed pitches, and sneaky fastballs. The Bulls have last licks in the seventh, the score tied, 9-9. With two outs, Nick strolls to the plate. I drop my notebook, wipe my palms on my shorts, and pick at my nails. "C'mon, Nick. You got this," I whisper. The softball gods hear me, and Nick belts a double into the right-centerfield gap. Up next is the man who was on death's door twelve hours ago: Darryl Shonjon. From the top step of the dugout, the Aging Bulls stand and cheer.

"All we need is one pin, Rodney," bellows Sal, his reference to a classic Miller Lite commercial drawing a chuckle from everyone except Hank, the only Bull too young to remember 1982, who assumes Sal is talking about Pittbase, not Dangerfield.

Darryl looks back at his teammates and adjusts his prescription glasses. "Watch and learn, boys." Then he taps his bat on the plate, winks at Valentino Timms, and rips a single right through the pitcher's beautiful, brawny legs.

I jump out of my seat. Nick tears around third and beats the throw home. I grab my head with both hands, knocking my shades off their perch. "Oh my god! We won! We won!"

The Bulls barge out of the dugout and storm the field. Half of them embrace Nick at home plate, half tackle Darryl at first base. I reach down behind my seat and pluck my glasses off the ground. The handful of spectators sitting in my section looks at me cross-eyed. I scoff, cup my hands, and scream as loud as I can into my makeshift megaphone—the same way fans used to scream for me. "Way to go, Shonjon!" I yell.

He looks up at me, flashes a smile, and raises a fist. I keep my phone in my pocket and take a mental picture of the moment.

The on-field celebration carries over into the parking lot, where many beers are chugged, and many Bulls are hugged. An inebriated Hank ricochets through the crowd, brandishing a bottle of Casamigos, slurring in a high-pitched drawl like an Alvin & The Chipmunks record playing at half speed. "We're... moofin' on to da... U.S. shamshimship series, baby. Hee-hee, lessee how... we do... against big, bad Oregon and... da tourneemint's bessss player, Race McIntyre. Oooh, he's... soooo... scary."

"Who's that?" I ask a hammered Hank.

"Who... dat?" he repeats while clutching my shoulder in an attempt to stay vertical. "Errrr-one knowsssssss... Race. He's tearing... up... the tourney, hee-hee-hee."

Back at the hotel, the Bulls commandeer a fleet of high-top tables at the Ruby Slipper Lounge while the One Hit Blunders end their show with Dave Mason's soft rock '70s smash, "We Just Disagree." Slate stands on a chair and waves his arms, conducting a chorus of geriatric gamblers and middle-aged businessmen, until a sing-along breaks out. I sit with my back against the wall, sip a beer, and smile. Slate dances over, takes my hand, and urges me to join the fun, but I've never heard the song in my life and don't budge. (In 1977, Barker Avenue B-Boys would've blared Kool Herc, not Dave Mason, from their boomboxes, and that was twenty years before I existed.)

I return to my beer, listen and learn, and by the third chorus, I know most of the words, something about good guys and bad guys.

After the One Hit Blunders conclude their set, the Pastafarians set up their instruments. Next to me, Wink and Sal stand together speaking in low tones. I turn away but bend an ear as Wink whispers to the team manager, "We have to stay a couple more days now. What should we do about finding Biff?"

"Don't worry, he'll turn up," Sal says in a hush. "But think about it this way; if he doesn't turn up, at least we'll go home with a great story."

Through a haze of cigarette smoke, Cousin Stu enters the lounge with three gray-haired men in pinstripe suits and makes a beeline toward me. I peek over both shoulders, praying the men are looking for someone, anyone, else. I tap Sal on the back, and he spins around as his cousin approaches.

"Sal, we gotta talk," Stu says through a frown, his three companions looming behind him, scowling like rejects from a *Goodfellas* casting call.

"Sure, what's up?" Sal says, moving between me and Stu.

"It's about your team and the tournament," Stu says. "Vegas is setting a line on your series with Oregon. The head oddsmaker wants a word with you. It'll be quick. Follow us."

Sal sets his Stella on the high-top and stares me in the face. "If I'm not back in twenty minutes, call security."

"Seriously?" I say.

"Nah, I'm busting balls." Then he whips out his wallet. "Here's my card. Give it to Darryl to pay the tab."

After Stu and his henchmen escort Sal away, I sit with Darryl at a table near the stage as the Pastafarians cover UB40's "Red Red Wine," featuring Rodney on the steel drums.

"Here's Sal's Amex," I tell the hero-of-the-day. "He wants you to settle up the tab."

Darryl takes the card and grins. "Figures," he says. "I hit a walk-off and they still treat me like their accountant."

"Need a drink?" I ask as he rattles the ice in his glass.

"You don't know me very well, do you?"

I smile and say, "I'll be right back."

Standing at the bar in the back of the lounge, waiting to be served as I watch Rodney rock it onstage, I realize I've been in the same clothes for thirteen hours. I'm thinking I might head up for a shower when I hear a familiar voice.

"Can I help you?"

I turn and face Russell, and I decide to stay.

He's dressed in white linen, the top three snaps on his short-sleeved shirt undone, the cross on his gold necklace glistening against his perfect skin. He's taller than I remember, cuter, his curls cut tighter, from a recent shape up, I guess. His glossy smile would make an orthodontist blush. His dimples are disarming.

"Oh, hey, thanks again for your help at the pool," I say as if suddenly remembering who he is, as if I haven't been thinking about him for three days.

"Don't mention it," he says, tossing a towel over his shoulder, creating a breeze sending the scent of his Tom Ford Body Spray my way. It smells like he's wearing poetry.

"You know, I never paid you for that drink."

"You're good." He leans in, and our eyes lock, while the bar between us chaperones. "The first Razzamatazz is always on the house."

I smirk and order two vodka tonics. Russell hooks me up and then looks to help another customer. Before he steps away, I say, "What do I owe you?"

"You're with the Aging Bulls," he says. "They've got you."

I leave a five-dollar tip and return to Darryl, who's leaning back in his chair, tilting his head, and shaking an empty glass above his gaping mouth. I slide one of the V&Ts in front of him and wink.

He holds his glass high. "Here's to me, Mr. Clutch." And the sound of our laughter contaminates the air, infecting us both.

"I'm glad you feel better," I say.

"Me too," he says. "Last night was strange."

The reggae group finishes their set, and we polish off two more vodka tonics while losing ourselves in conversation for the better part of an hour. The Ruby Slipper has nearly emptied but won't close till 2 a.m. Our herd has thinned, and when Bryson and Bo bolt, the only other Bull remaining is Rodney. After dapping up the three Vitos, he dashes off stage and approaches our table. Shimmering in sweat, he hugs Darryl and gives me a fist bump. "You know, I like to see you two hanging out together," says the Trinidadian. "I knew you'd become friends, man, right from the very start."

"You've got good instincts," I say.

"And Darryl," Rodney says, "I don't know what Webb did for you, but I'm glad you're healthy, man. He must've used some powerful, magical shit on you."

"Yeah, I don't know, but I do feel great," Darryl says, stealing a glance at me.

After Rodney says goodbye, Darryl and I sit silent. The room has cleared. I tap my nails against an empty glass and stare at him as he scratches his palm.

"So?" I say.

He lifts his chin. "So what?"

I put my forearms on the table and lean in. "You saw her, didn't you?"

"Saw who?"

"The woman by your bed last night," I say.

He removes his hat and glasses, places them on the table, and rubs his head. "I don't know what you're talking about."

"You do so," I say. "Don't lie to me."

He lets out a long breath, like he's been holding it in for years, then he looks at me with tired eyes. "Red kimono?"

"Yes."

"Yeah, I saw her."

July 2 notes:

This afternoon, the Bulls got a huge win against Florida to move on to the U.S. Finals. For the first time, I'm not nauseated when I say, "We're staying a bit longer in Las Vegas." Biff Nerby still hasn't come back from his hike, but at least Darryl recovered from his sickness, thanks to a magical remedy Webb concocted and a mystical force he conjured.

With a little help from his friends, Darryl got his groove back today and got the game-winning hit. I admit, I haven't been this excited in a while, probably not since I got my book back from Clete, but that was more relief than anything. I'm not sure what's changed. But I know to feel excited, you need to feel comfortable, and to feel comfortable, you need to know you belong.

Today's interview is with the man of the hour, Darryl Shonjon. For our conversation, we sat alone at a table in the hotel lounge after celebrating with the team. A big man with a big laugh, fifty-five-year-old Darryl is originally from Brooklyn, shares first base duties with the equally-limited Leo, and vaguely resembles Idris Elba after a really, really bad night's sleep.

Me: So, how's it feel being the hero?

Darryl: Nothing I'm not used to.

Me: Seems like you're a man who enjoys celebrating, always the last one to pack up in the parking lot after games, and now here in the lounge.

Darryl: I've been the last to leave many times. But I will never be the first to leave.

Me: Tell me about your illness yesterday. What happened?

Darryl: Ugh. I never felt so sick in my life. Head was killing me, skin was burning up, couldn't keep anything down, dizzy as hell. For a minute there, I felt like Fred Sanford, thought it was the big one. Coming to join you, Elizabeth.

Me: And Webb's the reason you're still with us, huh?

Darryl: Dude saved my life. I know Slate gives him a hard time, but I owe that guy.

Me: So, tell me about your last name. You got a line of apparel like the other Sean John?

Darryl: I'm all substance, no style. But just like Biggie needed Puff, the Bulls need Shonjon.

Me: Are you worried that Biff's still missing?

Darryl: Can we just focus on me here? It's kind of my night.

Me: Of course, sorry. What do you think of the tourney?

Darryl: Honestly, I didn't think we'd get this far, didn't think we'd win a game, didn't think we'd score a run. I'm amazed we made it to Vegas, period.

Me: What does being on the Bulls mean to you?

Darryl: This team's just comfortable, you know? They keep me grounded, keep me laughing when life gets stressful. No judgments, just laughs. I can count on any of those guys for anything, and they can count on me.

Me: What's your role?

Darryl: Well, I broke the color barrier on the Bulls, and I brought Rodney on board. So, I guess that makes me our Chief Diversity Officer.

Me: You know, I just, um, I think—

Darryl: What's up? Why so serious all of a sudden?

Me: It's just, I know you're kidding, and I wish I could laugh about that, but I never knew how to handle my feelings about race. My dad used to say, "Deal with that stuff, or it'll deal with you." But I never really talked to him about what that meant.

Darryl: Your pops was right. But dealing with those feelings isn't easy. It's easy to bury them. I can't say I haven't done that. I think some of us laugh to keep from crying, or from putting our fists through a wall, oldest coping mechanism in the book.

Me: Do you still bury your feelings?

Darryl: Listen, Izzy, there are three men of color on this team, along with a bunch of white dudes. That's a typical ratio, but it never gets easier. I grew up in a Black neighborhood and got bused to a white private school, did my best to fit in, but felt I didn't belong anywhere and got used to that feeling, didn't have much of a choice. So, every day I'd walk to the bus stop in my school uniform and my friends on the block would talk smack, like I wasn't one of them. Then I'd get to school, and kids would call me the

N-word. Did it bother me? Yeah, still does, 'cuz I still hear stuff like that today. It's like I'm stuck in seventh grade with grown-ass adults acting like they wanna beat me up at recess. But I don't have any answers. Sometimes I think we gotta be okay just being okay.

Me: I know what you mean.

Darryl: How do you deal with it?

Me: I try not to let it bother me, but it does. It's all that stupid stuff, like a guy a few weeks ago who said I wasn't really Latina because my playlist consisted of too many rap songs and no mariachi music.

Darryl: Wow, original.

Me: So, what are our chances of winning?

Darryl: The tournament or the battle against racism? 'Cuz I can tell you, the odds of the Bulls winning the tourney are slightly higher, and our team stinks.

Me: Any final words of wisdom?

Darryl: Yeah one last thing, if people got beef with me 'cuz of the color of my skin, that's their problem. They can get angry all they want, but I'm not down with all that hate. It's like that corny Dave Mason song. Ain't no good guy, ain't no bad guy, only you and me, and we just disagree.

Me: Think that's true?

Darryl: Nope. There are definitely bad guys.

Darryl and I are the last ones to leave the lounge. As we head toward the elevator, an elderly man in a ten-gallon hat hobbles in before us. We quicken our pace and hustle through the door just in time. The man takes one look at us and hops out.

"What floor you on?" Darryl asks.

"Six," I say.

"Okay, Big Time," he says. "In your D-luxe apartment in the sky, while the rest of us slum it on three."

I blow on my nails and say, "Just press the buttons, Shonjon."

We reach his floor, and after he steps off, he holds the door. "Hey, thanks for the talk," he says. "See you tomorrow."

On the couch in my room, after transcribing my conversation with Darryl, I wonder if the mostly white readers of *Mature Living* will care about his story. I admire that he's found a way to stay strong, but he shouldn't have had to. Once, during a lecture on emotional suppression, my psych professor said that *walls* are built to be strong, not people.

Too tired to shower, I change into sweats, slide into bed, and grab *All That You Had* and open it to where it's marked, just past the midpoint. Whenever I get halfway through my book, I always worry about the main character. She's so far from home but so close to finding her father, at a crossroads, with no idea which way to go. The girl knows her dad left on the day she was born. Now she needs to find out why.

DAY ELEVEN

I WAKE UP SUPER early, open my laptop, and review my notes and interviews. I still don't know what I'm doing with this story, but at least I have plenty of options—which is more than I could say after my four years at Northwestern.

Following graduation, I left Chicago and moved back to the Bronx, back to our shell of an apartment. I waited tables at Café Isabel while applying for jobs at media companies and news-papers. The market was crammed with over-qualified dynamos whose writing abilities ran circles around mine, I assumed. As my prospects dwindled, I came to a familiar conclusion: I wasn't good enough.

In the course of six months, I landed zero interviews but gained an inbox full of rejection emails and twenty extra pounds packed onto my thighs and hips, which I blamed on my abuelas back in Venezuela. (Every dish on our restaurant's menu came from their recipes, and each of my three squares a day included several empanadas.) I looked horrible, and I felt worse.

On top of it all, Ava developed type 1 diabetes. Without health insurance, my mother had difficulty affording insulin and doctors' appointments. At fourteen, my sister struggled socially and at school. Mami stretched herself thin to cover our needs but didn't have the money or time to succeed. She managed the café every day and worked the graveyard shift at a nursing home four nights a week. I wanted to help more, but until I brought home a paycheck, I was useless. Trapped in a life not meant for me, I watched the world go by, without it watching me at all.

When I got my first job offer, I jumped all over it like it was a belt-high fastball. *Mature Living* magazine was a dying publication, based in Manhattan, with dwindling ad revenues and a shrinking subscriber base of elderly readers. My receptionist position wasn't what I'd hoped for, but it was full time, with benefits. I respected my new boss, Kay, an angular woman, abrupt but authentic, who said if I answered calls for a year, she'd let me start writing for the magazine.

I didn't love that desk job. My salary was a notch above minimum wage. The work was soul-sucking and simple. But if I wanted to be a "real" journalist someday, I had to pay my dues. Besides, I was finally able to help Mami with the bills.

So every Monday through Friday, I got on the subway, went to that gig, and watched my dreams run further out of reach. I put my personal life on hold, made no friends, and logged fifty-hour weeks on top of my night shifts at Café Isabel. And whenever I felt like quitting, I could hear my father yelling, "Let's go, Izzy! Put your whole heart into it."

Easier said than done, Dad.

Now, I'm finally ready to put my heart into this assignment—not sure about my *whole* heart though. Once I finish reviewing my notes, I make a cup of coffee and try to draft an opening paragraph to my story, but I still haven't found the right angle. All I know at this point is that I'll be painting the Bulls in a mostly good light, not because I feel obligated but because it's accurate.

At 7 a.m., I take an overdue shower and get dressed, then I fall back into bed and stare at the ceiling, my tangle of wet hair soaking the pillow. On the wall opposite the bed, above the mirror, another quote mocks me: *If at first you don't succeed, try, try again. Then quit. There's no point in being a damn fool about it. – W.C. Fields*

While on my way to breakfast, another group of folks with nametags on their chests shuffles past me in the lobby, quiet and somber. The men wear dark suits and ties; the women wear black dresses. A sign by the front desk reads: *The Emerald Outpost Welcomes the FDA.* I approach a young bellhop and ask, "These people work for the Food and Drug Administration?"

"No, ma'am," he says. "They're with the Funeral Directors of America. Got their convention here the next three days."

And just when I thought the black cloud had lifted.

Outside the Taj Meh Hall's double doors, Nick leans against a wall and hides his face while talking on his phone, slouching like he spent the night on a cinderblock cot. He hangs up when he sees me, shoves the cell into his pocket, and fixes his hair. "Hey, good morning," he says, chipper and cheery, his eyebrows dancing on his high forehead. "What's up?"

"Your Verizon bill," I say. "You've been on the phone since the day we met."

"Tell me about it," he says, his brows sitting this one out, his body loosening.

"Everything all right?"

"Yes, but not really," he says. "Just stuff going on with my mom."

"Wanna talk about it?"

"Trust me, you don't want to know."

In the ballroom, the Bulls and I eat breakfast, rejoicing over the victory against Florida, and Darryl's heroics, and the late-night celebration. When Wink brings up Biff, the vibe in the room deadens. I can't speak for anyone else, but I'm concerned about the lanky shortstop and assume the worst. His disappearance isn't normal, but then, nothing about the Aging Bulls is normal.

I'm still eating when the double doors burst open, and I drop my fork, sending egg crumbles onto the carpet. A stocky man in a tan suit walks into the center of the room carrying a white cardboard box with *Nerby Evidence* written on the side in black Sharpie. "Good morning everyone, my name's Detective Fogarty," the man says with a toothpick on his lip. "I'm looking for a Mr. Sal Rucosa."

I place my hands on the table and sit still, remembering how Papi taught me to act in front of law enforcement.

Sal steps forward. "That's me, Detective. How may I help you today?"

"Just need you to identify an item for me," he says. "And I'll ask your whole group to set aside a few hours tomorrow to meet me at the station for questioning." As he scans our faces, his gaze lingers on Rodney, Darryl, and me.

Harold squirms in his seat. "What do you m-m-mean, q-q-questioning?"

Fogarty shoots him a look. "Someone tell *A Fish Called Wanda* here that he'll speak when spoken to." The detective opens the box and presents a ripped T-shirt covered in blood. "My men found this Yo La Tengo concert shirt in the desert, near a coyote den about two miles from here."

A collective gasp goes up in the ballroom.

"Look familiar to any of you?"

"Possibly," Sal says, moving in closer to examine the evidence.

I put my hand over my mouth and turn away, recalling Biff in that shirt during our interview. Noticing my alarm, the detective walks over and crouches next to my chair. The smell of his cologne is cloying as he whispers into my ear. "I know your kind, young lady. If you have anything to tell me, better tell me now."

I look dead ahead, try to keep my voice calm. "I don't know anything, sir."

Fogarty flicks his toothpick onto the floor and moves into the center of the room again. "By this time tomorrow," he says, "we'll have our DNA results back from the lab. I strongly suggest none of you leave town between now and then." After shaking Sal's hand, the detective packs up his box and departs the Taj Meh Hall, eyeing me as he goes.

I get up and pour a glass of water to steady my nerves, then sit alone at a table far from the door. Even though the detective was pig-ignorant, he still made me nervous, like all police officers do.

Darryl pulls up a chair. "You all right?"

I stare at my glass. "Yeah."

"Hey, I don't know what that guy said," Darryl says, "but you've got nothing to worry about."

"I know."

"And don't worry about Biff either. Wherever he is, he's fine."

"Right," I say, unconvinced. "But there's something else."

"What?"

"Our interview last night," I say. "I'm sorry it got so personal. I won't use that stuff in my story."

"It's okay."

I scratch my lip and look across the room. "The last thing I wanted was to make you uncomfortable."

"Hey, Izzy." Darryl waits for me to face him. "Use whatever you want. I'm glad I said what I said."

Before I can exhale, Leo's voice cuts the air. "Alright, team," he says, gliding toward the double doors, "I'd like to introduce a special guest who'll be delivering a motivational speech for us this morning."

"Fine, as long as it's not Rupacava," Slate says before covering up as Rocco tries to plant a kiss on his cheek.

"Believe it or not, our guest is even less inspirational than Rocco," Leo says, grabbing one of the handles. "Please put your hands together for—"

He opens the door.

The Bulls erupt and stampede toward the ballroom entrance, arms raised in exaltation, hooting and hollering like they've won the World Series. Darryl and I stand by our table, on our tiptoes, stretching our necks, peering through a sea of paunchy dad bods.

When our "special guest" sheds the love of the mob and enters the room, Biff Nerby wears a smile wider than the Hoover Dam. I hurry over to him and wrap him in a hug. And behind his dark sunglasses, I think he might be crying.

The clamor grows and questions fly till Leo takes charge again. "Okay, Biff, will you please tell us where the hell you've been?"

Biff tucks in his baby-blue polo and adjusts his glasses. "Well, I started a new job in Florida this week," he says. "I thought it started in August, but I got my months mixed up."

"Classic Nerby," Bryson says.

"I'm managing a time share company," says Biff. "Well, not really managing the whole company, just kind of looking after the property. Actually, I'm more on the maintenance side of things. But it's super cool. I get to set my own hours and everything."

"Why didn't you answer our calls and texts?" I ask. "We were really worried."

"Would you believe me if I told you I lost my phone?" he says.

"Yes," the rest of us say.

"We thought you were dead, you fucker," Slate says before taking off his Maryland hat and lashing Biff across the arm. "They found your bloody shirt in a coyote den."

"Oh, that's a funny story," says Biff, rubbing the scrapes on his arm. "I cut my hand on a cactus and used my shirt to stop the bleeding. Then I tossed the shirt in a hole because it was disgusting and gross, and it was really hot out anyway, so I didn't really need a shirt."

Benny takes off his Celtics hat and lashes Biff across the other arm.

"Are you playing with us today?" asks Sal.

"No, I've got meetings," says Biff, rubbing his new scrapes. "My company's home office is in Vegas—so weird, right?—and I'm here for two days of training, flying back to Florida tomorrow. But hey, good luck against Race McIntyre. I remember watching him play with the Pawtucket Red Sox when I was in college. My dad was friends with the GM, and they used to take me into the clubhouse after games. Race and I had a few beers together back in the day."

"Hey, Nerby, we're glad you're alive," Slate says, "but everyone stopped listening to you after the coyote story."

I click a photo of Biff as he starts his little lawnmower laugh. "Ha-ha-ha-ha-ha-ha."

And it's the sweetest sound I ever heard.

Later, when we arrive at Big League Dreams, it looks like we took a wrong turn and ended up in Boston. The Fenway Park replica at the facility is a dead ringer for the real thing: a mini Green Monster in left with a tiny CITGO sign beyond; a little triangle indention in the centerfield wall; and a puny Pesky Pole in right. Everything but 37,731 drunken Irishmen throwing haymakers and chanting, "Yankees suck!"

The forecast calls for rain, but only a wispy cirrus sails in the sky. (Nothing like the cloud that had hung over Fenway for eighty-six years, until Game 4 versus the Yanks in 2004, when Dave frickin' Roberts stole second and exorcised the "Curse of the Bambino.")

Twenty minutes before the first pitch, I sit in my front row seat and watch Race McIntyre run wind sprints along the third baseline. When he finishes, he limps to the on-deck circle near home plate and swings a giant bat with two weighted donuts choking the barrel. I get a good look at him, his intense green eyes, his shoulder length brown hair streaked with gray, his body lean and muscular and broken, a combination of Jacoby Ellsbury and Crash Davis.

I never heard of him till this week, but he looks familiar. I take out my phone and Google his name. Wikipedia tells me he's a forty-five-year-old minor league legend, a former five-tool outfielder, a first-round draft pick who finally got a cup of coffee with the Red Sox in 2011 after toiling for fifteen years in their farm system. He played one inning in The Bigs, got one at-bat, and struck out looking.

"This guy actually played in the real Fenway," says Hank, who's been leaning against the wall in front of me for who knows how long. "I remember watching him play that one game for the Sox, felt bad for the dude. He waited so long for a chance and never took the bat off his shoulder. I always wondered why he didn't quit sooner."

In a surprise start, Rocco toes the rubber for the Bulls. (Vinnie's fallen ill and gave Sal every excuse in the book why he can't play except for a note signed by Epstein's mother. But in his defense, a bug *has* been going around—called "McIntyre-itis"—affecting pitchers only.)

When Rocco plunks Race with a fastball in the first, he stares down the Oregon stud and booms, "You can't hit me if I hit you first." After five innings, Rocco has nailed Race in the buttocks three times on three consecutive pitches. On offense, the chaps from Walnut Gap cobble together a mixed bag of at-bats. Wink and Sal smack two hits apiece, while Bo and Harold each strike out twice. The Bulls are up 2-0 in the sixth when Bryson takes a mighty swing and clubs a two-run homer. As the ball sails over the Green Monster, a gruesome groan lumbers off Lowdan's lips, and he crumbles to the ground. The crowd goes silent.

I cringe as Bryson staggers to his feet, grabs his lower back, and hobbles to first, where Rodney, who singled ahead of him, helps his comrade around the bases. When they reach home plate, Bryson collapses. The attending EMTs cart him off the field and load him into an ambulance. Harold hops aboard to soothe his friend. The Bulls (shaken, not stirred by the incident) hang on for a gutsy 4-2 victory.

Instead of celebrating in the parking lot afterward, we jump into the Anonybus and hightail it to Desert Springs Hospital. On the way, we watch *Eight Men Out* while praying the Bulls have at least eight men available to finish the tournament. When we get to the emergency room, an icy receptionist wearing too much makeup tells us Bryson is recovering from surgery and can see only two visitors at a time. Slate leans over her desk and whispers into her ear. She winks at him then hands out passes to everyone. "Your friend is on floor sex, er, um, I mean floor six," says the blushing woman. "Room sexty-sex, oh gosh, um, sixty-six."

I roll my eyes, and the Bulls head toward the elevator. As Sal passes by, I tug on his shirt sleeve. He spins around. "What's up, Iz?"

"I'm gonna wait down here," I say.

"You sure?" asks Sal.

"Yeah, I'll go up later and ask Bryson if he's up for a quick interview. Plus, I need to check in on things back home."

"I'm sure Lowdan's pain meds are kicking in now," says Sal. "He'll be primed and ready for your interview. He won't remember it, but he'll do it."

After the Bulls go upstairs, I call Mami and Kay, need to know how my mother's feeling and what my boss has heard about the magazine's chances of survival. Neither answer, so I leave messages. Twenty minutes later, the Bulls pour back into the reception area.

I walk over to Slate. "How's he doing?"

"He's fine, almost shit himself when I gave him his homerun ball signed by that McIntosh guy."

"You found the ball Bryson hit? And Race McIntyre signed it? Are you serious?"

"Fuck no," says Slate. "I took a ball out of the equipment bag, and Benny forged the signature. Lowdan will never know the difference."

"You're a horrible person," I say, punching him in the shoulder.

"Yup, and in twenty seconds, that receptionist will agree." He grins like a fox about to prance into a henhouse and says, "Gotta go break a promise." And he struts across the room.

I can't stomach the soap opera and head for the elevator. I get off on the sixth floor, stroll down the hall, and pass two giggling nurses. "He claims he's not Rob Lowe," one of them says, "but I got a selfie with him anyway."

When I walk into Room 66, Bryson is lying in bed, propped at a forty-five-degree angle, tubes creeping out of his arms, wires attached to his chest. His gauzy eyes are half-open, and he holds a yellow softball in his hands. All around, monitors whir and beep. A small guitar leans against a wall in the corner.

"Hey, slugger," I say, approaching his bedside.

"Hey, Izzy. Thanks for showing up."

"You good?"

"Think so, can't feel much." He untangles a tube around his arm and shows me the ball Slate gave him. "Look at this," he says. "The guys brought me my homerun ball, signed by Race McIntyre."

I don't have the heart to tell him the truth, and I can tell he doesn't want to know it anyway. "I have no idea how they found that," I say. "You hit that thing a mile."

"It was a pretty good shot, wasn't it?"

I point to the guitar in the corner. "Is that yours?"

"No, Harold borrowed it from pediatrics." He extends his arm and contorts his face. "Mind, oof, handing it to me?"

I oblige and give him the instrument. He stares at the *El Toro* tattoo on my wrist. "That's pretty cool," he says. "For your dad, right?"

"Yeah," I say and step away from the bed.

As Bryson tunes up the guitar, caring for it like a wounded kitten, he winces with each turn of the tuning pegs. "You like, oof, Pink Floyd?"

"Not really, sorry."

Wearing a smile made of string, he strums a few chords and sings in a broken whisper. "Hello? Is there anybody, oof, in there? Just nod if you can, oof, hear me. Is there anyone at home?"

I sit in a brown leather chair by the window. The air conditioner next to me hums along with the song, and I listen till I'm comfortable and numb.

July 3 notes:

This afternoon, the Bulls prevailed against Race McIntyre and the Oregon Lions. The victory was just what the doctor ordered, right after she ordered a CT scan for Bryson Lowdan's back. The poor guy twisted his spine into an Auntie Anne's pretzel while smacking a two-run homer late in the contest and was probably flirting with an anesthesiologist when Wink caught the final out of the game. Immediately following the win, the Bulls and I rushed to the hospital only to find that BL's on the DL for the rest of the tourney.

Bryson's a fifty-four-year-old outfielder (big bat, average arm, good hair, aforementioned bad back) who grew up a few towns over from Walnut Gap. He's kept a low profile since we've been in Vegas, but I've seen him pound his share of rum & Cokes, destroy his share of sushi platters, and break his share of rules (the liquor locker at Skat's didn't pick itself last night). After Slate, Rocco, and Vinnie, the Bull most likely to hit up Leo for bail money would be Bryson. He's reliable and resourceful, like a favorite kitchen gadget; you never notice when he's not there, but when you need him, you can always find him crammed in the back of the drawer.

When I interviewed him, Bryson was reclining in his hospital bed, hopped up on pain meds, strumming a guitar. Not every chord was perfect, and he didn't know all the lyrics. But he knew enough.

Me: Have you always played guitar?

Bryson: Since high school. It was a good way to pick up girls back then. Now it's just a hobby. I only play classic rock mostly, reminds me of the good old days. I'm not great at it, but it relaxes me.

Me: You look pretty relaxed now. How'd the surgery go?

Bryson: The doctor said it went as well as could be expected. But she wants to keep me here for at least ten days. The nurses give me a lot of attention, which is nice.

Me: So, your teammates just left. What do those guys mean to you?

Bryson: We've got a great group. They're the best, and they're really funny too. I can't keep up with their wittiness half the time, but every now and then I'll sneak in a joke and get a few laughs.

Me: You were having a great tournament. How do you feel now that it's over for you?

Bryson: It sucks. I knew my back wouldn't get through the whole thing. But I feel like I contributed, and that's all I can do.

Me: I know you enjoy yourself in the postgame parking lot. You'll miss that the most probably, right?

Bryson: Oh yeah, that's the best part. It's great making fun of everyone and making fun of yourself too. Which reminds me, did the guys make fun of me because I wasn't there after the game today?

Me: No, we didn't hang in the parking lot today, but Slate got a few jabs in on you during the bus ride here.

Bryson: Whooaaaa!

Me: What's life like for Bryson Lowdan off the field?

Bryson: Girls' softball dominated my life for a long time, like a lot of us who coached and watched our daughters play. I've got two who played, and the youngest hopes to pitch in college next year.

Me: If it weren't for your kids, there'd probably be no Aging Bulls, huh?

Bryson: Yeah, all of us have daughters. Isn't that crazy? That's how we all became friends. And growing up, it was only me and my older sister. And my dog is female too. With all the women in my life, the Bulls are like my brothers.

Me: It's quite a life you've made for yourself.

Bryson: And this is the perfect way to spend it. Not in the hospital, but I mean playing ball with these guys. What about your life, Izzy?

Me: Mine? I've spent my whole life waiting for it to begin.

Bryson gets a Facetime call from his family, and we wrap the interview. I say goodbye, leaving him with his wife and daughters. Halfway down the hall, a teenage boy with a backpack over his shoulder turns a corner and scuffs toward me, sneaking a peek into each room he passes. As we get closer, he slows down, and we both stop.

"Um, hi," the boy says. "Do you know what room Bryson Lowdan is in?"

"Yeah, sure, it's Room 66," I say. "Last door on the left."

"Okay, thank you," he says, putting his head down and walking away.

After he takes a few steps, I say, "Hey, how do you know Bryson?"

The teenager stops and pivots. "Oh, I'm his son."

"You have a name?"

"Oh, yeah, I'm Zach."

"Wait, Zach, how long have you been in Vegas?" I ask.

"I just landed," he says. "I go to college in Colorado, and I'm working there this summer. My mom texted about my dad, and I wanted to see if he was okay." Zach puts his hands in his pockets.

I nod and smile. "That's really nice of you. He'll be happy you're here."

"Okay, well, bye." He drops his chin and heads down the hallway.

On my way to the elevator, I think of the Bulls and their

families, how we've spoken ad nauseam about daughters but not about sons. And that gets me thinking about my own family, how fractured we are without Papi.

I call an Uber and go back to the Emerald Outpost. After ordering room service and transcribing my interview with Bryson, I find a pen and open my journal. For the millionth time, I try to write about my father's death, how much I miss him, but as usual, I can't.

When dinner arrives, my veggie quesadilla tastes like it came from a 7-Eleven, isn't even close to authentic. Mami used to say, "Food should be prepared with love, but not all recipes call for it." And I remember one day, twenty years ago, at Café Isabel with my parents. Snow blanketed the Bronx, and the restaurant was empty, but Papi always kept the place open, no matter the weather. Mami led me into the kitchen, where she rarely let me go, and sat me at the counter. Standing on a stool, she reached high for a spiral notebook. She opened it to the very first recipe, written in pencil, traced over in pen. She said her mother used to make empanadas for the kids in her village to bring to the beach. Then Mami whispered the secret ingredient to me, and we gathered what we needed: corn dough, shredded beef, black beans, and fried plantains. We mixed the beef, beans, and plantains. We flattened the dough with our palms, smoothed the edges, added the mixture. Mami behind me guiding my fingers, we folded the dough and pressed it closed. When we finished, she dabbed my nose with flour, took my face in her hands, and kissed my forehead. Her lips lingered on my skin. "These empanadas are made with lots of love, Isabel," she said. "Just like you were."

DAY TWELVE

UTSIDE THE WALLS of the Emerald Outpost, the dreary morning sulks while morbid questions clang inside my head like the tolls of a bell. *If Mami dies, what will I do? How will I take care of Ava on my own?* Back and forth, the questions clang.

As I coax myself out of bed, a chill sprints up my spine. I stagger to the thermostat and turn off the AC. After drawing the curtains, I open the sliding door and step onto the balcony. Clouds gather, the sky growing darker than my thoughts. On the street below, cars and floats roll past, clad in red, white, and blue. People wear uniforms and carry signs, stroll to the sounds of a marching band, its horns and drums swaying in sync, daring the clouds to rain on their parade.

In the bathroom, I wait by the sink while the faucet water warms. After a minute, I flick my fingers under the stream. "Shit!" I pull my hand back. The water is freezing, colder than before. I cringe, shake my arm like it's covered in bees, but the sting in my hand stays. Thunder rumbles in the distance.

On television, a meteorologist says July rainstorms are rare in Vegas, that it hasn't rained in a month, that the town can sure use it, but that "Mother Nature should've picked a different day." A news anchor agrees and wishes America a happy birthday, gushes about "the greatest country in the world," boasts that every U.S. citizen has a right to life, liberty, and the pursuit of happiness. He claims all men are created equal.

Happy birthday, Papi.

I snatch the remote and change the channel, scroll through the guide, hoping to find something my father would've liked. I land on *Aliens*, the '86 sequel to the '79 blockbuster. Stretched out on my belly, my head at the foot of the bed, I imagine my parents watching that movie. I see them in my mind, snuggled in front of the TV in our apartment, a VHS tape grinding in the VCR, Papi laughing at the scary parts, Mami holding his hand. I think of the love they had for each other, the strength they showed, how they must've felt like aliens in the States after leaving Venezuela, must've viewed their new life like a sequel, must've known sequels usually flop.

At the start of Ripley's nightmare scene, I retreat to the other end of the bed. Sitting against the headboard, knees bent, I hold a pillow to my chest and bite the inside of my lip till I taste blood. When Ripley awakens in a hospital fifty-seven years after getting lost in space, I grip the pillow tighter. As a monster grows inside of her, I close my eyes, unsettled by the monster inside of me, the one that tells me I'm nothing.

I skip breakfast and spend the rest of the morning in bed.

In the afternoon, when I walk into the fake Fenway, the first thing I notice is the red, white, and blue bunting hanging over the walls along the baselines. In the stands, hungry kids pledge allegiance to the smells of grilled hot dogs and baked apple pie. A fife and drum ensemble, off beat and out of tune, struggle through wonky versions of "God Bless America" and "Yankee Doodle." A compact woman with a busty voice, squeezed into Daisy Dukes and a Stars-and-Stripes halter top, butchers the national anthem, belting out the "rocket's red stare" and "bombs thirsting for air."

The morning storm clouds have morphed into an angry, churning, floating ocean. A bald eagle, clasping the game ball in its talons, swoops out of the fluffy black sea and glides onto the field, landing on the arm of a falconer. The falconer, in turn, gives the ball to the Bulls' starting pitcher, Vinnie Shalers, who waves and salutes to the cheering crowd.

I note Vinnie's cockiness and take photos as he dances and wriggles around the circle like Foghorn Leghorn hopped up on Adderall, bopping to a song playing in his brain. He's bounced back from his "illness" and—with the Bulls ahead in the series—decides on a risky strategy: throwing strikes to Race McIntyre.

"Yo, I watched that dude yesterday," Shalers had announced during pregame warm-ups. "That sucker was clueless. Plus, I'm a lefty, he's a lefty. I'll tie him in knots."

Four homers later, Vinnie's strategy doesn't seem like such a great idea. Each one of the "Race Tracers" (as announcers in the minors used to call them) are ripped down the line, miles over the puny Pesky Pole. If there wasn't a wall in rightfield, Harold would still be running to retrieve those balls. After five innings, the Bulls are down 10-0, and Rocco takes the circle in relief, wearing his catcher's mask and chest protector to avoid adding injury to insult. When poor Bo whiffs to end the game, earning himself the golden sombrero, striking out as many times as Race has homered, the shellacking is complete. Final score: 14-0. The Bulls line up at home plate, shake hands with the victors, and clop off the field with their tails between their legs.

Our heads hanging low in the parking lot, we're only half-way through our first beers when the threat of rain intervenes. The overall mood of the team, like the weather, has taken a turn. A zap of lightning crackles over a faraway mountain, and a roll of thunder follows a second later. The storm has arrived. As we pack up the coolers and gear, the skies open up. We scramble into the bus, safe and somewhat dry, while the heavens weep.

Slate mans the wheel, sober for the first time in twelve days, one day for each step he'll never memorize. I sit in the back with Bo and try to refill his drained spirits. The bus lurches forward, then it stops with a jerk.

"Sorry," yells Slate. "I think I almost hit a guy." He leaves his post and steps off the bus, disappearing into the blinding rain. Thirty seconds later, he comes back aboard, drenched and shivering. "Dominguez," he calls. "Get up here."

I walk up the aisle and squint out the windshield through wipers swishing at full speed. A dark, hooded figure stands tall in the downpour. "Who is that?" I ask Slate.

"Someone who really wants to talk to you," he says, handing me an umbrella from under the driver's seat. "Take your time. We'll be here."

On the bottom step of the doorway, I reach into the rain and pop open the umbrella. I turn and look at Slate. He brushes away the water on his cheeks and gives me a nod before I march into the storm.

The deluge crashes down, and the din fills my ears as I slosh toward the hulking shadow. With the umbrella held low above my head, I move closer through the wall of rain till I see two large feet strapped into leather Birkenstocks standing in an inch of water. Raising the front of the umbrella, slowly at first, I reveal the person's black shorts and Red Sox sweatshirt. I stop there for a moment. Then I tilt the umbrella all the way up, showing my face, and his.

"Race?" I say.

The giant removes the hood of his soaked sweatshirt, and his long hair gets wetter and longer by the second. He wipes the rain off his forehead and looks down at me, his green eyes watery. I step closer and offer him the umbrella. He takes it, holds it over both our heads, and keeps us dry.

"I don't understand," I say, rubbing my arms. "What's going on here?"

"It was my fault," he says.

"What are you talking about?" I ask. "How do you even know me?"

The bus headlights pierce the downpour and shine onto his face. Race squints into the glare. "I followed your softball career," he says. "Thought I recognized you today sitting by the dugout. The Yankees hat tipped me off." His lip curls and he points to the bus. "When I shook hands with those guys after the game, I asked if it was you."

"Okay, stalker," I say, ready to run. "What do you want?"

"We met once before, a long time ago," Race says. "The day of your dad's funeral."

I sweep the cobwebs off a memory tucked into the back corner of my mind, and I look at Race McIntyre like he's a ghost. "You were the man at the cemetery?" I ask. "You played against my father in Venezuela?"

He nods and looks at his feet.

"What did you mean before?" I say. "What was your fault?"

He sniffles and meets my eyes. "His injury."

"What about it?"

Race sucks on his lips like he wants to keep the rest of the words inside, but they fight their way out. "It was a meaningless game, the end of winter ball," he says. "We were nineteen. I tried to score from first on a routine single, a dumb move just to impress the scouts. The centerfielder bobbled the ball, and I tore around second. I turned my head, saw the guy toss a lollipop to short, and I hauled ass. My third base coach threw up the stop sign, but I didn't care. I was halfway home when I saw your dad rip off his mask and catch the relay throw. He stood there, blocking the plate, holding the ball tight in his mitt, waiting for the easiest tag he ever made." Race exhales and watches the raindrops fall off the edge of the umbrella.

"You ran him over, didn't you?"

He doesn't look at me. "I should've gotten into a rundown," he says. "Might've made it back to third, but I was a stupid kid and kept going. Lowered my shoulder. Went for his knees." The aging ballplayer stares past me and whispers, "I don't know why I didn't slide."

A clap of thunder punctuates his statement, and the rain picks up. I imagine my father lying motionless in the dust, his lifeless dreams beside him in a heap.

I look over my shoulder at the bus, make out Slate's silhouette behind the foggy windshield. "I don't know what to tell you," I say, turning back to Race.

"I just wanted you to know the truth."

"I should get going."

"Yeah, me too." He gives me the umbrella and covers his head with his hood.

As I walk away, the rain lets up. Thunder whimpers in the distance. Standing by the bus door, I close the umbrella and glance back at Race.

"Hey, Isabel," he calls.

"What?"

"He held on."

"Who?"

"Your father, El Toro. He didn't drop the ball. He tagged me out."

I step onto the bus.

When we get back to the hotel, it's 5:45. The rain has ended, but the sky is darker than before. I go up to my room, shower, and order a soup and salad from room service. While I wait, I dial my mother.

Me: How are you feeling?

Mami: Fine, but I can't talk now, Isabel.

Me: Okay, I can call back. What's going on?

Mami: Nothing. I'll explain later.

Me: All right. Are you sure you're okay?

Mami: Sí, I'll call you tomorrow.

My mother doesn't always make sense, and I know this won't be the last time she hangs up on me, leaving me to wonder if we'll ever mend our strained relationship.

After dinner, I get a text from Rocco asking if I want to go on an Escape Room adventure. Due to a severe lapse in judgment, I say yes. At 7:30, I zigzag through a morbid maze of funeral directors in the lobby and crawl into a black Suburban with Rocco, Harold, Webb, Nick, and Hank. I've never been to an Escape Room and have heard mixed reviews, everything from "scary" to "easy" to "impossible" to "cheesy." I don't know what to expect but feel comfortable with the four smartest Bulls—plus Rocco, who springs for the Uber XL and our forty-dollar per person Escape Room entrance fee.

Ninety minutes later, I stumble onto the Las Vegas strip, gasping for air, after escaping from a virtual ax murderer who trapped me and the Bulls inside a simulated creepy cabin buried deep in an imaginary forest. If it wasn't for Harold's big brain, Webb's competitiveness, Nick's resolve, and Hank's unexpected logic, Rocco and I would've needed elephant tranquilizers to ease our panic attacks.

On the strip, Fourth of July hoopla erupts, and the street is littered with obnoxious drunks setting off fireworks and waving flags. Rocco bops and stomps to the beat of a Keith Urban song blasting out of a passing convertible. "Yo, this celebration is lit!"

he says, taking his phone from his pocket. "I'm canceling our Uber back to the hotel. Let's hang out!"

"You can," says Webb. "I gotta rest for tomorrow's game."

"I'm beat," Nick adds. "Knock yourself out, Rupacava."

Harold and Hank keep quiet but follow the others down the sidewalk. I take two steps in their direction, more than willing to call it a night.

"Oh no you don't, Izzy," Rocco says behind my back. "You've got an interview to conduct."

I freeze, turn, and nod. "Why not?"

"Great," he says before looking down the street and yelling to the other Bulls. "Yo, fellas, we'll catch up later." They're already out of earshot.

We duck into a cigar bar called The Americana and find a table near the window. "I'll grab a couple of brewskis," Rocco says.

He pushes through the smoke and blends in with well-coifed white men wearing Brooks Brothers shirts and drinking bourbon at the bar. I scratch a make-believe itch on my ear and squirm in my chair. I tug on my blouse and button an extra button on top. Rocco returns with two tall glasses of Bud. We clink them together, and I spill some of mine on the table.

"Happy Independence Day," he says before taking a ten-second sip.

"Yeah, you too."

He burps and notices the mess I made. "I'll get something to wipe that up." He leaves again and comes back with a handful of cocktail napkins and two more beers.

July 4 notes:

At the start of the tourney, there were seventeen Aging Bulls, and no one gave them a snowball's chance in Vegas to win. Now there are fourteen, and they have even less of a chance. Clete, Biff, and Bryson won't be riding in on their white horses to save the day. Yet still, despite injury and adversity, the Bulls are locked in a stalemate against an unbeatable foe.

Today's interview is with starting catcher Rocco Rupacava, a fifty-four-year-old wrecking ball of chaos. He's a brash, opinionated contrarian, a combination of Knute Rockne and Julian Assange, a former high school football player who helped the Union Farmers win a New Jersey state title back in 1985. I'm guessing Mr. Rupacava didn't spend a lot of time in concussion protocol, and if you heard him talk, you'd swear his name was Rocco Balboa.

We shared a couple of beers at a bar called The Americana. Rocco was chatty, warm, and generous. During our conversation, the guy was an open book, one with lots of Amazon reviews, not all of them glowing, but I enjoyed reading his story and formed my own opinions. As we spoke, I got to know a devoted family man who'd been knocked down and counted out before, and I felt for him, the same way I felt for Rocky after Clubber Lang destroyed him in two rounds.

Me: Enjoying tonight's festivities?

Rocco: Oh yeah, baby. Nothing better than July fourth. We should pick up some M-80s later and put 'em under Hetan's pillow.

Me: Were you as nervous as I was in the Escape Room?

Rocco: Not for a second. I had total confidence in Nick, Hank, Webb, and Harold. I knew they'd get us out. I didn't have as much confidence in Nick and Hank though. Or in

Webb either. So basically, yeah, we would've been screwed without Harold.

Me: What happened in the game today?

Rocco: Listen, once in a blue moon, Shalers throws a clunker. McIntyre got lucky and ran into a few fastballs right down the pike, simple as that. But Vinnie's a tough S.O.B., and Race won't see those same pitches tomorrow.

Me: What does being on the Bulls mean to you?

Rocco: Honestly, Izzy, I don't know what I'd do without the Bulls. This is the best group of guys I know. I've thought long and hard about the meaning behind this team, and it really comes down to three simple things: We are who we are. It is what it is. And we do what we do. Does that make sense to you? 'Cuz no one else seems to understand me when I say that.

Me: Sure, whatever. What about the postgame parking lot? Can you tell me why that's so special?

Rocco: We solve all the world's problems in the parking lot. If people would just listen to us, the world would be a better place.

Me: What's your role on the field?

Rocco: Starting catcher, backup pitcher, team philosopher.

Me: What's your life like off the field?

Rocco: I'm all about pride. I'm proud of my buddies, proud of my work, proud of my beautiful wife, and proud of my daughter. Those two ladies, they're my everything.

Me: What were you like as a kid?

Rocco: Oh, I was a handful. Hard to believe, I know. God, it's funny, I was just thinking about a recurring nightmare I had as a kid. I'll never forget it, always the same thing, me alone in a big city, turning down a dark alley, and getting abducted by a giant shadow. I always had the feeling someone was out to get me, knew early on I had to be a fighter.

Me: Rough childhood?

Rocco: No, it was actually pretty great. I mean, it wasn't perfect, but none of us had that. That's what's great about this team. On the Bulls, we get a mulligan, another crack at our childhood.

Me: What have you learned from being on the Bulls?

Rocco: I've learned that when times get tough, people will have your back. We've got each other's backs on this team. I'm proud to be a Bull, just like I'm proud to be an American. I'd do anything for these guys. They can lean on me, and I can lean on them, and they know I'd fight as hard for them as I would for this country.

Me: You're really lucky.

Rocco: We're all lucky, Iz.

Me: Not all of us, Rocco. I mean, I'd love to believe people would have my back whenever I asked for help. But in this country, people like me don't lean on others. We get leaned on, and then we get pushed aside.

I'm not sure how much he missed, but when I look up for his response, Rocco is sleeping, chin on his chest. I reach across the table and tap his shoulder. His eyes pop open as he raises his glass. "To a night we'll never forget!"

Rocco's slumber, reasonable or not, reinforces a self-con-sciousness I've always fought, the voices in my head telling me nobody cares what I have to say. Like the boys in seventh-grade who laughed at my ideas for our class science fair. Like the girls on my club team who scoffed at my captain's speeches.

Back at the Emerald Outpost, just before midnight, I change into baggy sweats and a *Dora the Explorer* T-shirt I thrifted in the Village for three bucks. I'm not tired, too wired from the Escape Room and my conversation with Rocco. Slouched on the couch with a bottle of water, I settle into *The Wedding Singer* on HBO.

Knock! Knock! Knock!

"Yo, Iz, you awake?" Rocco's voice crashes through the door like a battering ram. "Let's hit Skat's for a quick pop."

After realizing it isn't a nightmare, I get off the couch and go to the door. "It's late, Rocco," I say. "I'm going to bed."

"No, you're not," he says through the barrier. "C'mon, just one more."

"I've had too much to drink already. I've got nothing left."

"Listen to me, you're capable of a lot more than you think," the Bulls' catcher says, sounding like he's motivating Shalers during a bases-loaded jam.

I shake my head and look down at my outfit. "I'm in sweats and a kindergartener's T-shirt. I can't go anywhere dressed like this."

"Sure you can. You'll be back here in a half hour, tops."

"Ugh." I grab my phone, Yankees hat, and room key. I unlatch the door and confirm an earlier discovery: there's no easy escape from Rocco.

DAY THIRTEEN

OON AFTER I started working for *Mature Living*, Kay made
good on her promise. Though I'd been answering phones for
only two months, she rumbled into the reception area one
day and stuck a Post-It note on my computer screen. On it, she'd
scribbled the name Dottie Willoughby.

"I'll send you an email with her contact info," Kay said.
"You're finally getting your big chance, Dominguez. Don't shit
the bed."

My debut article on Dottie—and her celebrity look-a-like
rutabagas in North Jersey—was entertaining and well-con-
structed, but my mother might have been the only person who
read it. Kay was semi-impressed and continued to give me
monthly assignments. She liked my piece on a toboggan club at
an assisted living center in the Catskills, as well as one about a
retired couple on Long Island who renewed their wedding vows
every Christmas since 1977. And I grabbed her attention with
a suggestive yet tasteful exposé: "Sex and the Octogenarian."
(Mami didn't buy that issue.)

A year passed, and after putting in what certainly felt like
my ten thousand hours, I was ready for another job. Writing
vanilla stories that appealed to Baby Boomers had cramped my

budding style. Using language they could easily digest with their Ritz Crackers and Ensure had quieted my natural writer's voice, which wasn't very loud to begin with.

Fishing for a new opportunity, I sent my work to other magazines, multimedia companies, and every newspaper in New York, but I got no bites. Scrolling through Instagram each day, I compared myself to white college classmates (bad idea, I know) who had less journalism experience but still landed better gigs, and I couldn't help but guess (bad idea again) that if I'd been a Caucasian male, I'd be writing for *The Atlantic*. I should've known their lives weren't as perfect as their social media feeds claimed, but the rational part of my brain wasn't at the top of its game.

All I needed was a better job with a boost in salary, and then I could help more with my family's finances and find a place of my own. I was suffocating in our apartment; my mother treated me like a kid; my sister wouldn't leave me alone; and the walls closed in, crushing me with photos of Papi, his eyes following me everywhere, reminding me of all that I wasn't.

But at least my dad can't see me now, waking up in the Funnymoon Suite after a night on the town with Rocco, my back sore, my head pounding. I'm lying in a tangle of sheets on the floor next to the couch, purple stains all over my Dora shirt. If I didn't know Biff was in Florida, I'd say he slipped me another gummy.

I try to piece together broken memories from the night: the Escape Room, the fireworks, a bad Keith Urban song, The Americana, my interview with Rocco, my room, *The Wedding Singer*, a knock at my door, a drink at the bar.

Following a trail of purple stains on the carpet, and what smells like Sour Patch Kids boiled in bile, I inch toward the closed bathroom door and wait outside. I gather my guts and twist the handle, peek inside and gag. Purple goop is all over the place, vomit coating every white subway tile on the floor. I can't reach the Advil on the counter to calm the calamity in my cranium, can't reach the Listerine to wash the taste out of my mouth.

Where's my phone?

I scan the entire hotel room, scour the carpet, search all surface areas, and find the cell between the couch cushions. The only clues about last night are fifteen texts, and five missed calls, from Leo Tarriso. He sent his first text at 2 a.m., the last just before my phone turned up. Each message contains one of the following exclamations: Where are you, Izzy?! Are you okay, Izzy?! Tell Rocco to call me ASAP, Izzy!!

I call Leo.

Seconds later, a flurry of knocks at the door triggers my PTSD. I jump off the couch, praying Rocco hasn't shown up with Egg McMuffins and a jug of Mimosas. Leo rushes in with bags under his eyes, his skin whiter than ever. He oozes concern. I haven't seen anyone this worried since Kate McCallister realized Kevin was missing in *Home Alone*.

"Do you remember anything?" Leo asks. "Anything at all?"

"Nothing," I say. "Ugh, I feel like such an idiot." I plop onto the couch, stretch out, and cover my face with a throw pillow.

Leo sits next to me. "Well, I can tell you what I know," he says. "And it's a good thing you're sitting down."

"Oh, god."

"At 1:45 last night," Leo says, "you called me and asked if I'd walk you down the aisle."

"What? I don't wanna hear this." I cover my ears and shut my eyes.

"So after you called, I woke up Benny and we cabbed over to the Viva Las Vegas Wedding Chapel, arrived in the nick of time."

I stiffen and stare dead into Leo's worn-out face. "Please tell me you're joking."

"Have you looked at the pictures on your phone?"

"Holy shit, there's evidence?" I offer Leo my phone. "I can't look."

He takes my cell. "You gotta face this, Izzy," he says. "It's not easy, but it's not the end of the world."

Regaining my composure, and a smidge of posture, I push the hair away from my eyes and watch as Leo swipes on a dozen recent selfies. All of them feature me in my baggy sweats, Dora shirt, and Yankees hat: the outfit I wore to Skat's twelve hours ago.

"Oh. My. God."

Leo swipes onto a selfie of me on top of the bar, bookended by Rocco and that cute bartender, Russell, each of us holding a giant Razzamatazz and mugging for the camera with puckered purple lips.

He swipes onto a selfie of me preening, piggybacking on Russell somewhere on the Vegas strip, glassy-eyed Rocco photo-bombing us from behind, sticking out his tongue, brandishing a bottle wrapped in a brown paper bag.

And my head sinks into my shoulders.

He swipes onto a selfie of me planting a fat one on Russell's cheek at a chintzy wedding chapel, an obese Elvis impersonator hamming it up in the foreground, throwing up a peace sign.

"That's all of them," Leo says.

"What? No shots of me with a missing front tooth?" I ask. "Or toting a kid named Carlos in a Baby Björn?"

Leo convinces me to rest on the couch while he cleans my bathroom floor. When he finishes, he hands me three Advil and a glass of water. "Here, take these," he says. "Then take the longest, hottest shower in the history of long, hot showers, and you'll feel a million percent better."

"Promise?" I ask.

"No," he says. "But I guarantee you'll feel at least thirty-six percent better." He smirks and points to the Advil in my hand. "Things will turn around, Izzy. But first, you gotta take your medicine."

I swallow the pills.

When Leo leaves, I get off the couch, collapse onto the bed, and pull another pillow over my face. I want to go downstairs and find Russell to apologize for whatever I did, hear what he remembers, but I'm too ashamed. After letting loose a muffled scream into the pillow, I sit up and whip it at the bookcase, knocking over another framed quote: *Tragedy is when I cut my finger. Comedy is when you fall into an open sewer and die. – Mel Brooks*

While my current situation is tragic, there's nothing comedic about the weather. Yesterday's storm didn't do diddly to cool off the city. At the fake Fenway, the scoreboard temperature flashes 108 degrees. In this kind of heat, chickens lay omelets and robins pull worms out of the ground with oven mitts. It's so hot, the vendors at Big League Dreams can't even serve chili dogs.

The Bulls warm up, taking BP whacks, throwing long toss, running wind sprints, working up a sweat. I lean against the fence down the rightfield line, away from the team, can't look anyone in the eye. I'm not sure if Leo or Benny told the others what happened to me last night, but I'm afraid of what they might think.

Fans file into the park, pouring through the turnstiles like water bursting from a dam. Till now, no Bulls game has drawn more than a hundred spectators, but the U.S. final—a do-or-die affair featuring Race McIntyre—has attracted every softball fan in Vegas willing to sit in a convection oven for two hours. A buzz cuts through the heat as the crowd settles into their seats. I imagine all of them whispering about me, pointing at me, and I want to disappear.

But the buzz isn't about me.

As I pass by the stands, I overhear fans sharing breaking news: Race isn't on the field, at the park, or anywhere, apparently out of commission with a calf injury. With just fifteen minutes till the first pitch, the best player in the tournament, the one everyone has come to see, is a no-show.

I duck into the Bulls' dugout where Leo and Benny have cornered Sal. At first I assume they're telling him how I almost married Russell, but when I move closer, I realize their conversation revolves around the missing Oregon superstar. "Dude, just tell us," Benny whispers to Sal. "You were with those mafioso characters at the Ruby Slipper the other night. Did they put a hit on Race?"

"Are you serious?" Sal says, stifling a laugh. "You think Race McIntyre sleeps with the fishes?"

Leo looks over both shoulders. "The oddsmakers are giving us no chance. We're eight-and-a-half run underdogs, but that was assuming McIntyre would play."

"Guys, I'm like Shultz on *Hogan's Heroes*," says Sal. "I know nothing."

"God, you're old," says Leo.

"There's no way anyone bet on us," says Benny, his shifty eyes on the lookout. "If we cover, Vegas will win millions. Can we get into trouble for this?"

Sal chuckles. "I'm not in on the fix, fellas, and I didn't make Race an offer he couldn't refuse, even though I *am* Sicilian." Then he turns to me and says, "Izzy, have you heard anything?"

"Yeah." I step in closer. "There's a rumor flying through the stands that Race pulled a calf muscle and told his team he couldn't walk."

"That's the most ridiculous injury excuse I ever heard," says Leo. "If any of us said that we'd be laughed off the team. Sal, tell us the truth."

Sal lifts his arms to the heavens before crossing himself. "As

God as my witness, I had nothing to do with this," he says. "Now, let's get out there and win." Then he rubs his hands together. "Those guys whacked us yesterday, and revenge is a dish best served cold."

I sink into my seat and open my notebook. Vinnie throws his warm-up pitches, looks strong and confident in the circle. Starting at first base, Leo whips pregame grounders to his fellow infielders, shouting encouragement to all. In their dugout across the diamond, the Lions slouch on the bench, lost and tentative, unsure of themselves without their leader. Race's absence means the Bulls have a shot, but I wish he was here. After our conversation in the rain, I'd like to see him again and thank him for his honesty. I'm still angry, but I want to forgive him.

From the onset, it's clear Vinnie doesn't have his best stuff, but the Bulls' outfielders save his ass. When Oregon's first batter leads off with a bomb to left, Hank plays the ball off the mini Green Monster like Carl Yastrzemski and holds the guy to a single. With two down and the bases jacked in the third, Harold charges a low liner in right, lunges, and snares the ball off his shoestrings. In the fifth, Webb scales the wall in right center and robs the Lions of a three-run homer, preserving a two-run Bulls' lead. And in the seventh, Benny turns back the clock (along with Oregon's hopes for a comeback) and pegs two runners out at the plate, thanks to a pair of textbook swipe tags by Rocco.

On offense, the second base rotation of Nick and Wink chips in with RBI doubles. Clueless Bo strikes out again, for the seventh time in the series, but manages a run-scoring bloop. In the end, the bettors in Vegas lose a bundle, and the Aging Bulls win 5-4 to advance to the World Championship.

In the parking lot afterward, the celebration equals history's most joyous occasions: the surrender of Germany in '45; man's first flight at Kitty Hawk; and the discovery of fire by Homo erectus. Oktoberfest and Mardi Gras have nothing on us. The only comparison might be the Running of the Bulls in Pamplona.

"We're not done yet!" Rocco yells after ripping off his jersey and climbing on top of the Anonybus. "Let's win this whole fuckin' thing!"

In between toasts and cheers, the players mock each other, spearheaded by the man who sees himself as the horns. "Hey Bo, I wouldn't mind your batting slump," Slate says, "if you didn't throw like you have no fingers."

Saving Loth from Hetan's wrath, Sal steps in and assembles everyone together. "As you know, we're down to fourteen players," the Bulls' manager says. "None of us planned to be here this long, but we won't be home now for another week. Anyone have a work conflict?"

"I'm all good," says Benny.

"No problem here," says Wink.

"I can stay," says Leo at the same time as Darryl.

"Who are we kidding?" says Sal. "Our employers know we're all useless."

"Especially those of us who are our own bosses," Webb says. "I'm sure Slate and Hank agree with me on that."

"I love you, Ucho," says Slate. "But you're not funny, so stop trying."

"I've got bad news," says Nick, who's been quiet during the ruckus. "I have to leave tomorrow night. Work and personal reasons."

"Are you serious?" Rodney says.

"You can't leave n-n-now," Harold says.

"So what's the *bad* news?" Slate says.

When we get back to the hotel, my head's throbbing, but I agreed to go to a Toto concert with Sal and Benny and need to get ready. Cousin Stu gave Sal three backstage passes for a meet and greet, and I can't bail. Not just because I told the guys I'd join them, but because Papi loved '80's music, and Toto was his favorite band. He claimed they were the most underrated group in the history of music.

I decide to wear something special, something other than jeans or shorts. I rifle through my closet and pluck out the only dress I packed, knee-length and raven-black, with a sunflower print. Instead of wearing a ponytail, I let my hair down and brush it out. I slip into black heels and put in hoop earrings, the ones I avoid when I don't want to look Latina.

Benny texts me and Sal, says he's running late and will meet us at the concert. Outside the Emerald Outpost, a warm evening breeze sweeps away my headache as I wait with Sal for our Uber. When our driver arrives in a Dodge Charger, Sal opens the door for me, and we sit in the back, chatting like old friends. We talk about the big win. We talk about his wife's homemade lasagna. We talk about how he just binge-watched *Euphoria* with his two daughters. We laugh a lot.

Our driver stops at a traffic light and coughs. He's a red-headed man, mid-thirties, with a thick neck. I catch his eyes, narrow and dull, in the rearview mirror. He doesn't look away. The light refuses to turn green. The driver winks at Sal in the rearview. "Looks like a spicy one, amigo."

"Excuse me?" Sal says.

"Nothing." The driver leers at me again as the light turns green.

"Hey asshole," Sal says, "eyes on the road."

The driver faces forward and says something under his breath that sounds like, "She looks affordable too."

"That's it," Sal says, smacking the driver's headrest. "Pull over. *Now.*"

"What's your problem?" the driver says.

"You're the problem," I say.

The driver stops and lets us out, knowing better than to

ask for a five-star rating. Sal and I walk three blocks without speaking.

"I'm sorry about that," he finally says, his face as red as a stoplight, his sky-blue shirt seeped in sweat.

I shrug. "It's okay. Thanks for having my back."

He stares at the ground, walks between me and the street. "You know, Izzy, when I was in high school, something happened," he says, putting his hands in his pockets. "I still think about it."

"Yeah?"

"It was a fight between some mamalukes I knew from Jersey City and a Cuban kid, new to the neighborhood," he says. "Those dudes, friends of mine, they jumped the kid, pinned him down, and started whaling on him." Sal slows his pace. "I remember standing there watching, right there in the street."

"What happened to the kid?"

"I dunno." He looks at the sidewalk. "But I should've helped."

Sal falls silent as cars zip past us on the strip. After we walk another block, I say, "Hey, how about I get your interview now?"

July 5 notes:

Sal Rucosa is the reason I'm here. He's the one who sent Kay the *Bull Slurham* video, the guy who talked me into coming on the trip. In the past two weeks, he and the Bulls have looked out for me. They've opened up for me. They've let me in. I haven't trusted many people in my life, especially men, for a lot of different reasons. But I trust these guys now.

I interviewed Sal while strolling the Vegas strip on our way to a concert. Fifty-nine-years-young, he's a silver-haired goombah from Jersey City, more complicated than he lets on, happy enough in the background. He's more Salvatore Tessio than Don Vito Corleone, more Abe Vigoda than Marlon Brando. On the field, Sal fills in wherever he's needed. Off the field, he tolerates the grief attached to running a team. He speaks up when necessary but doesn't get too deep. If he hasn't totally locked up his past, he's at least guarding the door, and as we walked and talked, I got the feeling he just wanted to keep moving.

Me: Looking forward to the concert?

Sal: Yeah, why not? Toto released their debut album when I was a sophomore in high school. Pretty sure "Hold the Line" played at my first keg party.

Me: Congrats on your big win today. How are you feeling?

Sal: Like we got extremely lucky.

Me: So what really happened to Race McIntyre?

Sal: Honestly, I have no idea. When someone disappears, why do people always blame the Italian guy?

Me: I'm sorry, you're right. We should blame Slate Hetan for all suspicious activity on this trip. How do you tolerate him?

Sal: Yeah, I don't know. All I can say is, and please pardon my French, he's a dick, but he's our dick.

Me: What does this team mean to you?

Sal: It means an extra twenty emails I have to send every week between March and September. Ha! Seriously though, it's not twenty emails. It's more like forty. I look at the Bulls like a dysfunctional family. We got all kinds of guys on the roster, and most everyone adds something different, while only three or four subtract. But we enjoy each other's company, and we enjoy the competition, and we all enjoy beer. I guess that's about it.

Me: Do you like managing the Aging Bulls?

Sal: It's fine, but if I didn't do it, someone else would. But they'd suck at it, and then I'd still have to do it, because without me, the whole thing would fall apart. I'm either a glutton for punishment or the only competent member of the team.

Me: What's your role on the field?

Sal: Defensively, I play wherever I'm needed. Offensively, I'd say I'm the best power hitter on the Bulls, a crucial bat in the middle of the lineup, and a straight-up RBI machine, but my hypocrisy only goes so far.

Me: What would you do without the Bulls?

Sal: Some call me a creature of habit, a homebody, a hermit at times. These guys have brought me out of my shell a little bit. I think running this team scratches my itch for organization and control, even though the Bulls are disorganized and uncontrollable. Without this team, I'd probably just spend the extra five hours per week rewatching *The Wire* and *Breaking Bad*.

Me: No one expected the Bulls to get this far. How do you explain it?

Sal: We're in the Senior Men's Softball World Finals. Think about that. You can't make it up. Who knows how we'll do in the next series, but we'll lean on each other and figure it out. Then when it's all over, win or lose, we'll have a few beers, and we'll have no regrets.

Benny never makes it to the concert, texts Sal something about losing track of time with Slate at the hotel bar. Too bad because the guys from Toto are as smooth as advertised. After the show, Sal and I flash our passes to security and go backstage to meet the Yacht Rock legends. I snap an "ussie" with them and immediately text it to the Bulls group chat.

"Benny's gonna be so jealous," Sal says.

I study the picture and laugh. "He won't be jealous of your dorky smile."

Sal looks at me, a glint in his eye. "Oh, Izzy," he says, showing a playful side I've come to love. "Wanna make a TikTok video?"

"Um, no," I answer in record time.

"Yeah, terrible idea," Sal says. "I was kidding anyway."

"Can you imagine what the Bulls would say?" I ask, shuddering at the thought. "We'd never survive the ridicule."

Sal grins. "Maybe not, but at least we'd be miserable together."

Back at the Emerald Outpost, we stand by the elevator and rehash the night. When the door opens, Sal holds it for me. "You heading up?" he asks when I hesitate.

"In a few," I say. "Gotta take care of something first."

Men notice as I glide through the lobby. I straighten my sunflower dress, keep my chin up, and stride across the casino floor, leaving a trail of perfume. When I get to Skat's, I spot Russell washing wine glasses behind the bar. He doesn't notice when I slide onto a stool in front of him.

"How's the Razzamatazz?"

"It's super sweet," he says before lifting his head and beaming. "But it'll kick your butt if you're not careful."

I giggle and say, "Hey, I'm so sorry about last night."

"It was my fault too," says Russell, his dimples doing most of the talking. "But I don't remember much, except that it was really nice to be with you."

I tuck my hair behind an ear and plunk my elbows on the bar. "Maybe we can start over, like with an old school date."

Russell puts a finger to his cheek. "You know, I think I can score tix to the Pastafarians."

"Awesome," I say. "Mind if I bring some friends? They're super old and kind of obnoxious, but they grow on you after a while."

"If that's what it'll take to see you again, then I insist."

His comment makes me blush, and I smile, certain that the team already approves of Russell. *Yes*, I think, *the Bulls will be okay with me and this boy.*

As I leave Skat's, I'm damn sure that my next kiss will be better than my first. The elevator whisks me up and away, and I relive a childhood moment with Roberto LaMotta—who lived one floor below me with his mom and three older brothers. He was bold and loud, dashing for a nine-year-old, had pimples on his forehead and fuzz on his cheeks. On the last day of third grade, after school let out, he and I went back to our apartment building and snuck up to the roof. The afternoon was dreary, looked like rain. Self-conscious in jean shorts and my least favorite shirt, the green one with spaghetti straps, I couldn't stop shaking. I knew what we both wanted, and I was nervous. Plus, Papi would be home from work in ten minutes, ready to take me to Reiss Field. I remember Roberto grabbed my hand and led me behind a short concrete wall. He drew me in close, and I got lost in his boy smell. When a raindrop fell on my shoulder, he kissed it off, and I pushed him away. He pulled me back, pressed his lips against mine. Then an old man shouted. It was the building superintendent. He looked me dead in the eye, yelled that he'd tell my mother, and I scrambled off the roof and into my apartment. Later that night, when I got home from the field, Mami slapped me and sent me to my room, forbidding me from touching another boy till after my quinceanera.

DAY FOURTEEN

Just when I think Vegas can't get any hotter, the morning proves me wrong, the weather app on my phone predicting a high of 110 before sundown. As I scroll through news headlines, one from *The Onion* addresses the heat wave sweeping across the Southwest: *U.S. to Install Fans in Debt Ceiling.* Luckily for the Bulls, the World Championship series won't begin till tomorrow.

I take out my journal and write an entry on Russell, a tally of pros and cons. Not surprisingly, it's a lopsided list, the only cons being that he lives in Vegas, and I'll soon be going back to New York and my family, a world away. Even so, I'm not quite ready to give up hope. One of the last times I felt so open to possibility was during my senior year at Long River Prep, when I was choosing a college. I turned to a pros-and-cons list back then, too.

On my eighteenth birthday, only fifty blank pages remained in the four-hundred-page leather-bound diary Senora Rojas had given me six years earlier. I had a month till national signing day—when I'd need to commit to a college softball program. The toughest two questions I faced: *How far away from home should I go? Would Mami and Ava be okay without me?* Having narrowed it down to three schools, Arizona, Villanova, and

Northwestern, I agonized over the choice, knowing that wherever I landed wouldn't be perfect.

> ... *Why I should play for Arizona: the weather, great
> competition, 24% Latino students, cute guys, party school, an
> opportunity to prove myself on the field. Why I shouldn't play
> for Arizona: too far away, not a great pre-med program, huge
> campus, party school, might not play much, not academically
> challenging... Why I should play for Villanova: only two
> hours from home, decent competition, good playing time, great
> academics, prestigious. Why I shouldn't play for Villanova:
> too white, too cold, pre-med just okay, boring town... Why I
> should play for Northwestern: Chicago, chance to start right
> away, Big 10, great academics, good pre-med program, best
> journalism school, Will Peterson. Why I shouldn't play for
> Northwestern: kind of far from home, weather not great...*

After I close my journal, a group text pops up from Sal with
a breakdown of the team's plans for our off day: Bo, Rodney,
Harold, and Wink have booked a hot air balloon ride, scheduled
for 10 a.m. (and they have room for one more). The rest of the
guys plan on hitting the links. Their tee time is at eleven. I've
never golfed before, but I want the extra hour in bed and reply
to the group that I'll tag along on the course but won't play. A
second later, I get a call from Kay.

Kay: I don't know what you did, Dominguez.

Me: Huh?

Kay: People are calling the office, asking about "Izzy and
the Miracle Bulls" and when the next issue is coming out.
I'm getting emails about it too, but I don't understand.

Me: Me neither.

Kay: Well, assuming there *is* a next issue, I'm making this the cover story now.

Kay hangs up and I do a little dance around the suite. My first cover story! Even though it's only *Mature Living*, it's still a national magazine. I skip down the hall, past the ice machine, and wait for the elevator. When it doesn't arrive, I take the stairs to the lobby. I'm psyched and a bit nervous about getting this opportunity, but I have no idea how it all happened.

At breakfast, I tell the guys at my table about my call with Kay, how people are asking about "Izzy and the Miracle Bulls," and how none of it makes any sense.

"Hey, that story better include our crazy night on the town," says Rocco, scratching his ear with a spoon.

Leo slides the salt and pepper shakers closer to me. "And don't forget to write that I almost had to draw up divorce papers for you and Russ," he says. "You two make a really nice couple, by the way."

Bo shrugs.

"Way to go, kid," says Vinnie, gnawing on a slab of under-cooked turkey bacon like it's a chew toy. "Congrats on your big chance. No one's rooting for you more than we are, except for your family of course. I mean, we're sort of your family now too, but not exactly, you know what I'm saying. But kind of, like a little bit."

I break into a huge smile as Vinnie's gibberish has Rocco and Leo in hysterics. Across the table, Hank turns away and sips his coffee before I can catch his eye. Just then, my phone buzzes; my mother is calling, and I excuse myself.

Mami: I need you to come home, Isabel. I can't do this by myself anymore.

Me: But you told me to stay, and my assignment isn't over yet.

Mami: My first treatment's pushed back again. I'm exhausted, and I'm worried, and Ava's sugar levels have been high. I don't know if her glucose meter is working. I asked you to check it before you left.

Me: I'll be home soon. I promise.

Mami: We need you now.

Me: I can't right now. I just need a few more days because—

Mami: Isabel, listen to me. For once, please listen. It can't always be about you. This is about your family. ¡Oyeme! I know you loved your father more than me, and I know—

Me: What? That's crazy, Mami. Why would you say something like that?

Mami: I know it's the truth, Isabel. The way you look at me, the way you always looked at me, I know you wish I were the one who died.

My mother begins to cry and hangs up. I can't believe what she said, and I don't know what to do. My family needs me, but Kay and the Bulls need me too. I can't help but feel that no matter what choice I make, it'll be the wrong decision.

When we get to the golf course, the place is empty. The clerk in the pro shop says not many folks golf on days when the heat index is double their average score. I join Nick in a cart. Hank and Darryl jump into one of their own and fill out our group. The foursome in front of us (Slate, Vinnie, Benny, and Leo) run into trouble on the first tee box when the starter sees Vinnie waddle to the ladies' tee with his cutoff sweats around his ankles after duffing his drive. I notice just in time to snap a picture. Vinnie spends the rest of the afternoon waiting on the bus while the others in his group form a sixsome with Webb, Rocco, and Sal.

Through the first five holes, I try to get ahold of my mother, but she doesn't answer my texts or calls. I pay no attention to the guys golfing, still thinking about what Mami said. Was it true? Had I secretly wished she died instead of Papi?

On the sixth hole, Darryl and Nick order drinks from a middle-aged blond-haired woman working the snack bar, and Hank takes Nick's spot in our cart.

"Izzy, I have to tell you something," Hank says. "I know why your story is getting so much attention."

"You mean the story I haven't even written?"

"Yeah, but we know it'll be great, and we wanted to help."

"And?"

"And somehow, with my limited software knowledge and Harold's hacking skills, we sort of acquired a list of names and sent out an email blast."

"Any chance that email included the phrase 'Miracle Bulls'?"

Hank nods as a salty waterfall pours off his dome.

"How many people on that list?"

"Um, maybe ten thousand, give or take." He cringes and leans away from me.

"Well, that explains it," I say, debating whether or not to punch Hank in the nose. "The only reason people are interested in my story is that it was jammed down their throats by two egg-heads who still play Mastermind and wear secret decoder rings."

Nick gets back into our cart and the round continues. My heart rate in overdrive, my tolerance level spiking, I don't care when Darryl scores a hole-in-one on ten. *Dumb luck.* I don't care when Nick's chip shot clocks Hank in the head on twelve. *Serves him right.* But I do care when Mami finally texts me back on fifteen. *About time.*

Mami: Sorry about before, just having a really bad day.

Me: We need to talk.

Mami: I didn't mean what I said.

Me: I know, I love you.

Mami: Just come home when you're ready…

I stare at my phone for a minute then plunk it into the cart cupholder while Nick parks under a desert pine by the sixteenth tee box. "Hey, I'm leaving tonight," he says. "And you still haven't gotten my interview. Wanna chat now?"

I'm too frustrated with my mother to care about an interview with Nick, but I don't know how to tell him. "Don't you want to finish the rest of the round?" I ask.

"There's only three holes left," he says. "Come on, we'll go to the clubhouse and start a bar tab for the group."

We drive back, step into the bar, and sit at a table for two in the corner. "You a wine drinker?" Nick asks.

"Sure."

"Great, they have something here I think you'll enjoy." When our waiter comes by, Nick orders two glasses of Petit Verdot from Venezuela.

"Look at you, all boujee," I say, and he laughs.

Nick sits up tall and straight, a telephone pole dressed in khaki shorts and a pink polo. His eyebrows, arched and plucked, are prettier than mine. Not one hair on his handsome head is out of place. When our wine arrives, he sticks his nose into his glass and takes a small sip. "Mm, that's good."

I follow his lead. "Mm, yeah, really good."

He puts his glass down. "So, how's the family?"

"They're fine." I take another sip.

Nick looks at me and waits.

I cave. "Except for my sister, Ava, who's not exactly fine. She has diabetes, and it's been tough on her and my mom."

Nick sighs and nods. "My daughter has diabetes too," he says. "She's older now, but we've dealt with it for a long time. It's manageable, but it's not easy. The key is to acknowledge your sister's feelings and build her independence. It's hard on the whole family, but you need to be patient and as supportive as possible."

"Good advice," I say. "Got a cure for cancer?"

"Oh, Izzy," he says, tilting his head. "Is it your mom?"

Over Nick's shoulder, a group of men at the bar stare at me. When the shortest of them winks, I scowl at him. He laughs, slaps one of his buddies on the back, and staggers toward our table.

"Don't even," I mumble.

The little man brushes past Nick's chair and stands over me, his hairline receding by the second, his pug nose all in my business. "What are we celebrating here?"

I lean away from him, glance at his wedding ring, and lift my chin. "Celebrating your wife's fascination with the Napoleon complex."

"Whoa, good one," the guy slurs with booze on his breath, and he puffs out his chest. "Cute *and* funny. I love that combo."

Nick rises from his seat. "Hey fella, beat it."

The drunkard stumbles backward. "Who the hell are you?"

"I'm Nick Chinsola."

"Ray Kinsella? The dude from *Field of Dreams*?"

"What? That's not even the same name," Nick says. "And it's a fictional character, dumbass."

The short man squints, studies Nick's face. "But you've definitely got a Costner-esque thing going on, might be the jaw line." He pulls a business card from his wallet, hands it to Nick and says, "Ever consider a career in Hollywood?"

"Well, I did a little acting after college."

"Yes, yes, I can tell," the man says. "Gimme a call, Ray, and I'll make you a star."

"Um, it's Nick."

"Of course. Nick."

The talent agent puts his wallet into his pocket and knocks over my glass. "Oh, shit!" he says as the Petit Verdot pools in the middle of the table. "Where's your waiter?"

"Don't worry," Nick says in a deep whisper. "If you spilled it, he will come."

July 6 notes:

Along their yellow brick road, the gang from Walnut Gap has completed an impressive trifecta—beating Oregon, Florida, and West Virginia—slaying the Lions and Tigers and Bears. Oh, brother. Tomorrow, when they face-off against the most dominant team in the tourney, the Dominican Republic, the Bulls will realize they're not in Kansas anymore.

My interview today is with Nick Chinsola. On the field, he's a decent hitter and infielder. Off the field, he's a decent family man and friend. The Bulls joke that Nick reminds them of a foosball player, chiseled and stiff, easily manipulated, controllable. But I see him as sturdy and strong, forward-facing, dependable. Since we met, I sensed a softness under Nick's painted-on veneer. I thought if he were hiding something, he might be ready to let it out. He probably thought the same about me.

Me: So you were an actor? Were you any good?

Nick: That was my dream, but I didn't go the distance, and I'm a realtor now, so there's your answer.

Me: What do you think about the tourney so far?

Nick: C'mon, Izzy. We don't have to talk softball.

Me: I just have some basic questions.

Nick: Izzy, stop. Tell me what's going on with your mom.

Me: She's sick, starting chemo soon. I don't know if I should stay or go home and help. I don't even know how to help.

Nick: I'm so sorry. Actually, that's why I'm leaving. My mother needs me too.

Me: What's wrong?

Nick: She's just getting old, turning ninety-eight soon, and I'm running out of ways to help her. But I have to keep trying.

Me: That can't be easy.

Nick: It's not, but we need to take care of our parents; that time comes for all of us. And relationships between parents and children are never easy; they're all so different. A mother and son don't have the same bond as a mother and daughter. Same with fathers. What I have with my daughter is a lot different than what I have with my son.

Me: Is your father still around?

Nick: No, he died a while back. My parents were totally opposite. My dad was smooth and charismatic, loved life. He didn't put any pressure on me. But my mom wanted me to be somebody important, and I knew I couldn't meet her standards. For a long time, I tried to be an impossible version of myself.

Me: Same. The pressure from my dad was nothing like the pressure from my mom. He pressured me to be a great player because he thought it'd make me happy. My mother pressures me to be perfect to make her happy, or to make me stronger, or maybe to strengthen us both. I'm not sure, but she makes me nuts. Like years ago when I told her about my anxiety, and she said, "Stop making that shit up, we've got *real* problems to deal with." Deep down though, I admire her. She's been through a lot, and I think she's doing her best. But still, she's got me shook.

Nick: What?

Me: Worried.

Nick: Oh.

Me: It's like, I know she loves me, but she drives me insane.

Nick: Funny how everyone's parents show love in different ways. Some show it with money, or affection, or neediness. Others by putting pressure on us. They might do it because they want what's best for us, or because they're acting out of guilt. But what I'm learning is that we can't take on their guilt, and we have to let go of our own.

Me: Yeah, I'm just in a bad place, and I don't know what to do. It's this feeling that won't go away, like a cut that won't stop bleeding. I'm thinking I should just forget my stupid dream, move back to the Bronx with my mother, and figure out the next sixty years from there.

Nick: What's your dream?

Me: It used to be to write a novel, which seems impossible now. Guess I'd settle for being any kind of writer, but that might not be in the cards.

By the time our golf contingent gets back to the hotel, the sun has set. In the lobby, I run into Cousin Stu, who says the front desk has a message for me. A receptionist tells me that a staffer at Big League Dreams called and said they found my notebook at the park, said I must've left it there yesterday. I jump into a cab, and my driver carves through the night.

At the facility, I ask the cabbie to wait while I motor into the main office, a smallish building next to the knockoff Yankee Stadium. Inside the office, the facility manager gives me my notebook. He's a jolly man with a horseshoe of hair and a round face, weathered and worn from twenty-something years of semi-retirement in the Las Vegas sun, I assume.

"Thank you so much," I say, holding the notebook to my chest.

"You're very welcome, little lady," he says.

I take two steps toward the door and stop. "Can I ask you a question?"

"Shoot."

"When do you turn out the stadium lights?"

"Gonna hit that switch in about an hour."

"Would it be okay if I went onto the field for a minute?"

The man smiles. "Gate's still open, dear."

After telling the cabbie he can leave, I hurry to the stadium, push open the gate, and step out of the shadows. The field lights beam down like the lights at Northwestern's Drysdale Field, the ones I played my final game under five years ago. I cross over the first base chalk line and onto the diamond. *Papi would've loved this place.*

Gazing up past the lights, into the clear night sky, I think of how I compartmentalized my father's death, telling myself that it was okay because nothing else could be taken from him, or from me. As if that were true. I kick the dirt near the first base bag.

"Hey, kid!" A voice flies out of nowhere.

I jump back, swing my head around, and look across the diamond. "You gotta be kidding," I whisper.

Out of the third base dugout, Slate Hetan appears, a six-pack of beer in one hand, two softball gloves in the other. "Wanna have a catch?"

"You asshole!" I yell, throwing my arms up. "You scared the shit out of me."

"Sorry, but that was kinda funny," Slate says, unfolding his pirate smile. "You should've seen your face, looked like Sornecki running after one of those four-thousand-foot bombs Shuheg coughs up."

I roll my eyes. "What are you doing here?"

"I could ask you the same thing."

"I asked you first."

"I asked you second."

"Why do you have to be so complicated?"

"I'm not," Slate says. "You just don't know simple when you see it."

We walk toward each other and meet near home plate. He drops the six-pack and flings one of the gloves at me. I don't flinch, and it bounces off my thigh and falls to the ground.

"Pick that up," he says. "Let's get loose."

"I haven't played catch in a million years," I say, dusting off the mitt.

"Leo and Darryl haven't caught a ball at first base in a million years, but it doesn't stop them from trying."

I place my notebook on the dirt and stay at the plate while he moves ten yards down the line toward third. We toss the ball back and forth, slowly to start, like how Papi threw to me when I first fell in love with the game. Slate's glove is too big for me, keeps slipping off, and the cracked leather on the inside scratches my fingers. My reaction time isn't what it used to be, but I catch all of his throws in the webbing, barely feel them hit my glove.

He takes twenty steps back. "Okay, hotshot, show me what you got."

"Hey," I say. "Get closer."

"You kidding me? Throw the goddamn ball, wuss."

My half-ass lob bounces and rolls to his feet. He snatches the ball off the dirt, flips it up in front of his chest. He squints in my direction, like he's lost me in the lights, before finding his focus again. "You know, you're not that hard to figure out."

"What?"

"You act tough," Slate says, "like you don't need anyone, always shoveling yourself out from under the shit life dumps on you. You wear that brave face, but inside you're just a scared kid." He flips the ball up again. "What are you trying to prove anyway?" He winds up and fires the ball at my head. I flash my glove in front of my face to escape a broken jaw.

"What the actual fuck!" I scream.

"Good hands, dude. Now answer me."

"Okay, psycho, want to know what I'm trying to prove?" I pound the ball into my mitt and stomp toward him, stopping halfway down the third baseline. "I want to prove that everything my father did for me wasn't a waste. Giving up baseball, moving to the States, practicing with me every day, coaching me all those years. I want him to know I appreciate what he sacrificed, and I want him to believe I was worth it." I whip the ball at Slate. "But he's dead."

As I return to home plate, Slate doesn't say a word. When I stop and face him again, he paces five steps back and waits till I'm ready.

And we keep throwing. And throwing. And throwing. Each time, the ball hits square in the pocket of my glove, but my right arm is aching now. My shoulder's sore, and my elbow's stiff. He takes ten more steps back.

"Stop!" I yell. "That's too far."

"Shut up."

"Gladly."

We play catch in silence. *Pop. Pop. Pop.* The ball keeps rhythm, smacking the center of our gloves like the chops of an axe against a stubborn araguaney. My arm loosens up, and I put more mustard on my throws.

"That's better," Slate says after catching the last of them. "We're good now." He grabs the six-pack and heads toward the dugout. I snap up my notebook and follow him. On the wooden bench, he rips two beers from the plastic binding, wipes off the dusty cans with his shirt, and hands one to me. We take long swigs, our parallel gazes aimed at the field.

Slate sighs and leans back, rests his head against the cool concrete wall. "You know, when I was a kid, not many people liked me."

"Shocking," I say.

"But not for the same reasons you didn't like me." He gazes into his beer can like it's a crystal ball. "Kids made fun of me all the time because I had dyslexia," he says. "They called me stupid when I had to go to a special school, and I was terrified that I'd never have any real friends. When I thought of my future, I saw nothing." Slate drains the rest of his beer and cracks open another. He takes a sip, and I see the hurt in his eyes.

"Sorry," I say, wishing I could say more.

"Then when my dad split, I was all fucked up," Slate says. "Felt like I had to be the man of the house at twelve years old. That was really hard, but I tried. I had no one to talk to about it, but I kept putting myself out there." He takes another sip. "Even after getting married and having kids, I still didn't know if I'd have any true friends and wasn't sure I deserved any."

I stare at my Nikes.

"When Benny and I formed the Bulls, it gave me what I never had, what I always wanted." His smile returns. "Now I've got a family, and friends, and friends who are family. And I've got you. And you've got us."

I size up my beer, hoping it'll speak for me, and set it down between us on the bench. "You know, it's really nice of you to open up," I say. "But whatever lesson you're trying to teach me, it's not enough."

"Dude, all I'm saying is you're not alone," Slate says. "Don't be afraid, and don't give up on yourself. This quitting thing, it's a hard habit to break once you get started. Throw yourself into the world, Dominguez. If you fall apart, fuck it. We'll be there to pick up the pieces."

The stadium lights go out, and the desert air grows cold. Slate and I share a Lyft back to the hotel, talk only about softball, stay inside the lines.

Safe in my room, I dive under the covers but can't fall asleep. After flicking on the bedside lamp, I take *All That You Had* off the nightstand and open it to the beginning of the third act, the section where the protagonist loses her way and an unexpected character points her in the right direction. I flip one page, then another, and my shoulders tense. Because now the girl knows where to find her father, but her biggest challenge lies ahead.

DAY FIFTEEN

ON A DRIZZLY Monday at *Mature Living*, forty-eight hours before the Aging Bulls and I left for Vegas, I sat at my desk drowning in a stack of expense reports when Mami called and cut right to the chase: "I have breast cancer."

No sooner had I hung up than the other shoe dropped. From the far side of the cubicle wall, Steve in advertising called out to me. "Isabel, Kay wants everyone in the conference room. Pronto!"

I was dazed going into that meeting and even more dazed coming out. Nothing Kay said registered in my brain after her opening statement: "The magazine will be ceasing publication after the next issue."

That night, after Ava went to bed, I sat on the couch with Mami and told her the bad news, then she told me the rest of hers. The oncologist had recommended chemotherapy and radiation treatments, beginning as soon as possible.

"How are we going to do this, Isabel?" Mami asked, her voice quavering.

"Don't worry," I said. "I'll get another job."

"And if you can't find anything, what then?" she asked. "My

hospital bills will be too much, and what about Ava's insulin? And your student loans?"

"I said I'll find something."

Of course, I haven't found anything, but now that the magazine might survive, we might be okay. I'm eager to share the news with Mami, but I also don't want to get her hopes up in case things don't work out.

In the ballroom at breakfast, Harold brings me a raspberry Danish.

"What's this for?" I say, taking a seat.

"It's for your b-b-base. You need something in your stomach, but you sh-sh-shouldn't eat too much. I did a comprehensive w-w-web search."

"On what?"

"Riding a roller c-c-coaster. I've been terrified of them all my life, but I think I'm ready to give it a try. I was h-h-hoping you'd come with me."

I accept the Danish and take a bite. "Okay," I say. "But why me?"

Harold glances around to make sure no one's listening. "Because if I chicken out, I d-d-don't want any Bulls there. It would get back to Hetan, and he'd n-n-never let me hear the end of it."

Harold's logic, as always, is rock solid. "Count me in," I say.

After breakfast, I hail a cab to take us to a hotel called New York-New York, home of the Big Apple Coaster, a rip-off of Brooklyn's Cyclone. When we get to the hotel, I step out of the car and immediately feel homesick. To my right, replicas of the Statue of Liberty and the Empire State Building loom. To my left, the coaster's steel rails twist in the sky like a giant frozen snake.

"You okay?" Harold asks.

"Yeah, thanks," I say.

We're first in line for the coaster, which opens at 11 a.m. Temps have already cracked the century mark, with a high of 112 predicted. It's so damn hot, I consider asking Lady Liberty to lower her arm. While we talk and joke and sweat the time away, a queue forms behind us.

"Look at all these p-p-people," Harold says five minutes before the ride opens. "I w-w-wonder if I'm the only one s-s-scared out of his socks."

I tilt my head and say, "Everyone's scared of something." Then I flinch when my phone buzzes. It's a text from my sister.

Ava: heard you and mami had a fight

Me: Yeah, is she okay?

Ava: yup fine now

Me: What about you? How you feeling?

Ava: awesome

Me: How do I know you're telling the truth?

Ava: you don't lol, but why would I lie?

Me: Haha, see you when I get home sis.

The gates open. The fraidy-cat Bull and I rush into the front seat of the yellow coaster. "Don't be nervous," I say. "The Big Apple's no match for us."

And I see my father and me, sixteen years earlier, on a sunny day in Brooklyn, rushing into the back seat of a red coaster, Papi saying, "Don't be nervous, Izzy. The Cyclone's no match for us."

Harold's hands tremble, and I pull down the safety bar. "Keep your head back," I say. "And don't forget to breathe."

My hands tremble, and Papi pulls down the safety bar. "Keep your head back," he says. "And don't forget to breathe."

The Big Apple jerks forward. *Click. Click. Click.* "Oh, no," Harold says.

The Cyclone begins a steep climb. *Clack. Clack. Clack.* "Oh, no," I say.

Halfway up. "I wanna go b-b-back, Izzy!"

Almost there. "This is scary, Papi!"

At the top. "Don't look down, Harold!" And then—

Down and up. My hair in my face. Down and up. My stomach in knots. Down and a loop. Harold howling. The world below me. Twist, and down, and up, and level. Catch my breath. Where's my breath? Then down and up, and down and around. Me and my father and Harold and me. Then down and up, and down and up, and around and around and around. Then level and brakes and over. *Hissssssss.*

It takes a full minute to pry my forearm from Harold's grip, and he's either wearing a huge grin or his facial muscles are permanently extended from the centripetal force of the ride.

Before heading to the game, the team gathers in the hotel parking lot, where Benny tears open a huge cardboard box filled with T-shirts. "Designed these myself," he announces, displaying one of the gray shirts to the group. On the front: a cartoon bull holding a mug of beer in one hand, wearing a mitt in the other, under the words *Aging Bulls*. Written on the back: *U.S. Senior Softball Champs!*

"Nice to see your art degree finally paying off," Darryl says.

I help Benny distribute the swag, XLs and Larges for most of the guys, a few Mediums mixed into the bunch. I pull out a Small, chuckle, and hold it up for Benny. "No way this fits any of you."

He smiles. "I know. That's yours."

On the bus, we're ready to roll, but one Bull hasn't yet boarded. "Where's Rodney?" I ask, and a tremor of worry undercuts the mood.

Sal gets out of his seat. "Oh yeah," he says. "I saw Rodney this morning. He said he turned down an offer to play full-time with the reggae band for the next three days so he could keep playing in the tournament. I told him I was placing him on the DL, effective immediately."

Hetan looks up from picking a scab on his knee. "You *what*?"

"Dude," Sal says. "It's his dream. He can play with us anytime. I told him to grab his drum and get to band practice. Executive decision."

The Bulls are clearly bummed to lose their biggest cheerleader, but the consensus is, Sal did the right thing. Still they have no Nick, a solid hitter and infielder, who left the night before to take care of his mom. Plus their best pitcher, Clete, went home to his family. Bryson's big bat is resting comfortably in the ICU. And no one knows for certain where Biff is (including him), but he's not coming back. Twelve available, if not quite capable, Bulls remain.

"It's fine," Sal says. "Darryl and Leo will rotate at first, as per usual. Harold and Bo will switch off in right field. Slate's still at short. Me at third. Wink takes over full time at second. And Vinnie pitches. If he needs Rocco to relieve, they can flip positions."

We arrive at Big League Dreams and haul the equipment across the lot toward the facility's crowning jewel, the knock-off Yankee Stadium, where the best-of-three World Finals will take place, where Slate and I faced off last night. The building's familiar concrete façade invites me inside, and on the field, the interlocking *NY* spray painted behind the plate welcomes me home. More than ever on this trip, I feel like I belong.

Judging by their long faces and slumped shoulders, the Aging Bulls feel like they *don't* belong. Everyone knows the tourney's international representative, Los Gigantes del Dominicano, is formidable, indestructible, unbeatable (and every other *-able* or

-ible in the dictionary). The DR Giants are led by snobby third baseman Mateo Glassiendo, a Jose Altuve clone and the odds-on favorite to win MVP, at least since Race McIntyre got knocked out of the running. His team has won all six of their games so far, all by more than seven runs. They swept all three of their series, annihilating teams from Japan, Netherlands, and Venezuela. They haven't made an error. At this very moment, I bet the tournament director's practicing how to say "Congratulations" in Spanish.

The stadium is packed. Before the contest begins, Glassiendo puts on a show during BP. By the end of the third inning, he's hit two of the longest home runs anyone can remember. After his second bomb, he rounds second base, looks over his shoulder at Slate, and yells something in Spanish. Hetan charges, and the benches clear. No one throws a punch. But on offense, the Giants deliver a flurry of roundhouses and lead 14-1 after five.

And it gets worse. With a Dominican runner aboard in the top of the seventh, Benny lays out for a liner in right center and smashes into Webb's knees. Both players crumple, crushed like empty beer cans in a parking lot. The crowd gasps. The Giants laugh. The ball rolls to the wall. Benny lies facedown on the grass, as if asleep in a poppy field. Webb staggers to his feet, retrieves the ball, and heaves it toward the infield well after the DR plates their final two runs. When Bo goes down looking for the last out of the game, the Bulls have been pounded, 16-2.

Later, around a lifeless circle of beach chairs in a parking lot made of lava, spirits are chillier than the bag of ice on Benny's left shoulder. Fidgeting with my phone, I sit between Darryl and one of the beer coolers. He leans over, grabs two Stellas, and hands one to me. We crack them open, and the sound echoes in the silence.

"Look at it this way," Darryl says to the group. "Our tanks might be empty, but our coolers are full."

No one laughs. Not even Hank. And he laughs at everything.

"If this is the end," Leo says, "it's been quite a journey." He leans back in his chair and holds up the T-shirt Benny designed. "And you gotta love these really awesome shirts."

"Those shirts are my final contribution," says Benny, wincing while adjusting his icepack. "My arm's shot. I can't play anymore."

"Anymore?" Webb says, holding two frosty tallboys against his swollen knee. "Like you ever could."

"This ain't the end," says Slate, rising out of his seat after two tries. "We just need a jolt, a kick in the ass, some kind of boost."

"If Clete were here," Vinnie says, "we could borrow some of his HGH."

"Or his Preparation H," Sal says.

"I got an idea," Slate says with conviction, like someone who has ideas often. "How about Dominguez takes Benny's spot?"

"What?" I say, sitting up straight, certain I misheard him. "Are you nuts?"

Slate turns to me. "Shut up, I know how good you are," he says. "You were a stud in high school, played D1 in college."

"But I'm a girl, if you haven't noticed," I say. "And this tournament is for old men."

Leo backs me up. "Technically, she's right."

"Fuck that," says Slate, who's spent the last two weeks—and probably most of his life—scoffing at technicalities. "The kid's got an arm like Kelly Leak, and she's the best athlete here. She'll take Benny's spot in left center. We can't put Ucho there, 'cuz he'd overthink it and probably have a nervous breakdown."

Webb throws his hands up, but I'm the one having a breakdown. Playing catch with Slate was one thing, but the thought of actually playing in a game has my heart thumping. I feel faint and dizzy. My throat tightens. It's not just that I think I'll embarrass myself, though there is that. It's more about being on the field with guys who are old enough to be my father. And I get that it doesn't make any sense—I played for years after Papi died—but the thought of doing so now is paralyzing. I feel like something terrible will happen. I feel like I'm losing control.

"You can't force me to play," I say, raising my voice. I stand and look at the rest of the sitting Bulls. "You guys are on my side, right?"

They're looking everywhere except at me, and no one makes a peep. I shake my head. "You know what? Screw all of you," I say. "I never should've come on this stupid trip." I toss my backpack over my shoulder and board the Anonybus.

"You're playing, Dominguez," Slate calls. "Your team needs you."

"This is *not* my team," I yell over my shoulder.

Back at the hotel, I storm off the bus, hurry through the lobby, and make a beeline for the casino. I track down a waitress and order a shot of vodka. *Who needs the Bulls?* And another shot. *I don't owe them anything.* And another. *What do they know?* And another. *Who do they think they are?*

I purchase $200 worth of chips at the cashier booth, head to the roulette table, and lay it all on six black. And lose. I fire back another vodka shot and decide to book a flight to New York first thing in the morning. They can't make me play if I'm not here, and I already have plenty of material for my story. But it's no longer going to be a favorable depiction of the team; nope, now I'll be calling them on their Bull-shit. I zigzag toward the cashier again, my Discover card burning a hole in my back pocket.

"Izzy," a voice calls from behind. "You okay?"

I swing around, teeter, and spy two Harolds. "Get away from me, Hapnets," I shout, swatting at him, missing by a mile. "What kind of dopey name is that anyway? Hapnets. Pfft."

"Hey, c'mon," he says, reaching for my arm. "Let's sit somewhere."

"Get off me!" I push away from him, stagger backward, and land on my butt. The casino goes quiet. A thousand eyes drill into my heated face. Like high rollers who put it all on the line, gamble and lose, I bury my head in my hands. And I cry.

Harold crouches next to me. "It's gonna be okay," he whispers.

"How do you know?"

He helps me up and ushers me to Stuffy's 24/7. I sit across from him in a back booth, wearing the same clothes I wore while calming him on the Big Apple rollercoaster nine hours ago. He showered and changed after the game, has on jeans and a button-down shirt.

A spunky waitress in pesto-green slacks and a white blouse skips over to our table. "What's happening, Mr. Hapnets?"

"Hi, Laney," Harold says.

"Welcome back to Stuffy's, high calories at low prices, good in the gullet, better on the wallet. Will you two be enjoying our $7.99 all-you-can-eat special?"

"We're not that hungry," says Harold.

"You sure?" the waitress says. "It's called *Buffet the Appetite Slayer*, and it's to die for. Maybe you and your daughter can split one."

I glare at the girl. "Excuse me, but he's not my—"

"Thanks, Laney," Harold says. "Just two coffees, please."

"Sure thing, sweetie. Be right back."

I drop my head and rake my fingers through my hair. "What's wrong with me, Harold? I'm such a wreck." I squeeze my eyes shut.

"Hey, don't sweat it," he says. "You had a little too much to drink."

"I just don't want to play," I say. "And Slate really pisses me off sometimes."

"I know, Izzy," he says. "But whether you play or not, you

gotta take it easy on yourself. You don't deserve the abuse. No one does."

I stare at him and smile. "Guess what, Harold?"

"What?"

"Your stutter's gone."

July 7 notes:

I just drained five shots of vodka and three cups of coffee. That's the kind of day I've had. But the Aging Bulls haven't fared much better. This afternoon, they were pulverized in Game 1 of the World Finals by the DR Giants and their stud third baseman, Mateo Glassiendo. In the process, the Bulls' best defensive player, left centerfielder Benny Eggan, injured his shoulder. Now the team wants me to play. There's a better chance of my father coming back to life.

Today's interview is with Harold Hapnets, whom I spoke with at Stuffy's 24/7, while he helped me sober up. Harold's a respectable, credible, nourishing soul. If he were a buffet selection, he'd be the house-smoked salmon at the Waldorf-Astoria. (In contrast, Slate Hetan would be the three-day-old mystery meat at Golden Corral.) Harold's a fifty-one-year-old website designer, a Bull who bats near the bottom of the order and plays rightfield, when he plays at all. He's kind, smart, and a little nerdy. In college, he probably rocked a mullet and banged his head to Iron Maiden and Twisted Sister. But he's clean cut now.

While in Vegas, Harold has befriended an old acquaintance of mine, Dottie Willoughby. Two of the warmest people I know, Harold and Dottie have become cold-hearted slot machine addicts. For ten days, they've pumped one-armed bandits with coins, certain they'd be winners after every try. And that's exactly why I don't gamble.

Me: Sorry, I'm a complete mess.

Harold: And I'm sorry I talked Hank into blasting out that promotional email without your permission.

Me: It's fine, I know you were trying to help.

Harold: You know, Izzy, I've read some of your articles. You're really talented.

Me: Thanks, but I wouldn't bet on my writing career if I were you, unless you're the luckiest man on earth.

Harold: Well, I'm down a few hundred on the slots, but there's still time to make it all back. Our friend Dottie though, she hit it big right before she left yesterday. Talk about a hot streak. Wow.

Me: So what happened in the game?

Harold: Other than getting crushed and losing our best outfielder, not much. Which reminds me, we could use another player now.

Me: There's zero chance I'm playing tomorrow. I'm not on the roster anyway, so it doesn't matter, and I really need to go home.

Harold: I get it. You should do whatever feels right.

Me: That's the problem. So, what's your role on the Bulls?

Harold: I'm an old guy who understands his limits, and I'm definitely not the best player out there. This game isn't easy for me, but now I appreciate how hard it was for my daughters playing in high school and college, pitching against great hitters, hitting against great pitchers. It's pretty scary stuff.

Me: As scary as the roller coaster?

Harold: That's a different story. But thanks again, I couldn't have done that without you.

Me: What's life like for Harold Hapnets off the field?

Harold: It's all about family for me. Got three great kids and a loving wife. In that department, I *am* the luckiest man on earth. It's not like playing the slots, where you pull a lever and cross your fingers. In real life, you make your own luck, and with family, you gotta keep playing. You can't just walk away from the game.

Me: You can't make your own luck if the game's rigged though.

Harold: The way I look at it, Izzy, luck is just thinking you're lucky.

Me: I wouldn't know.

Harold: Dottie and I talked a lot about luck this week, luck and karma, and how they're related. Before she left, she gave me fifty bucks and made me promise to use it on her lucky slot machine. She really likes you, by the way, kept telling me how witty and smart you are, how she's proud of you and thinks you're a wonderful journalist. She said when you first met, you made her feel special.

Me: Dottie wouldn't say a bad word about anyone.

Harold: She also told me she's been in your shoes. Said she lacked confidence when she was younger, was afraid to stand up to the men at her job, doubted herself all the time. She wanted me to tell you that the world has more faith in you than you might think. Surround yourself with good people, she said, seek out healthy relationships, and just keep showing up.

At the desk in my suite, I close my laptop and stare out the window. The lights in the distance, strung along the strip, outshine the stars above. The dull moon hangs low. I pop three Advil but doubt they'll keep my mounting headache at bay. At 11:15 p.m., I get a group text.

Sal: Whoever's awake come to the ballroom now. Urgent!

After deleting the message, I head downstairs, thinking it'll be the last time I see the team before I bail in the morning. I'm still angry that they're trying to make me play, but after my evening with Harold, I don't want to leave on a bitter note. By half past eleven, every Bull not named Clete, Biff, Bryson, Nick, or Benny has converged in the Taj Meh Hall. They occupy two round tables while I lean against the wall by the door, staring at my phone, pretending to read a Bleacher Report article on the Yankees' farm system.

"Okay, looks like most of us are here," Sal says. "I just want to let you all know we've been in touch with the tournament committee and—"

"Can I say something?" I interrupt.

Sal holds up a finger. "Sure, Izzy, one second." And he continues. "Before play began a couple weeks ago, the committee bent the rules and allowed us to add a woman to our roster as long as she wasn't a pitcher."

My eyes become saucers, and I shake my head. "No, no, no," I say, moving toward Sal. "Do *not* tell me I've been on the team this whole time." I get in the manager's face. "You added my name without asking me?"

"It wasn't my idea, but yes, you've been on the Bulls from the start," he says, cheeks turning red. "The committee said our team was so bad, The Queen and Her Court could play for us, and we still wouldn't win."

Steam shoots out of my ears. "How could you do this?"

"Izzy," Sal says, "I'd never ask you to play unless we were desperate."

"What next?" I say. "Are you gonna quit and make me run the team too?"

"I wouldn't put it past me."

Gritting my teeth, I glare at the man I once trusted. "I hate you, Rucosa."

"I know you don't mean that." Sal picks up a large plastic bag off the floor. "Here, I bought different sizes," he says. "You know, just in case."

I look inside. The contents: three pairs of black softball pants and three pairs of blue cleats. "No way," I say.

As I turn toward the door, Benny jets into the ballroom carrying his glove and his filthy Bulls jersey. "Sorry I'm late," he says, offering up the items to me. "I know you wore number six too, and you can use my glove if you want."

"She should probably use a mitt that works," Webb says.

"I won't need a glove," I say, "because I'm not playing."

Slate gets out of his chair. The other Bulls go quiet. He heads straight for me, taking his time, and stops at my side. Shoulder to shoulder, he leans in and whispers, "Grow up." Then he's gone.

I drop Benny's jersey and glove into the bag with the pants and cleats, sling it over my shoulder, and leave the ballroom. Thirsting for another drink, I pass the slots in pursuit of a waitress.

Weee-oooo! Weee-oooo! Weee-oooo!

I jump at the jackpot siren and quicken my pace. Ever since we arrived at the Emerald Outpost, that sound has put me on edge, taking me back to my childhood on Barker Avenue, the constant sirens of police cars, fire trucks, ambulances. Those neighborhood noises never bothered me until a sunny September morning when I was four. Mami couldn't take me to work that day because I had the flu, so I stayed with Senora Rojas and her daughter Pia in the apartment down the hall. Before Mami left, she said, "Isabel, be good. No fussing." On the couch, with a box of Kleenex and a warm blanket, I practiced my English watching *Bob the Builder*, while Pia rolled around on the carpet with two plastic fire engines. Her father wasn't home; he was working. The toy sirens wailed, and Pia rolled, and the telephone rang. When Senora Rojas rushed into the living room and changed the channel, I heard more sirens and yelling. People were running, and two towers were burning. Then the towers collapsed, and Senora Rojas screamed and rushed back to the phone to make a call. "Pick up! Pick up!" she shouted. The real sirens wailed, and the toy sirens wailed, and I never saw Pia's father again.

DAY SIXTEEN

SINCE I'VE BEEN in Vegas, the days have gotten hotter and hotter, new numbers leapfrogging the old like slash marks on Paul Bunyan's growth chart.

"If I'm right, and I'm always right," says the morning show's weatherman, "we'll miss our record high by one degree today. For goodness sake, people, stay inside!"

Ready to return to New York, I click off the TV, open my suitcase on the bed, and dump in my clothes. Then I remember I haven't booked a flight. At the desk, I hop on my laptop in search of a one-way trip while the plastic bag of softball gear lounges next to me on the floor. JetBlue flights are full for the next two days, so I can't use my leftover credit. The cheapest available flight I find costs $720. I try to book it, but my Discover card gets denied. So does my corporate card. Pacing the room, I wear out a path between the suitcase and the softball stuff. Eventually I realize I'm overreacting. All I have to do is lie low until the Bulls leave for the game. It's not like they're going to drag me onto the bus.

Unable to ignore the plastic bag, I feel the tiniest bit bad about not helping out the team, and I don't know why I brought the gear back to my room in the first place. I decide to drop it off at the breakfast buffet before any of the guys get there, but when I pick it up, something stinks. I take out Benny's jersey, sniff, gag, and chuck it. The shirt lands on the back of the chair, the number six staring back at me.

What did my grandfather tell me when I visited him in Venezuela? "Life sends us messages in the form of numbers, Isabel. When you receive the number six, that's your guardian angel saying you need to make a change for the better. That number is special, mi cielita, because it represents the unconditional love your angel will always have for you."

I never believed in magical numbers, but looking at that jersey, I can't help remembering the pride I felt whenever I put on a uniform, whenever I wore my dad's number. I wipe my eyes. The panic that seized me yesterday has mostly subsided. On the desk, next to the lamp, is another framed quote: *No one ever said life was fair. Just eventful. – Carol Burnett*

I head into the bathroom, fill the tub, and squeeze half a bottle of body wash into the warm water. Kneeling on the bathmat, I wash every fiber of that Bulls jersey. I scrub the grass stains off the letters, scrub the mud stains off the number. When it's clean, I take it out to the balcony, lay it over the rail, and there in the Las Vegas sun, it dries.

When I meet the team in the hotel lot wearing my softball uniform, the Bulls are clearly surprised, but they try not to show it. They hide their smiles, acting like it's perfectly normal. I do the same.

"Where's Bo?" asks Sal, counting his sheep. "We can't leave without him, but only because he usually drives."

"Oh, I just remembered," Hank says. "I texted him this morning, needed him to fix a little *situation* I had with my toilet. He said he had to go home for a family emergency."

"Nice of you to tell us, Henry," says Vinnie.

"Nice of *Bo* to tell us," says Sal.

"I don't believe this," says Harold. "We're dropping like flies."

"Speaking of dropping flies," says Webb, putting his arm around Harold. "You're our only right fielder today."

"Yep, without Bo, we have only one sub," Sal says. "And none if you count Leo and Darryl as the same person."

"Let's go," says Slate. "We got a game to play and some drinking to do."

"Okay, I'll drive," says Leo.

"No!" yells Benny, hopping onto the bus and jumping behind the wheel. "I may have lost an arm, but we don't need to lose our lives."

As the rest of the Bulls board the Anonybus, I lag behind. Vinnie waltzes over, Foster Grants clasped to the collar of his guinea tee, a bulky UPS package in his arms. "You getting on, Izzy?"

"Do I have to?"

Vinnie laughs. "You know, I was gonna give this to you at the stadium," he says, "but now's good too." He hands me the package. "For you, kid."

I look at him sideways and rip it open. Inside: the Wilson A2K glove I saved up for in high school and used in college. "My mitt," I say. "How? Where?"

He smiles. "I asked your mother to send it," he says. "Thought you'd rather use your own glove. Hope you don't mind."

"Of course I don't mind." I slide my fingers into the leather.

Vinnie leans in. "Hmm, looks like Mom oiled it up for you too."

I pound my fist into the soft pocket. "Feels strange."

"You're gonna be great out there today," Vinnie says, putting on his shades.

"What if you're wrong?"

"Listen," he says, "you're the best softball player I've ever seen. You got the skills and the experience. I know it's been a while since you laced 'em up. But it'll all come back to you, I promise."

I take off the glove. "The best player you've ever seen?"

Vinnie squirms. "I mean, um, the best player I ever read about, heard about," he says. "You know, I read things and hear things, stuff like that." He slaps me on the shoulder. "C'mon, let's go." And we climb aboard.

Thirty minutes till game time, the stadium hums with activity. Vendors bark, selling beer and brats. Fans cheer, waving flags and fists. While the Bulls play catch and hit balls into a bow net, I sit alone on the outfield grass, stretching my hamstrings. A shadow appears on the ground next to me, and I look up. Mateo Glassiendo stands over me and yawns. His smeared-on beard, like charcoal on his cheeks and chin, veils pocked skin. His heavy eyes hint at a rough night's sleep. I get to my feet.

"What are you doing here, *vaina*?" he snarls.

I know the term. Mami uses it when she hates someone so much she refuses to speak their name. The word means *nothing*.

I answer, "Estoy en el equipo." (I'm on the team.)

He turns and spits, then runs his eyes up my body. "Deberias estar en la case de tu padre lavando su ropa y preparando su cena." (You should be at your father's house washing his clothes and preparing his dinner.)

I try to ignore him as he saunters off. When I get back to our dugout, the Bulls have Wink surrounded. "I'm just telling you what I *think* I heard," the second baseman says, hands up as if under arrest. "The guys were groaning about getting no sleep last night."

"Who was?" I ask.

"The Giants," Wink says. "They were talking mostly in Spanish, but it was something about loud noises outside their hotel. They kept saying *grua, grua*."

Everyone looks at me. "That means crane," I say.

Everyone looks at Vinnie. "Hold on a minute," he says, taking a step back. "Yeah, I might know a few construction workers around here. So what? I take no responsibility." He crosses his arms and sits on the bench. "Plus, I don't buy that story. Cranes aren't that noisy."

A roar explodes in the stadium, and the fans chant: "El Toro! El Toro! El Toro!" I look to the field, where some wacko dressed as a bull turns cartwheels in front of home plate. Hearing my father's nickname filling the ballpark makes me shiver.

"Hey, look, we got a mascot!" Rocco yells.

"Ask if he can play first base," Darryl says. "Leo and I are both gonna pass out at some point today."

Our "mascot" wears a brown and white costume of soft fabric, with a long tail, a large head, a black snout with a gold ring, and two fuzzy horns. He prances around the bases, sliding into each bag. He jumps on top of the Dominican dugout and dances a jig. He pulls down the umpire's shorts. The Bulls point and laugh. The fans roll in the aisles.

The Giants complain and yell, "¡Mata ese toro!" (Kill that bull!)

Five minutes till game time, the mascot gallops over to us and high-fives the human Bulls standing in a line outside our dugout. I stay on the bench behind them. The fake bull spots me, jumps into the dugout, and sticks out his hoof to shake my hand. I scoot away. He trots closer, his furry arms spread wide for a hug.

"Leave me alone!" I say.

Once the game is under way, the Giants play like they're stuck in manure. Groggy from the night before, distracted by our mascot, they make a ton of errors, including three by Mateo Glassiendo at third. Their pitcher, who hasn't walked an opposing hitter all tourney, hands out eight free passes. As for us, Webb hits an inside-the-park grand slam. Rocco smashes four hits and drives in seven runs. Leo crushes a ball off the leftfield wall and turns an easy triple into a stand-up double. Harold owns right field, catching six fly balls and dropping only one. And me? I suck. In four at-bats, I ground out twice to the pitcher and pop up twice to second. In left center, I misplay two singles and overthrow three cutoff men; Webb backs me up on two other balls that sneak under my glove, preventing three more unearned runs. I catch one shallow fly ball but think it's the third out of the inning and don't throw home as a runner tags up and scores. I haven't played this poorly since first grade. But we win 13-8 and tie the series.

In the parking lot, I lean against the bus and nurse a Stella. The Bulls sit in their silly circle of beach chairs and celebrate the victory. Vinnie gets up and opens a cooler. "Who needs one?" he asks his mates and looks back toward me. "Izzy, you good?"

I nod.

He grabs two beers and joins me by the bus. "Hey, I got an idea," he says. "Why don't you interview me for your story?"

I look across the lot at the stadium. "Maybe later."

He puts his arm around me. "Nah," he says. "Let's do this right now." And we wander away from the Bulls.

July 8 notes:

This afternoon, the DR Giants tried to put the Aging Bulls out to pasture, but the Bulls snatched Game 2 of the World Finals. The tournament champion will be decided tomorrow, but I won't be on the field. I played today and never looked like such a loser in my life. No offense, but I felt like Rodney, like softball was a foreign concept, like I'd never swung a bat or caught a ball before. Even the dumb mascot freaked me out. The Bulls don't need me. Win or lose tomorrow, they'll do it on their own.

After the game I interviewed Vinnie Shalers, a fifty-one-year-old pitcher from Staten Island. He's a little guy, close to my height, but he stands taller than I ever will. Vinnie's an instigator, an agitator, original as a fingerprint. He could be a hero or a villain, a heavy or a sidekick. He's thoughtful, and he likes to talk. A lot. He's sugary sweet and painfully irritating—an ice cream headache of a man—and I doubt I'll ever meet anyone like him again.

Pitching in Vegas so far, Vinnie has succeeded one day and failed the next, teetered between saving his butt and falling on his face. In every game he plays, no matter how hard he gets hit, Vinnie Shalers can't wait to throw his next pitch.

For our conversation, we strolled the Big League Dreams parking lot, near a replica of Yankee Stadium. Our bus, parked in the distance, was the only vehicle left on the grounds.

Me: I'm sorry about the game. I didn't help you at all.

Vinnie: Listen, Izzy, as a pitcher, I'm used to my fielders and hitters having an off day once in a while, and I understand it's part of the sport. As opposed to when Clete pitches and gets discombobulated every time a Bull pops up or makes an error. I'm more of, how should I put this, a "genteel" competitor.

Me: How would you rate your pitching performance so far in the tournament?

Vinnie: I mean, not to brag, because I don't really like to brag, but I'd give myself a solid 7.75 out of ten. Actually, let me amend that, if I may, and give myself an 8.45, due to the high level of competition. Maybe a 9.15, somewhere around there.

Me: Did you coach your daughters in softball too?

Vinnie: Of course, all three of them. My youngest, Harley, actually started out playing baseball against the boys.

Me: What advice did you give her?

Vinnie: I used to tell her she's just as good as them, even better than most. Told her to be assertive, act like she belongs, and that if she did, her talent would follow. She was nervous early on, but I used to pitch to her every day, hit her grounders and stuff, and I saw her confidence grow and grow. God, we spent so much time together for so many years. Now she plays softball in college, and I still get to see her sometimes, just not every day anymore.

Me: You should fly her out here to take my spot.

Vinnie: You know, Izzy, I have to confess, and you may not want to hear this, but I'm the one who told Sal to put you on the roster before the trip began.

Me: You what?

Vinnie: Look, please don't be mad. It's just that Harley and I saw you play when you were in high school. The first time we went to one of your games, you made a diving stop in the hole and threw the batter out at first by two steps. Harley was amazed, and she loved you, Izzy. You became her idol that day, and you were the best player we ever saw.

Me: You tricked me into coming because you thought I'd be a ringer? Well, look how that turned out. Hope you're happy.

Vinnie: Nah, it's not like that. I just knew the only way I could play with you in a real game was if we added you to the roster. I just wanted you and me to be on the field together, that's all I'm saying.

Me: Why?

Vinnie: To be honest, Izzy, and this might sound crazy, but hear me out, I just wanted to feel like I was playing with Harley again. Just one more time, me and my little girl, kicking the same dirt, smelling the same grass, giving each other a little nod after making a play. Trust me, if your dad were still with us, he'd do anything to be on a ballfield with you again.

Me: If he were still with us? His ghost haunts me every day, Vinnie. That's why I lost it when the bull mascot showed up at the game. When the crowd was chanting "El Toro," it was too much, you know? It's all too much.

Vinnie: If you don't mind my asking, how did your father die?

Me: A car accident, thirteen years ago, and I still can't believe he's gone. It's like it's not real, you know, like he's still here. Sometimes I forget, then it all comes back, like today. I mean, I get it, people die all the time. I just wish it didn't hurt so bad.

Vinnie: I'm so sorry, Izzy. Listen to me though, I know it's hard, but we should be grateful for those relationships, you know what I'm saying, the special ones like what you and your father had, because not everyone gets that kind of love. Yeah, it sucks that he's gone, but maybe think of it this way: it only hurts as much as it was worth, and if you love who you lost, you'll never lose who you loved.

I've been to Papi's grave only once since his funeral. I was nineteen. It took an hour-and-a-half, by train and bus, to get from Barker Avenue to Calvary Cemetery in Woodside, Queens.

Mami had buried him there because Calvary is the biggest cemetery in the country, and she wanted him to have lots of company. I went alone that summer day to apologize to my father after I quit playing softball. For an hour, I sat on the grass in front of his headstone, talking to him, hoping he heard me. "It wasn't the same without you," I told him. "I couldn't do it by myself. I'm so sorry, Papi. Please say you understand."

The birds sang. The wind blew.

Back in my hotel room, I listen to my recorded conversation with Vinnie, laugh out loud, cry a bit, and try to forget how poorly I played this afternoon. After showering and getting dressed, I text the Bulls to ask if anyone wants to get together for dinner. No one responds.

I go down to Skat's, expecting to see my teammates, but they aren't there. I sit alone at the bar and look around for Russell, but a waitress tells me he took the night off. I down my vodka tonic, flip a buck onto the bar, and head to the Ruby Slipper, where the One Hit Blunders are belting out "Steal Away" by Robbie Dupree. The Bulls aren't there either, or at Stuffy's, or in the casino. By now I'm sure the team is avoiding me after my dreadful game, and I don't blame them.

Up in the Funnymoon Suite, I order fries and a strawberry sundae for dinner. After midnight, I change into my sweats, brush my teeth, and pick up my room service tray. As I'm putting it out in the hall, the elevator door opens, and Slate steps out.

"Hey!" I say.

"What's up, Dominguez?" He moves toward me with a mitt in his hand.

I smile. "You lost? This is a high rent district, you know."

"You left your glove on the bus, nitwit." He tosses it at me.

"Thanks," I say. "Where were you guys tonight?"

"Oh, um, we went to visit Lowdan in the hospital," he says. "Figured you'd be busy writing or something."

"Huh. Did you get my text about dinner?"

He pauses. "Shitty cell service, I guess."

I nod. "Yeah."

"Well," he says, looking at the wall. "I'm hittin' the sack."

From my doorway, I watch him head toward the elevator and press the button. When the door dings, he looks back at me.

"Goodnight, Izzy," he says and disappears.

"Hey, Slate?" I call, but the door is already closing—on his hand.

"Ow, shit!" He peeks out at me. "What do you need, kid?"

I bite my lip. "Wanna have another catch?"

Slate grins. "Meet me in the parking lot in five."

DAY SEVENTEEN

To quote one of my heroes, the poet Amanda Gorman, "There is nothing so agonizing, or so dangerous, as memory unexpressed, unexplored, unexplained, and unexploded."

It was 2008, a Monday in July, the day after my team won the New York City championship. School was out for the summer, but my mother woke me up early. It was cloudy outside and dark in my room, but I could see she was crying. Three-year-old Ava stood behind her in the hallway. She was crying too.

"What did I do wrong?" I asked.

It took Mami a long time to answer, but finally she said, "Papi's gone."

I rubbed my eyes. "Gone to work?"

"No, Isabel."

To stock our family's restaurant for the week, my father drove to New Jersey every Monday and Wednesday before dawn. A friend of his, Mr. Tanner, managed a wholesale warehouse in Fort Lee and gave Papi a big discount on produce. My dad used to say a smile can go a long way, but he never got to smile at Mr. Tanner that day.

The policeman who called Mami that morning said a truck driver on the George Washington Bridge fell asleep at the wheel and swerved into Papi's van. Both vehicles flipped, the officer said. Her husband had died at the scene, and she needed to ID his body. The cop also said the other driver had been treated and released from the hospital.

I used to think about that man all the time, the truck driver who killed my father. I wondered if he knew what he did, that he stole a life, ruined a family. I wondered if he cared, or if he forgave himself, or if he lost any sleep. I wondered if he had a daughter and if she ever wondered about me. For eight years, I carried a hatred for that man, lugged it around like a heavy chain. Then one day, during an argument with my mother, after I told her I was quitting softball and transferring out of pre-med, she told me the truth. The truck driver hadn't fallen asleep and swerved into Papi's van. It was the other way around. Mami had lied, and I'd blamed the wrong man the whole time.

At 5 a.m., the hotel room is ghost-quiet, but my mind is noisy. I shuffle into the kitchenette, make a cup of coffee, and step out onto the balcony. Warm mug in one hand, cool rail in the other, I welcome the morning. High above, an airplane slices through purple clouds layered into the whipped cream sky. The wind billows my hair. My final twenty-four hours in Vegas have arrived, along with the championship game. After my catch with Slate last night, I know I'll play again today; I won't let the team down by quitting, even if it means embarrassing myself. A part of me is actually looking forward to getting back onto the field.

Back east, it's ten past eight, the morning bustle under way. I slip away from my balcony bliss and go back inside to check my phone. The weather app indicates a record high of 118 degrees. Then I get a call.

Kay: Bad news, Izzy. Corporate is shutting us down after all. You'll get two weeks' severance, and your benefits expire at the end of the month.

Me: No, it can't be. They can't do that!

Kay: Well, they did. No need to keep working on that story.

Me: What am I supposed to do now?

Kay: If it were me, I'd enjoy my last day in Vegas and then start looking for a job on the bus ride home—maybe in a different industry. I'm sorry, Izzy.

I spend the morning alone in my room, distraught, trying to reach Mami and Ava, though I dread breaking the news to them. At least I never got Mami's hopes up by telling her the magazine might survive. When my calls and texts go unanswered, I open my laptop to look at job postings but end up staring at my Bulls notes instead. So many notes, so many interviews, all of it wasted. I hate to think of abandoning the story just as I'm starting to figure it out.

At 1:30, I put on my uniform, grab my glove, and take the elevator down. When the door opens, I start across the lobby and almost bump into Russell. He's standing there with a duffle bag over his shoulder, his eyes red.

"Hi!" I say. "Something wrong?"

"Hey," he says. "The Bulls told me you'd be down soon. I just wanted to say goodbye."

"What? Why?"

"I'm leaving town," he says. "My Uber will be here in a sec. Got a GM job at a restaurant back east."

"Congratulations!" I say. "That's great, right? Back east where?"

But before Russell can answer, I hear a familiar squawk behind me and wheel around.

"Hey, Izzy, look who I ran into at LaGuardia!" It's Clete Shuheg, and he's with my mother and sister. Ava jumps into my arms. Mami follows.

"Oh my god!" I say, squeezing them tight. "What are you doing here?"

"Rooting for your team," says Ava.

As Clete smiles beside us, I peel my sister off me and turn to my mother.

"You should be home, Mami. What about your treatments?"

"I decided to start next week," she says, rubbing my arm. "I couldn't miss the big game."

She wipes her eyes as I laugh away my tears. "Thank you," I say, deciding not to ruin the moment by telling her that I'm officially out of a job.

"Look at you, my little girl in a uniform again," Mami says, taking a step back. "And wearing number six. Oh, Isabel, Papi would be so happy right now."

Ava peeks at the back of my jersey and sniffs the sleeve. "Gross," she says. "Has this thing ever been washed?"

I hug my sister again, kiss her forehead. It's been just a couple of weeks since I've seen her, but she looks older, so much like me. "I'm really glad you're here," I say.

"Well, it's kind of a special occasion," Ava says, grabbing my hand. "You know what tomorrow is, right?"

"Of course." I give her fingers a squeeze. "July 10th, the day Papi died."

"And Isabel, you know what today is?" Mami asks, her dark eyebrows arched.

"Um, the day *before* he died?"

"Sí," my mother says with a grin, "when you won the city championship." And she goes to a happier place in her mind. "I can still see the smile your father wore when he got home that day. He was so proud of you. Muy orgulloso."

The clamor in the lobby grows louder. The rest of the Bulls come over and, one by one, I introduce them to my family. Over the next five minutes, the guys give Mami and Ava the star treatment, and I wish I could give them a great end to their story, even Slate, especially Slate, maybe not Slate.

Then I remember Russell. I scan the lobby, but he's already gone. I feel awful that I didn't get to say goodbye and make a mental note to text him later.

"Okay, wheels up," Sal shouts. "Time to finish what we started, Bulls."

Rocco swigs the remains of a Bloody Mary. "Ahhh, yessir."

Clete taps me on the shoulder. "Hey Izzy, I'll drive your mom and sister to the park. We'll be pulling for you."

"You're not playing?" I ask him.

"No, I'll be watching with these lovely ladies," he says. "You got this."

Mami seizes Clete's arm. "Este caballero is a wonderful escort," she swoons.

Clete blushes and moves in closer to her. "I told you, I'm a happily married man, Maggy." And we all laugh.

I hug my mother again. "See you at the game, Mami."

Ava gives me a fist bump and winks. "Kick Glassiendo's ass, sis."

I sling my backpack over my shoulder and board the Anonybus. Without our regular driver, Bo, one-armed Benny slips behind the wheel again, making his contribution to the team by preventing Leo from driving.

I sit by myself in the front, in the same seat as when we began our journey sixteen days ago. The opening scene of *The Natural* plays on the TV above me, the movie's musical score rising, and the bus rolls out of the lot.

When we get to the stadium, the fans are so rowdy I can hardly hear Sal announce the lineup: "Ucho in right center and leading off, then Shalers pitching, Hetan at short, me at third, Rocco catching, Hank in left, Darryl at first base, Leo subs in, then Dominguez in left center, Harold in right, and batting last and playing second base, Wink Sillano."

Twenty minutes before the game, I sit alone in the dugout while the other Bulls stretch their legs and loosen up their arms. As I re-tie my cleats for the third time, Harold plops down beside me. He reaches into the back pocket of his cargo shorts and presents a cashier's check. "This is for you," he says smiling, "from Dottie and her lucky slot machine."

I take the check, look at it, and throw it back at him like it's on fire. "Are you crazy, Harold?" I say. "That's for a hundred grand."

He offers it to me again. "I know, but she insisted," he says. "She wants you to use it for something special, and she asked me to thank you for her."

"Thank me for what?"

"For being you."

I'm still staring at the check, speechless and astounded, when the sound of honking snaps me back to earth. Beyond the centerfield wall, the Anonybus pulls to a stop. The door opens and Rodney Pittbase pops out wearing his Aging Bulls jersey. I can see his smile from two hundred and fifty feet away. He climbs onto the hood and scrambles to the roof, lugging a big black case. In less than ninety seconds, he sets up a PA system and his steel drum kit. In the stands, the fans go wild, singing and dancing to Rodney's version of Jimmy Cliff's "You Can Get It If You Really Want" and Third World's "96 Degrees in the Shade."

For the second straight day, our fuzzy bull mascot appears, twirling to Rodney's grooves, staggering around the bases, slapping high-fives with kids in the front row, sneaking behind the DR Giants and stealing their hats. When the bull tumbles over the pitching rubber, Harold turns to me in the dugout.

"You can check my math," he says, "but I'd guess it's a thousand degrees in that costume."

"I still can't believe *this* math," I say, waving Dottie's check. "Will you hang onto this for me?"

Ten minutes before the first pitch, I run out to centerfield to limber up and calm my nerves. On my way back, Mateo Glassiendo leers at me from across the diamond and shoots me the bird. I shoot him one back. Then, nearing the dugout, I notice a large man sitting where I used to sit, wearing a Red Sox hat and T-shirt. He tips his cap and I do a double take. "No way," I mumble. "Race?"

"You wear that jersey well, kid."

"Thanks. How's the calf?"

"Weirdest thing," he says. "Healed up right after the Bulls beat us."

"What are you doing here?"

"I couldn't miss this game. I had to see you play." He looks into the cloudless sky, past the tall stadium lights that seem to shine even during the day.

I wait for his gaze to come back down. "My dad would really appreciate this."

"I can only hope," Race says, his long hair grayer than I remember. "Now get out there and make us proud."

I nod and walk back toward my team, my knees weak, my eyes wet. The Aging Bulls circle up outside the dugout. In his pep talk stance, Rocco sticks his hand into the middle of the group and shouts, "Let's go, right arms in here!" We put our arms in together, like spokes in a wagon wheel. While I wait for Rocco to give us a cue, all of the Bulls stare at me.

"What?" I ask.

"Since you're one of us now," Slate says, "we made it official." He smiles. "Turn 'em over, boys."

The Bulls rotate their arms. Imprinted on their wrists, each player has an *El Toro* tattoo, exactly like mine.

Slate tugs the brim of his cap. "We're all in this together, Dominguez."

Rocco finger-combs his sweaty mane away from his face and squats, his eyes demanding our attention. "Okay, listen up," he snorts. "Real quick, real simple. We are who we are. It is what it is. And we do what we do. Because we're the Bulls, and everyone wants to be us! So let's go out there and play like it!"

The day is hot, but not just any hot, a grease-fire-in-Hell's-Kitchen kind of hot. Before we take the field, I duck into the dugout for some water. The bull mascot stumbles in, points to his mouth, and collapses on the bench next to me. This time, I don't run away. I offer him the bottle, but he can't hold it with his hooves or drink it wearing a big furry bullhead. As I grab his horns, I feel like Daphne unmasking a villain on *Scooby-Doo*. I pull it off. "No way!"

"Yes," gasps Bo Loth, "way."

He looks like he's on the brink of passing out, his face drawn, his hair dripping sweat.

I hold the bottle to his lips. "I thought you went home?"

Bo guzzles the water and pants. "I'm the guy… huff, huff… who can build stuff and fix things, but on the field… gasp, huff… I can't build my confidence or fix my swing, wanted to help the team and… huff, gasp… lighten the mood… huff, huff… and could only think of this."

"Great idea," I say. "Sorry I blew your cover."

Bo closes his eyes, slides down on the bench. "Yeah, I would've gotten away with it too… gasp, huff… if it weren't for this sweltering heat."

On Vinnie's first pitch of the game, he takes a rocket off the shin, buckles, and crumples to the ground. By the time he gets to his feet and limps to the dugout, Clete is out of the stands, in his uniform, and all warmed up. The self-proclaimed "Nordic boy toy" is a bulldog in the circle and keeps the game scoreless for seven innings. We have last licks, and in the bottom of the final frame, Hank leads off, swings at the first pitch, and promptly pops to the pitcher. Up next, I take a strike, thinking I should work a walk. But on the second offering, I go for a ball at my eyes and fly out to right.

When I get back to the dugout, I'm hyperventilating. I throw my helmet onto the ground, and Sal approaches. "Pick that up and stay loose," he says. "If Harold gets on, you're gonna pinch run."

Our last hope, Harold, singles past Mateo Glassiendo at third, who slams his glove down in disgust. The fans hiss and boo. Glassiendo flips them off and grabs his crotch.

I put my helmet on again and jog onto the field. When I take Harold's place at first base, we slap hands, and he says, "Let's see those wheels."

Coaching in his sling, Benny puts his good arm around me. "We got two down," he says. "Take off at the crack of the bat, and if Wink hits a gap, try to score."

Wink steps to the plate. The crowd goes bananas. He digs his spikes into the dirt. I get ready to run. After five pitches, he's worked a full count but hasn't taken the lumber off his shoulder. On the next offering, I know I need to go. The pitcher winds up and delivers. Wink swings with all he has and slices a line drive to right center. The outfielder lunges, but the ball squeaks under his glove and rolls to the wall. I round second and chug toward third. My helmet flies off and nicks my heels. I stumble and then regain my speed. I lift my eyes and pick up Leo in the coach's box. His arm is a windmill, waving me around. The fans scream. The Bulls cheer. I make the turn, tagging third base in perfect stride. Out of the corner of my eye, I see Mami and Ava leaping out of their seats, Slate bounding out of the dugout. I fly down the baseline. Leo rushes alongside, shouting and encouraging.

And then my father is there. I hear him calling out to me.

"Go Izzy! Go! You got it!" I run like I'm a kid again, like Papi's chasing me around the bases at Reiss Field. Dust kicks up. I run hard. The sun beats down. I run harder. The throw comes into the catcher on one hop. Papi calls out again. "Faster, Izzy! Go!" The catcher gloves the ball and blocks the plate. And I see Papi in my bedroom doorway, my city championship trophy glowing next to him on the dresser. I hear his last words to me. My teammates cheer louder. I stick my left leg out, bend my right knee, and start my slide.

But in my heart, I'm already home.

Two hours later, in the center of the Taj Meh Hall, the Bulls gather around several coolers of beer. "We got this room all night," Sal says, "but I want to make a quick toast before we shower and change."

"Shower?" says Slate. "Why start now?"

"I guess this trip won't end with a *clean Slate*," Sal says, tossing me a look. "Now raise your glasses, Bulls." We close in tight, and our manager clears his throat. "As my Grandpa Luigi used to say: Here's to the nights we'll never remember with the friends we'll never forget."

"And if I may," Vinnie chimes in. "Like my Uncle Patsy used to say: I'd rather be with the people in this room than with the finest people I know." He lifts his beer. "To the Bulls."

"To the Bulls!"

As I finish my Brooklyn Summer, Mami and Ava stop by to say goodbye before Clete drives them to McCarran to catch a redeye back to New York. I grab my backpack, usher them to their car, and give them long hugs. My mother takes my face in her hands. "I love you, Isabel."

"I know you do," I say. "Love you too." And then I show her Dottie's check. "Put this in a safe place until I get home. It's a gift from a friend."

Mami looks at the check, then at me, then back at the check again. "Is this real?"

I nod. "Don't worry about the medical bills or losing the restaurant. We're going to be okay, at least for now."

She takes the check in both hands, carefully, as if it might break. Ava looks over her shoulder and gasps.

"I cannot believe this, Isabel," my mother says.

"Me neither," I say.

After they leave, I go back inside and hustle into the elevator, wanting to get out of my uniform and wash up before rejoining the party. Before the door closes, Wink jumps in with me. I laugh and say, "That's the quickest I've ever seen you move."

"Yeah," he says, smiling and flexing a bicep. "I'm more of a slugger than a speedster."

"You were incredible today," I say.

"Kinda proves that whole blind squirrel theory, huh?"

The elevator door opens to the sixth floor. "Oh, this is me," I say, stepping out. "Sorry we skipped your floor, catch you back at the party."

He gets out too. "Actually, I want to see something up here," he says and starts walking down the hall toward the Repenthouse Suite. "Come on."

Past the suite at the end of the hall, I follow Wink through a door with a sign that reads, *Employees Only*. "Wow," I say, "look at you, Mr. Rulebreaker."

"Yeah, that's me."

We start up a short flight of stairs. "I thought this hotel only had six floors," I say.

He looks back at me. "It does."

At the top step, the Aging Bull pushes open a door and holds it for me. An early-evening breeze, soft and warm, invites me onto the rooftop. The pinnacle of the Emerald Outpost offers a 360-degree view. Wink and I move around the edge. To the west, the sun settles above a bed of mountains. To the east, against a dusty backdrop, the lights of the strip awaken. From up here on the roof, with the skyline stretching before me, I can see the whole world.

July 9 notes:

If he were here, what would Papi think of the Aging Bulls? And what would he think of me? I wish he could've seen me play today.

For thirteen years, it was so hard for me to admit he was gone, but maybe he's always been with me, behind me in everything I've done. I know now that if I pay attention and open up, I can find him in other places. Like in the wind, or at a ballpark, or with the Bulls.

My final interview is with Wink Sillano. He's a fifty-two-year-old second baseman, originally from South Carolina, a college professor and book editor with delicate eyes—and a ginger beard ill-suited for his baby face. He's smart, quiet, calm, and harmless. If he weren't a Bull, he'd be a dolphin or a dove. I heard Wink might call it quits and retire from the team to begin another chapter in his life. And I wonder why any of these friends would choose to move on from one another.

Wink: Can you believe it's over?

Me: I know. Is it true you're retiring from the Bulls?

Wink: I'm leaning that way. It's been fun, but I don't think the team needs me anymore. They've got players way better than me.

Me: Something tells me those guys don't care about talent.

Wink: Maybe not. I don't know, it just might be time to move on. You played great though. Thinking about joining the Bulls full time?

Me: We'll see, but I might be in your camp, might need to focus on other things right now.

Wink: Did it feel good to play ball again?

Me: Better than I thought. But honestly, after yesterday's game, I was ready to burn my glove—right after setting Sal, Slate, and Vinnie on fire for forcing me to play.

Wink: I can empathize. What are your plans when you get home?

Me: I can't go back to my position at *Mature Living* since there's no more *Mature Living*. I guess I'll find another job at some other publication, or I'll just help my mother at the restaurant.

Wink: What do you *really* want to do?

Me: Tough to say now, but when I was younger, I dreamed of being a novelist. Writing was all I cared about, that and softball, but not so much anymore. I mean, I still think I'm good at writing, but I have a hard time believing my voice matters.

Wink: Like I tell my daughter, the two things that matter most are your dreams and your voice. You just have to be bold.

Me: Being bold isn't my strong suit. I'm better at failing.

Wink: Well, you're in luck, because writing involves a lot of failure. Every sentence, every plot, every book is flawed. Nothing ever feels done, and there's always a way to make it better.

Me: I wouldn't even know where to start.

Wink: Start anywhere. Just go for it, write like you played today. Whether we won or lost doesn't matter, because you gave it all that you had.

The second Wink says, "all that you had," I look harder at him, trying to wrap my head around a feeling I can't describe. I sift through my backpack, pull out my book, and check the author photo on the back cover. There he is, right where he's been the entire time.

I shake the book in his face. "You're Will Peterson?"

Wink smiles. "Well, that's my pen name," he says. "And that picture's ten years old, before I could grow a full beard."

"Oh my god! I love you! You're the G.O.A.T."

"That's nice of you," he says. "We're talking about books, not softball, right?"

"I've been reading *All That You Had* this whole trip," I say. "I mean, I've been reading it my whole life. I've read it so many times, I feel like it *is* my life."

"So what about your Bulls story? Any chance I could take a look?"

"Sorry," I say. "I never wrote it. And now there's no point."

Wink shakes his head. "That's too bad. You put in so much work. And you put up with the Bulls."

"Yeah, well, it wasn't easy."

We share a laugh, and then I look out at the Las Vegas skyline, ready to light up the night. "You know, when I first got this assignment, I was bummed. But this morning, when I found out the magazine was closing, I realized how much I wanted to tell this story."

Wink looks out at the skyline too. "*Wanted?*" he says. "Or *want?*"

And then, true to his name, he winks at me and excuses himself to get ready for the party. His question doesn't really register until I'm alone on the roof, and I realize he's right. I still want to tell the Bulls story, because now it's my story too. And just because it won't appear in *Mature Living* doesn't mean it can't appear somewhere else. And now that I'm not writing for the readers of the magazine, I can tell the story any way I want. I could even make it into a novel. I just have to go at it with my whole heart. *Todo mi corazón.*

I can't wait to get back to my laptop and back to work, but first I have a party to attend. I go down to my room, shower, and switch on the TV. As I get dressed, a local weatherman gushes about the day's record heat: "We've never seen anything like this, folks. Today was brutal, just unbearable, but we made history." On the news, kids splash in a wave pool at a local water park, and I'm transported back to the end of fourth grade, early June.

I was almost finished with my homework when I heard kids laughing outside on Barker Avenue and went to the window. Someone had opened the hydrant on the corner. My friends were skipping and splashing in the street. When Papi came home at four o'clock, I asked if I could play in the hydrant too. "We have work to do," he said, and we hurried to Reiss Field, where he hit me fifty groundballs, fifty flyballs, and threw batting practice for thirty minutes. Halfway done, tired and hot, I took a break and drank from my water bottle. Next to me on the bench, my father looked out at the field. Sweat dripped off his beard as he held his bat, gripped the handle, felt its weight, stared at the barrel like it was a photo of a long-lost friend. Normally Papi would hit me fifty more grounders and fifty more flyballs, then throw BP for another half hour before chasing me around the bases. But that afternoon, in that heat, he ended our practice early, and I ran the bases alone while he cheered me on, waiting for me to run into his arms when I crossed home plate.

Then, after we left that dusty field and got back home, my father played with me and the neighborhood kids on the street, splashing and laughing in the cool water. And it was the happiest day of my life. Until today.

THREE DAYS LATER

*D*ESPITE KAY'S ADVICE—AND thanks to Dottie's check—
I don't spend the bus ride home looking for a new job.
Instead, I focus on appreciating my final days with the
Bulls. And when I'm not hanging out with the guys, I hunker
down with my diary and tell my dad all the things I've been
holding inside ever since Senora Rojas gave me that first journal
on my twelfth birthday. I write about my fears, my hopes, my
dreams; my anger at him for leaving me; my appreciation for all
he taught me; my love for him, as strong now as it was the day
he died. And before I close my journal for the last time, I say the
goodbye I never got to say in person.

The Anonybus cruises east along Route 78, crossing the
New Jersey state line. After three days on the road, and twenty
days overall, we're almost home. Comfy on a matted-down
plush couch that stinks of Maker's Mark and butt sweat, I look
around at the disco balls, the plaid curtains, the purple carpeting. The Bulls are all sleeping, except for Wink, who's driving,
and Harold, who's playing Wordle in the backseat. Looking at all
these men, it occurs to me that our lives, mine and theirs, are like
empanadas and pepperoni nachos, softball and cricket. We're
not so different. I have my concerns (Mami and Ava, my resumé

and LinkedIn profile, my writing) and they have theirs (growing children and dying parents, downsizing and retirement, overdue colonoscopies). We don't share the same problems, but we all have them. And we're all just out here doing our best.

The Bulls wake up when Wink hits a pothole on the exit ramp, rattling coolers of empty cans. As we roll down the tranquil streets of Walnut Gap toward the Stillwater Softball Complex, century-old trees shade our bus from the summer sun. Wink veers into the parking lot, and a waiting crowd cheers, welcoming us home with banners and balloons. I press my nose against the window and see the families I've heard about—and daughters like the girls I used to write about, the ones with fairy tale lives, futures, and fathers. Now I feel like one of those girls.

The players pour out of the bus. Their loved ones swallow them up, congratulate them, hug and kiss them. Wink stays in the driver's seat, waiting for me. I grab my backpack and walk up the aisle.

"Well?" he says. "Am I ever going to see that Bulls piece or what?"

"I'm thinking it might be a novel now, but however it ends up, you'll be the first to read it, Wink," I say. "Or can I call you Will?"

He smiles. "Tell you what, when it's ready, you can call me your editor."

When I try to thank him, he just points me to the door, and I turn around. Out in the parking lot, everyone's waiting for me in a line. I can't help thinking of the receiving line at my father's funeral—the family, friends, and strangers whose hand-shakes and hugs didn't ease my pain so much as remind me that I no longer had a dad. The sight of this line has the opposite effect. Welling up, I take a moment to compose myself. When I step out of the Anonybus, the players hoot and holler like the knuckleheads they are.

"Listen up, folks," Sal calls out, quieting the crowd.

The Bulls and their families form a circle next to the bus, and Sal pulls me into the center.

"Before we all say goodbye," he says, "I'd like to announce that Isabel Maria Dominguez is officially on the Aging Bulls roster for next season."

Another cheer goes up.

"Hold on," Sal shouts. "I also have some bad news."

"Boooooo!" the crowd yells.

"All right, settle down." Sal throws his hands into the air like he's holding up a runner at third base. "The bad news is, in a year, Izzy will be a prize-winning journalist traveling the world, who won't make a single game and will forget all about us."

"Ayyyyyyy!"

I laugh and give Sal a fist bump. Then I face the crowd. "Thank you, Bulls," I say, "but I promise that I will never, ever forget you losers."

The goodbyes begin.

Clete charges at me with his arms out wide. I thank him for taking such good care of my mom and sister. He tells me that's what family's for and adds that he's happy they got to see him pitch. Next Bryson's wife introduces herself and her two daughters. She says once her husband recovers from surgery, they'll invite me over for dinner. I say I'd be honored and tell her about meeting Zach at the hospital in Vegas.

And the line rolls along.

The Bulls who couldn't make the trip, ringers Mac and JC, appear in full uniform, right where I left them twenty days ago. I tell them they nailed their scouting reports, except Rodney is even nicer than they said, and Slate is more annoying, and we high five. Next up, Benny gives me a one-armed hug and insists I keep his jersey; he says I deserve to wear six and he'll get a new number, maybe steal Ucho's. Webb follows Benny, and we string out a long goodbye. In Vegas, I connected with the spirit of the Bulls after watching Webb take care of Darryl, and I tell him as much. Darryl hugs me, and we laugh and hug again, and his beard scratches my face like Papi's did a thousand times before.

"I heard you were great," says Nick, walking toward me. "Sorry I missed it." He looks weary and thankful, like a man who just slept on his very first pillow. "Please give your mom a hug for me."

"I will, and do the same for me," I say before kissing him on the cheek.

Harold approaches with his family and says goodbye. The five of them look close and happy together, and I know for sure he's a lucky guy. When fellow egghead Hank joins the conversation, I thank both men for helping me with their impromptu email blast. Then Rocco rumbles over with his daughter, introduces us, and tells her I'm the best person he knows.

"It is what it is," I say, and we all laugh.

The line thins.

Bo gives me a bear hug and offers to trade me his 172-piece modular fixturing kit in exchange for hitting lessons. I tell him to keep the kit, the lessons are free. Up next, Rodney introduces me to his three children. I pull them aside and say they should listen to their dad because I'm pretty sure he knows the secret to life. After we hug and Rodney walks away, I'm certain that he loves the Bulls and belongs on the team more than anyone.

"Come over here, Harley," says a distinct voice behind me. "I want you to meet someone special." Vinnie taps me on the shoulder, and I turn to face an athletic-looking, college-aged girl.

"Izzy Dominguez? I can't believe it's you." She has bright eyes, a raspy voice, and her father's moxie. "You're why I play the game."

I shake her hand. "Nice to meet you, Harley Shalers," I say

as the girl beams. "I hear you're one of the best players Walnut Gap's ever seen. Must've had a pretty good coach."

Vinnie winks at his daughter and puts his arm around me. "Hey, thank you," he says. "I'm never gonna forget what you did for me, for all of us, know what I'm saying? We owe you, Izzy."

I wish Harley good luck in her college career, say I'd like to see her play someday, and suggest she have a catch with her father now and then to keep the old man out of trouble.

The sun dims, the air cools, and the Bulls head home with their families, pulling away in SUVs and sedans, honking and cheering. It's almost time for my train, but one Bull remains. I sling my backpack over my shoulder and stand with Leo Tarriso. Sniffling, he looks around at the empty lot, hands in pockets, nervous leg shaking.

I stand on my tiptoes and peck him on the cheek. "Goodbye, Mr. Tarriso," I say, holding back tears. "No offense, but I'm not going to miss your terrible driving."

He turns his head, wipes an eye. "Hey, I already apologized for hitting that pack of pigs in Toledo."

I laugh. "You mean that singular of boar?"

He puts his hands on his hips and furrows his brow. "You know, I thought our farewell was gonna be sad," he says, "but I'm not so sure anymore."

"You can't fool me," I say. "I already saw you cry, you big baby."

"Well, guess what?" Leo takes a set of keys out of his pocket and jingles them in front of his crooked nose. "This big baby gets to drive the Anonybus back to Trenton."

"Oh, god," I say. "Be careful. Vinnie needs that bus returned in one piece."

Leo chuckles, gives me a quick hug, then gets serious. "Listen, Izzy, if you ever need anything, please call me anytime."

"Don't worry, you'll be the first person I call," I say. "Because if you can get Rocco out of jail, you can do anything."

He ambles to the bus, gets behind the wheel, and calls out the window. "Hey, want a lift to the station?"

"Tempting," I say, waving goodbye, "but I'll walk."

As Leo starts the engine, my phone buzzes, and I check the text.

Biff: Wish we got to play together. You're the perfect Bull.

Me: Thought you said perfection was a myth? Lol

Biff: True, but by saying the "perfect Bull," it's like I was saying "perfect imperfection" which, if you think about it, makes perfect sense because there's nothing perfect about the Bulls.

Me: Sounds like you found that peyote.

Biff: Hahahahahahah

Leo shifts the Anonybus into gear and sputters away, revealing a black Jeep Wrangler, dented and dirty, parked in the next spot over. Leaning against the door with a six-pack of Miller Lite under his arm, Slate looks like a grizzled, tatted-out pirate.

"Hey kid, got time for a beer?"

I walk over, set down my suitcase, and drop my backpack. "I have no idea why," I say, "but I think I'm going to miss you the most."

"Impossible," he says. "You can only miss something that's gone, and I'm not going anywhere. We're teammates for life." Then he wraps me in a hug. "What's your name again?"

I jab him in the ribs. "You're such a jerk."

In the late-afternoon light, our shadows stretch out on the asphalt. He cracks open a beer and hands it to me as his *El Toro* tattoo rolls over the tendons on his wrist.

"Aren't you having one?" I ask.

"Nope," he says. "Got an early start tomorrow at the Blue Moose, training a new GM, met him in Vegas. You should stop by and say hi. He's really good with people." Slate smirks. "And he says you owe him a date."

I throw my arms around that old pirate's neck. "Thank you for everything," I whisper.

When I finish my beer, Slate gives me a ride to the station. I board the train and sit by the window. He's standing alone on the platform. I motion for him to go, but he doesn't budge, just waits by the track in his grubby baseball hat, smiling at me like he's hiding a secret. After the train pulls away, I pause a few seconds then look over my shoulder. Through a veil of sunlight and dust, the platform fades in the distance, and Slate disappears from my sight. But somehow I know he's still there.

EPILOGUE

$\mathcal{B}$E LIKE THAT tree, Izzy," Papi used to tell me. And after he died, I heard his voice whenever I looked at the old painting in our living room, the one that hung crooked above the couch.

But today, when I stare at that picture, the araguaney doesn't look the same to me. Not because its colors have faded in the afternoon sun pouring through our windows. Not because we moved the couch to the opposite wall to make room for the writing desk Mami gave me for my twenty-fifth birthday. And not because we replaced the painting's gaudy plastic frame. The difference is now I understand that there's nothing wrong with looking ordinary, going unnoticed, or being unspectacular. Because the people who love you will always notice and appreciate you, whether you're blooming or not.

"Be like the araguaney." That's what Papi used to say. But I no longer hear his voice.

I hear my own.

"We don't stop playing because we grow old.
We grow old because we stop playing."

—ANONYMOUS

ACKNOWLEDGMENTS

I could never write a book, or do much else, without my parents, who always encouraged me to shine; my sisters, who still do; and my brothers, who gave me the chance.

But no one deserves more appreciation than my wife, Jackie. Her belief in my ability, and her understanding of who I am, are the forces that keep me going. And she knows what Izzy knows, because she rose up through the same stereotypes trying to hold her down. The daughter of Spanish-speaking immigrants, Jackie struggled with her identity, with fitting in and finding her way. She grew up feeling the need to be perfect while fighting back the fear that she'd never be good enough. It's her story—and the stories of Latinas like her—that inspired me to tell this one.

Thanks to my kids, Caleb and Lucy, for being my fuel. They make me proud every day. If I leave anything behind in this world, it will be for them. But for Lucy especially, and daughters like her who grew up on the softball diamond, this book is a giant "thank you." For practicing hard and playing with your whole heart, for working through pain and pressure, for being fearless, for having fun. But mostly, for the hours we spent together, you and I, on the field or in the car or at the park playing catch, for the time I had with my little girl, time I may not have found anywhere else. Thank you, Lucy, for that gift.

Without my editor and friend, Will Allison, I'd be adrift on a sea of meaningless words and phrases. His genius astounds me. His patience rivals my own. His knack for dissecting a story, picking out the bad from the good, and prodding with purpose inspires me to be a better writer. My goal is to someday make his job easier. I rarely accomplish such goals.

Thank you to my beta readers: Celina Santos Herrero, Cindy D'Altorio Sherman, Andrea Soulellis Erickson, and Lara Pennington, who helped shape and tune the words on these pages. A debt is owed to all four, and a debt will be paid, probably in wine.

My endless gratitude goes out to everyone who read my first book, *You're Gonna Miss Me Someday.* I appreciate those of you who texted, called, emailed, or told me in person that you'd connected with my family's story, those who took the time to write a review or recommend the memoir to a friend. I wouldn't have had the confidence to start—never mind finish—book number two if it weren't for your support.

But if I had to choose one person, or entity, that made *Wave Her Home* possible, it'd be the group of friends about whom this book is not-so-loosely based: the Aging Bulls. We formed our ragtag team in 2014 and originally called ourselves the Raging Bulls, but after dropping every game in our rookie campaign, we quickly dropped the "R" in our name. The key to our success, we determined, was not to take ourselves too seriously, or seriously at all. That philosophy worked in our daily lives, so why wouldn't it work on the diamond? In this book, I embellished the personalities on our team and created caricatures out of characters. With our wealth of clownishness and dearth of on-field talent, it wasn't a stretch to turn fact into fiction. "We are who we are, it is what it is, and we do what we do," is just another way of saying, "We're all lucky to have eighteen best friends." We got to know one another while coaching our daughters, teaching them the life lessons softball can offer. Now, our bond solidifies while playing the game most of those girls left behind. We love the sport, and we love each other, simple as that. Oh, and we love drinking beer after playing the sport. If heaven exists, I hope the Bulls can meet there one day, like in the final scene of *Lost* when Jack turns up at that weird ecumenical church and reunites with his dead friends from the island. Yes, I'd like for my teammates to find each other again after we're gone, but not at a weird church. Maybe we'll meet in a celestial pub where cherubs pour bottomless glasses of Casamigos, or in some heavenly parking lot where an angel gets his wings whenever a beer's cracked open, or at a ballpark in the clouds where every diving catch results in a soft landing. Maybe we'll stumble out of a corn crop like in *Field of Dreams*, and just as those phantom players were led by Shoeless Joe, the Aging Bulls will be led by Clueless Po; that's Dave Ethan, or Slate Hetan, as he'll forever be known.

His nickname is "Po" for reasons not worth explaining, and none of us Bulls will ever meet beyond the pearly gates unless Ethan gets into the joint. What does Dave mean to our team? He's the key. He's the linchpin. He's the guy who'll have the idea to meet when we're dead, to throw the ball around, take a few swings, and drink some beers afterwards, but someone else will have to organize the whole thing. He's our Morris Buttermaker. A brute. A lout. A merciless wiseass with a heart of gold, who'll laugh at himself as quickly as he'll laugh at you, and he *will* laugh at you, a lot, so find an extra layer of skin somewhere. Actually, make it two. Dave invented the Bulls, pulled the idea right out of his head (insert joke here). He's an amazing father, coach, and friend. He's a man who falls in love easily, a rare and admirable trait. His greatest ability is creating teams and families, whether that's on the field, at work, or at home. Because for Po, team and family are synonymous. (Timeout: can someone please define "synonymous" for Dave? Thanks.) He doesn't overcomplicate life, once saying of the Bulls, "We don't want to be the worst, we don't want to be the best, we just want to hang." Basic. Easy. True. Po's got a way of looking at the world that makes everyone want to borrow his glasses, only to realize after they put them on, there are no lenses in the frames. He takes some getting used to, but once you know him, you understand he just wants you to be the best you can be. And he wants his teams, his families, to always stay together. This book would not be possible without the Aging Bulls, and the Aging Bulls would not be possible without Dave Ethan.

Thank you, Po, from all of us.

ABOUT THE AUTHOR

Ken Gagne is the author of *You're Gonna Miss Me Someday: A Memoir*. He grew up in Chicopee, Massachusetts. He and his wife live with their cat, Gary, in Maplewood, New Jersey, and are the proud parents of two grown children.

CPSIA information can be obtained
at www.ICGtesting.com
Printed in the USA
LVHW021546070922
727709LV00003B/346